DAMAGED, INCORPORATED

A MILITARY SCIENCE FICTION NOVEL

DREW AVERA

PROLOGUE
AN UNDISCLOSED MILITARY FACILITY IN SYRIA

The sun had barely begun to peek over the horizon and Staff Sergeant Roderick Ames was already dripping from head to toe with sweat. He carried his flak jacket in one hand as he jogged to the Commander's building in the middle of the camp. It was a prefabricated steel building much like the food trailers stationed just outside of the base.

The key difference between them was the armed sentries posted outside the door, and the coms antenna pointed towards the sky. Still, the resemblance was uncanny, and his mouth tended to water despite the fact the Middle Eastern Franchised Subway and Burger King were half-hearted copycats, which mostly served as a reminder of what an unlucky Marine might never see again once they left the protection of the base.

The franchises also refused to serve pork which prompted one knucklehead to tape up signs of protest depicting three strips of bacon and a close facsimile of "This is jihad" in poorly translated Aramaic. It got a laugh from the junior Marines. It also got the Commandant's attention.

But the "Pork Wars" wasn't why Ames was being called in for an emergency briefing at zero-dark-thirty.

"Ames, you're just in time," Major Joyner said as the Staff Sergeant stepped into the building. The air conditioning was cranked, and condensation dripped from the doorknob as Ames closed the door behind him. The accommodations were equal parts cramped and luxurious when compared to the dwellings the enlisted men shared. But envy was a distraction, and the world would be a much darker place with an equally uncomfortable Major Joyner in charge.

Ames stood at attention before Joyner and awaited orders.

The older man let out an exasperated sigh before saying, "I just received word that one of our friends from a three-letter-agency is following a lead. Unfortunately, it doesn't come cheap. I need you to take two duffel bags of unmarked bills to these coordinates." The man pushed a piece of paper with scribbled writings towards Ames.

Ames took it and shoved it in his pocket. "I don't understand, Sir. Are we playing ATM for the terrorists again?" he asked, in a failed attempt to hide his disdain.

"I beg your pardon?"

"I'm just saying, Sir. I'm not sure how these three-letter-agencies, and the people represented them, are helping us win this war. Every time we throw money at the enemy, they throw bullets at us."

The Major's brow furrowed as he winced. His eyes darted to the monitor on his desk and Ames followed his gaze. It was a live chat, but he couldn't tell with whom. The Major exhaled, "I'm sorry you had to hear that, Sir," Joyner said as he straightened the front of his uniform and swallowed hard. "I'll draft a letter of reprimand for his official record."

"Don't be ridiculous. Turn the monitor so that I can see the Staff Sergeant."

Joyner did as he was told, and Ames's eyes fell upon the familiar face of the Secretary of Defense. Craig Sanders was relatively new to the position and in recent years he to be involved in operations, and

2

Ames just happened to open his big fat mouth in front of the highest-ranking civilian in the DOD.

First impressions being what they were, Ames felt like a heel.

"Do you have an opinion you'd like to share with me, Staff Sergeant?"

"No, sir," Ames replied. His face flushed. Beads of sweat trickled down his back. He wanted to run away, pretend he never said anything, but he stood unflinching. Better to take what was coming like a man than to give the opportunity for the Secretary to think he was a coward.

"I get it," Sanders said, softening a bit. "You're a patriot, doing the hard thing and leaving everything behind to defend what this country once had. But you know you're not seeing the whole picture and it frustrates you to no end. If you can't verify an action, then how can it truly benefit democracy? You're spinning your wheels in a war that seems to go on forever. Does that sum it up?"

Ames nodded first, then answered. "Yes. It's a bit more complicated than that, but you're right."

Sanders nodded and shot him a sideways grin. "It's always more complicated. I was just like you. Look, Staff Sergeant, I know you're a patriot. The world owes you a debt of gratitude it can never repay. This country was founded by people like you, and though it might be different geographically than it was when it was founded, the guiding principles still abound. This money often does pay for terrorism, but we're constructing a puzzle and we don't know how many pieces we're dealing with. Maybe it's not the best play, but it's our only option to try and get the next piece locked into place. Do you understand?"

"Yes," Ames replied. It, again, was more complicated than that, but he kept it to himself.

"Good. Major, I'll leave you to it. I have another meeting waiting for me. I'll reach out soon."

The screen went black, and Ames stood in awkward silence with Major Joyner.

"I think I—"

"Don't ever embarrass me again, Staff Sergeant," Joyner spat. "I
don't care about your opinion. I don't care about your politics. And
I sure as hell don't care about your conspiracy theories. You're here
to do one job: and that's to do as you're ordered. Do you
understand?"

"Yes, sir," Ames replied, swallowing his pride.

Joyner wiped at his face, his jowls jiggling as he let out another
sigh. He looked like he was on the verge of a stroke, then again, he
always looked like that. He eyed Ames and spoke in a low, even tone,
"Get your detail together and roll out as soon as possible. Our asset is
waiting. Dismissed."

Ames gawked a moment, still taken aback by his encounter with
the Secretary of Defense. He hadn't intended for anyone other than
the Major to hear his protest, but he'd taken it too far. Spoke too
liberally.

And now he had to earn the Major's confidence all over again.

"I—"

Joyner's eyes darted up to Ames. "Did I stutter?"

"No, sir." Ames turned on his heels and promptly exited, biting
back the rage causing his heart to flutter madly. "I shouldn't have
opened my big mouth," he hissed as he darted under the low over-
hang leading into his company's tent. The Humvee was already
running while Jackson, his Sergeant and friend, leaned groggily
against the driver's side door.

"Hotrod," Jackson called, though the sleep deprivation took his
enthusiasm down a peg. "What's the scoop?"

"How many times do I have to tell you not to call me that
anymore?" Ames replied. A gentle eyeroll let Ames know Jackson
was in on his little joke. The truth was that Ames's recent promotion
put him in a position of higher authority. It was looked at as improper
from the gung-ho military types for there to be that much familiarity
between a squad leader and his men. But Ames recognized their
black and white way of looking at it was just a cover for their own

failed leadership ability. "Plug these coordinates into the GPS and get ready to roll."

"Roger that," Jackson replied. "Just the two of us?"

"No, send Lance Corporal Lin to retrieve some duffels of cash and ride shotgun. I'll take the gunner position."

Jackson nodded and pulled his radio to his lips to call on Lin. Ames hopped onto the Humvee and checked the .50 caliber mounted on top.

"Locked and loaded," he mumbled. *Probably won't see anything worth shooting, though.*

"These coordinates are an hour away. What time do we need to be there?" Jackson asked from inside the cab.

Ames squatted down, careful not to skin his shins against the metal grating on the turret stand. "Major said ASAP."

Jackson nodded and keyed his radio, "Lin, get a move on. This train is rolling."

"*Copy. On the way.*"

"Good kid, but slow like molasses," Jackson said grinning.

"Yeah, reminds me of someone I know," Ames replied with a smirk.

"Come on, I wasn't that bad."

"Right; you showing up late to muster for graduation was just something everyone dreamed. Is that how it is?"

Jackson shrugged. "It could happen."

"Just start driving as soon as his butt hits the seat," Ames ordered.

"Will do, Hotrod." Jackson winked.

Ames rolled his eyes and stood back up in the turret. The day had started like crap, but he was happy that the best part of his day was taking care of his squad. Major Joyner would get over his embarrassment eventually. Or he wouldn't. Either way, that wasn't Ames's responsibility. The squad was.

Lin yanked open the passenger side door and hopped in. The Humvee roared as Jackson gunned it, leaving a trail of dust where they had been.

T-minus one hour, Ames thought. *Then I can put this mission behind me.*

If hell is real, then it doesn't have anything on this place, Ames thought as he brushed sweat away with his sleeve. The Humvee groaned over the rocky terrain and for the first time in months, the Staff Sergeant wished he was driving. "You drive like my ex and aim for every pothole," Ames shouted down through the turret mount.

Jackson responded with something, but Ames couldn't hear it over the rumbling mass of armored steel.

"How much longer?" Ames asked, kneeling low enough to catch a glimpse of the GPS.

"Five minutes, Staff Sergeant," Lin answered. The kid still had the duffels in his lap, clutching them in his hands for dear life.

"Might as well be an eternity at this pace," Ames quipped, but no one heard him. He rose back to a standing position and saw a flicker of movement just over the horizon. "What is that?"

Ames pulled his helmet visor down and adjusted the zoom. He snapped the moving target and let the internal computer scan it. "Oh crap...we have incoming!"

Jackson accelerated and the Humvee lurched like a bull out the gate. Ames fought to maintain his balance as he gripped the .50 caliber and tried to aim for the incoming missile. He popped off a few shots and missed. Firing while aiming into the glaring sun made calculating by how much impossible. He fired twice more; each flurry of bullets accompanied by a torrent of expletives.

"Get us out of here!" Ames's heart hastened. There was no hope of evading. "We should have bailed."

It was too late for what should have been.

It was too late for regret.

It was too late for anything.

The blast turned everything silent, but Ames didn't have to

hear to know how bad the destruction was around him. The dull clash of steel erupting beneath him quaked his bones and rattled through his ravaged body. His head snapped in different directions with each tumble. He reached out for something to hold onto, but his arms weren't working. Another flip of the fiery behemoth revealed why.

Just like his hearing, they were gone.

The Humvee slammed to the ground a final time, teetering on its side as flames licked at Ames's body. He slumped forward, resting on the .50 caliber mount before his bloody frame slipped to the rocky earth below.

He blinked, trying to wake from his hellish nightmare. Instead, the sun stared mockingly.

There was nothing to wake from. And in that moment Ames knew for sure that hell existed.

Germany: four weeks later

Incessant beeping lulled Staff Sergeant Ames back to reality. Dry eyes opened to witness the dimly lit pock-marked drop ceiling of a sterile room. He moved to wipe the crust from his eyes, but only a weak, trembling stump responded.

And then he remembered that the nightmare was real.

"It was a Syrian missile strike," a voice said from the corner of the room. Ames shifted his head, but still couldn't get a good look at the man. For some reason the voice, and the ambience in the room sounded digital. It took a moment for it to register that he was hearing for the first time since the attack, then the man spoke again. "They took a lot away from you that day, but you're a fighter. I'll give you that."

"Who are you?" Ames croaked. His voice was sandpaper. As excited as he was to hear another person speak, the pain shooting at the dead ends of his stripped appendages dampened it.

That was all his life had become since he woke from the medically induced coma two days prior. He was hardly used to it.

"I'm the guy who's offering to give you your life back." The man rose and stepped into view. He reached down and touched a device attached to Ames's head, then the world went deafeningly silent again. A moment later, it returned. "My name is David Graham. This aural enhancement technology belongs to one of my companies and I'm in the business of rebuilding soldiers. What I can do for your hearing is only the tip of the iceberg. We can restore limbs, vision, speech...you name it."

Ames swallowed hard. He choked down the emotion bubbling just beneath the surface. "I can't afford this," he replied meekly.

Graham frowned. "I'm sorry, but I don't think you understand. The tech is already paid for. The only transaction I require is your continued service to God and country." Graham patted Ames's shoulder.

"Wh... who paid for it?"

"I did. It's a passion project of mine to help veterans when I can." Graham took a step back and paced the room. He clasped his hands behind his back as he walked. A man of confidence. A depiction of a military man if Ames's had ever seen one. "Patriotism was all but dead when I was a kid. The people who loved their country were forced into silence. The only people who wore their feelings on their sleeves were the ones trying to spark civil unrest. I lost my father to that madness. My mother followed shortly after."

"I'm sorry for your loss," Ames said. "I lost my father too."

Graham's eyes darted towards Ames. "We have common ground, my friend."

"I guess so?"

"If I'm being frank with you, I think we have a long way to go before we can build back our country into something reminiscent of what the founders intended. America isn't the same, geographically, or spiritually. We need to do better."

"You sound like a politician," Ames said as he struggled to sit up.

Graham moved towards the bed and adjusted the incline for him before responding. "I do have a political background, but I'm not that guy anymore. I learned that to affect change you can't be a cog in the machine."

"So, what does this service you require look like?" Skepticism oozed from Ames's voice, but Graham didn't seem to notice.

"I'm a member of an organization called The Order. We're a group of people who love our country and want to see her back on top. But the biggest issue we face is that laws were put in place to protect the crooked. That's why I left politics, the corruption, the betrayal, the hedonistic lifestyles. I was blocked before I was even sworn in simply because I was a man of faith."

"The Order? That sounds a bit ominous."

"What is the opposite of order?"

"Disorder," Ames answered.

"Chaos. It moves through everything and cripples it. The Order was created to halt the further demise of our nation. Our purpose is far from ominous."

"And you're offering me a job to facilitate that purpose?"

"I am, but I can understand if a person like you declined my offer."

Ames bit his tongue until he could hold it no more. "A person like me. You mean because I'm black?"

Graham spun to eye him. "No. I meant a triple amputee. I told you I thought patriotism was dead. The price you paid for your country has been steep already. Perhaps it's too much to ask for more?"

Ames swallowed the lump in his throat. "My service is all I have. If I lost my limbs and my ability to serve, then it's only a matter of time before I'm driven to complete what the terrorists started. If what you say is true, then your offer at least gives me hope to get back in the fight in some capacity."

A smile lit Graham's face, but soon faded. "I have to warn you, the pain you're experiencing now won't be the last. The procedure is difficult. We're developing technologies which grafts foreign material into your body. We'll be drilling into bone and hacking into your nervous system. Each person has varying thresholds for pain, but no one has been immune to it."

Ames clenched his jaw tight and stared forward. Contemplation painted a dark tint on his scarred face. No matter what decision he made, life was going to be hard. The real question was could he continue to live like *this*? His eyes met Graham's. "I don't care how much it hurts. Pain I can handle. Being useless I cannot. Sign me up."

Graham nodded as a smirk curled his lips. He stepped forward and laid a hand on Ames's shoulder. "Welcome to the team."

CHAPTER ONE

---

8 MONTHS LATER

Roderick Ames had never felt stronger. His newly developed cybernetics increased both his strength and endurance. And to his surprise, the nearly six-hundred-pounds of dead weight slung over his shoulders was no more cumbersome than hauling two sacks of concrete. As if that weren't enough, he was sprinting while carrying the load.

"Time," he said, on the brink of being out of breath.

"Three-nineteen. A new personal best," Doctor Heinric answered as he winked over his clipboard. The good doctor had been at every marked achievement the medically retired Staff Sergeant had made since he joined the team at Graham Tech. Turned out he was the closest thing to a father figure Ames had had in his life, save for a grumpy Gunny in his first platoon.

Ames dropped the test dummies to the ground. "I still think I can do better."

"And you will but give it time." Graham stepped up and gave an encouraging pat on Ames's shoulder. "How are these holding up?" He asked, referring to the cybernetic arms now surgically bound to Ames's body. The carbon fiber endoskeleton was fused with his bones and an outer sheath gave the appearance of a well-muscled brute. The technology even flexed like organic flesh as the appendages moved. It was a far cry from the claw amputees in years past used to be grateful for.

Ames was practically whole again.

"Better than the last pair," Ames replied. "There's less lag and I don't hear the whirring of the motors anymore."

Graham smirked. "I'm glad the dampening material is working. It's hard to be stealth when three out of four appendages are mechanical. How noticeable is the lag with this model?"

"There's maybe a quarter-second between my thought triggering any motion. I don't think it would be an issue with daily tasks, but maybe in a firefight there would be a delay. Is that something we can compensate for?"

Graham eyes Heinric. "Doc?"

Heinric peered over his clipboard and patted the well-worn pencil against his cheek. Ames noticed the chew marks near the eraser and wondered how such a brilliant man could have such an odd habit.

"I think it could be a software issue. I'll look at the coding. There may be a delay in the DI/AO computation."

"Oookay," Ames muttered as he glanced at Graham. It wasn't the first time he was lost in what people like Heinric had to say regarding his "cybernetic augmentations". The fact there was software inside him made him wonder how close he was to being a computer himself.

Each part of his body had something attached to it. The arms received synapsis responses from his spine via nanite fibers. His left leg received a similar input from the nerves in his hip and thigh. The Audiums in his ears were highly advanced ocular implants. He was mostly machine now but had little knowledge for how his new body worked.

Not that he was complaining. This beat laying in a bed waiting for death any day of the week.

"There's a reason he's paid so handsomely," Graham said with a smirk.

"I'll bet."

"Thank you, Doctor Heinric. We'll continue tomorrow. I need Ames to join me for a meeting upstairs."

"Yes, sir," Heinric replied, not looking up before he backed away, his eyes glued to his notes.

"This way," Graham said to Ames. "There's someone I want you to meet."

Ames followed Graham to his office. It rivaled any depiction of a multi-billionaire's lush aesthetic he'd seen in movies, right down to the indoor waterfall on the far wall. Hanging from the ceiling in the center of the room was an enormous monitor, and a familiar face.

"Staff Sergeant Ames, it's good to see you again."

Ames's jaw dropped as he stood before the Secretary of Defense. The last time they'd spoken he had questioned the man's orders. He half-expected to get an earful about that lapse in judgement, but instead Sanders appeared upbeat about seeing Ames standing before him.

"Thank you, sir. It's good to see you too." It wasn't a lie, but not entirely the truth. Ames was just happy to be alive. Who he encountered day to day was irrelevant.

"Secretary Sanders was telling me of a national security threat that might prove an opportunity for you," Graham said.

That piqued Ames's interest.

Taking that as his cue, Sanders spoke, "I have information about one of our own defecting. He's threatened to release sensitive information unless his demands are met."

"What are the demands?" Ames asked.

Sanders scoffed. "What most people in his situation demand...money."

"I have two briefcases filled with cash. One of them has a tracking chip. The other is wired with explosives. You'll have a neural link to activate either in the instance you feel it necessary," Graham said. "The tracker is only effective above ground, so bear that in mind."

Ames looked to the Secretary. "And what kind of information will he leak?"

Sanders locked eyes with Graham before responding. "I'm afraid that's above your paygrade but suffice to say that it could spark another civil conflict. We've hardly recovered from the last one, so we can't afford this information to be released."

Skepticism gnawed at Ames, but he wasn't about to question Sanders again. If this was that important, then he would have to have faith that what the Secretary said was true. Ames nodded and said, "I'll handle it, sir."

"I knew you would. I'll patch the coordinates for the drop to you, Mr. Graham. I trust you'll handle things from there?"

"I will, Secretary Sanders. Thank you."

"Take care," Sanders replied before the screen went dark.

Ames turned to Graham. "I see you have some friends at the top."

Graham smiled. "I have friends everywhere, but it seems the ones at the top are the ones who seek my help the most."

"Must be rough being the go-to guy for things like this."

"It can be overwhelming, but I would do anything for this country. Besides, we have you to help bring in the target. If you're successful, then there's no loss. If you fail, then my bank account will take a bit of a hit. Luckily, I can write that off in my taxes."

Ames didn't recognize that as a joke until Graham chortled.

"I'm sorry, I wasn't trying to be insensitive. Money isn't really an object for me at this point. I forget how much some people struggle with that. Please don't take that the wrong way."

Ames nodded, but something about that joke struck him odd beyond it simply landing wrong. *Is Graham so rich that he's that out of touch with reality?* Ames shook the thought away. *If not for this man's wealth, I would be relegated to wasting away in a bed at a VA hospital. If anything, he's a philanthropist.*

Graham stepped over to his desk and opened his incoming messages. He pressed his thumb onto a scanner and opened the encrypted message.

"That was quick," Ames said as he watched over Graham's shoulder.

"He likely sent it when I came to grab you," Graham replied.

Likely, Ames thought.

Graham read off the coordinates as he typed them into his computer and a large satellite image zoomed in on the location. "The target is at a facility in Baltimore, Maryland. I can have you there within the hour." He turned to look at Ames with a questioning glare. "Are you sure you're ready?"

Ames shrugged. "As ready as I'll ever be, I suppose."

Graham nodded. "Then let's get you suited up."

"You have a suit for me?"

A toothy grin flashed across Graham's face. "This is my favorite part. You'll see."

It was a snug fit, but Ames was pleased with how stretchy the material was. If he'd had armor like this in the Marine Corps, then life would have been much easier. "This is bulletproof?"

Graham nodded, "To an extent. I wouldn't suggest taking a .40 caliber bullet point blank, but a 9mm and smaller will bounce off like rice on a blanket."

"Hmm, I'd rather not test that theory if it's all the same to you."

Graham smiled. The tech giant had spent more than most people made in a lifetime to develop all this technology that went mostly unnoticed by the world. Why the military wasn't knocking at his door to get their hands on this stuff was mindboggling. "We did enough testing."

Ames tightened some of the straps along his leg and adjusted the height of his holster. Once he was satisfied, he turned to look at himself in the mirror. 'What do you think?"

"I think you make a *model* soldier after all," graham quipped.

Ames rolled his eyes. "You have the same sense of humor my dad did. Nothing but puns."

"What can I say, I'm easily amused, how does it feel?"

"Good," Ames replied. He moved and flexed in the mirror, trying to find pinch points that would constrict his movement. He found none. "Better than good, actually. Even with all these straps there's no binding. I have full range of motion. It's like wearing pajamas."

"It was designed to allow the body to move naturally. No binding or chaffing. You may also notice there's no noise from the garment as you move."

Ames shifted his body around to test that comment. "I hadn't noticed, but you're right. This should make stealth tactics easier."

"And there's something else," Graham replied.

Ames looked over to him. "What's that?"

Graham clasped bands over each of Ames's wrists and activated them. "You're never unarmed with these. They create a charge as your arms move and can discharge enough kinetic energy to knock a horse on its ass. If you keep charging them and hold onto something conductive, then you can essentially electrocute it."

Ames moved his arm in front of his face and watched small bursts of blue sparks form over his fingertips. His balled his fist and marveled as it glowed with blue, electric light.

"All it takes is a thought and you can send a charge into any combatant up to fifteen feet away. Try striking the column on the other side of this room."

Ames released the charge when he peered at the man liked he's lost his mind. "Are you serious?"

Graham nodded. The faintest of smiles curled the edge of his lips.

"All right, it's your building." Ames willed his hands to charge once more. He focused the cobalt orbs of energy and felt the power surging through him. The hairs on the back of his neck stood on end. He generated so much electricity that the clock on the wall stopped ticking. And then he thrust his fists forward and released it at his target.

The recoil sent him staggering back. His heart raced. A toothy grin spread across his face.

"How did that feel?"

Ames breathed heavily, not from the effort, but the elation. "That was the most amazing thing I've ever done. I've jumped out of planes into enemy territory to take out bad guys, but I've never done anything like that."

"I think you'll find that useful in the field."

"Indeed, I will. Do you have any more surprises for me?"

Graham chuckled. "Not yet, but if that excites you, then just wait for some of our newer developments to gain ground. Are you ready to go?"

Ames balled his fist and charged it again. Electricity pulsed and ozone burned around his hand. "Oh yeah, I'm ready."

"Then let's go."

Ames had jumped out of several models of aircraft during his service, but never had he strapped into an unmanned aerial vehicle. There was something wholly impersonal about it, but he clamped his mouth shut. He wasn't about to look a gift horse in the mouth and complain after everything Graham had done for him.

Besides, if the man could turn a triple-amputee into a super soldier, then surely, he could master developing a capable AI to fly this plane.

"*You'll reach the jump area in twelve minutes,*" Graham said through the com.

"Roger that."

The UAV lurched forward. There were no windows, but there was a monitor display on the forward bulkhead giving a pilot's view, if there was a pilot. The aircraft took off and shot skyward, climbing in altitude rapidly before leveling off. The G-forces were unsettling, so Ames closed his eyes and focused on his breathing.

17

The unspoken truth was he hated flying. Even with more than one-hundred drops under his belt, he was still a ball of anxiety during the flight. Most of his buddies in the Marine Corps thought he was lying when he spoke about how much it bothered him. They assumed if it was as bad as he said it was, then he wouldn't step foot on a plane.

But "hiding from your fears is giving in to them." His father said that many times before he died, and Ames tried to live those words as best he could to honor his dad's memory. He hoped the old man would be proud.

"*Six minutes.*"

Ames rose from his seat and strapped into the guideline leading to the ramp. A timer clicked down at the exit as he looked down at the metropolis.

Baltimore had risen and fallen half a dozen times, but its recent prominence was only achieved thanks to being taken over by a vast criminal organization with deep pockets. In many ways, Baltimore lay outside federal law, not because it wasn't still beholden to the government, but because no one within the city cared.

That was where a broken society led decades prior. Lawlessness always leads to destruction. The people down there just hadn't figured that out yet.

"*Two minutes.*"

A deep breath to calm his nerves, Ames took another step towards the ramp. He strapped the two briefcases full of cash to his leg harness. The wind whipped around him, momentarily making it hard to breathe as it rushed past in quick bursts. He unclasped the harness and held himself steady with a heavy grip.

"*One minute.*"

Time raced like the air caressing his body. He descended the ramp. Gray squares littered the landscape below. The warehouse where he would find his target drew near.

"*Go.*"

Ames released himself from the ramp and somersaulted as the UAV zipped away. He was in freefall at two-hundred feet per second. He watched his altimeter, clenching his jaw. The worst of it was imminent. The immediate tug of the leg harness when the chute deployed.

Right.

About.

Now.

Ames yanked the cord. As he expected, his newly assembled frame jerked harder due to the weight, but it felt no worse than when his body was wholly organic.

He took hold of the handles and directed his descent towards a small clearing near the warehouse. From his vantage Baltimore looked like a warzone. The gray squares he's seen before were now crumbling masses of half-burned debris. The structures left standing were on the brink of collapse. Only the downtown area appeared to have any life left in it, but these outskirts were no man's land.

For good reason.

The ground approached rapidly and pulled Ames from his distracted gaze. He was coming in hot.

Too hot.

"Oh crap," he muttered as he tried to correct his mistake.

Ames pulled down on both handles to slow his fall. He braced himself for landing and came in at an angle using his cybernetic leg as a shield. His leg drove into the crumbling asphalt and dug in like a trencher. He clamped his eyes shut as debris shot towards his face. He held them tightly closed until he surprisingly came to a standing stop. It was messy, but not as painful as it would have been without the augmentations.

"Thank God," he said under his breath before keying his com. "I've landed at the drop zone."

"Good. Keep the line open, but don't transmit unless you must. We don't know if he's capable of listening in."

"Roger that." Ames unkeyed the mic and removed his chute. "It's go time."

CHAPTER TWO

Ames arrived with the two briefcases in tow. The rundown warehouse was right off the water and smelled of mold and fish. He entered from the south side and kept close to the shadows. His lumbering frame took up most of the narrow aisles separated by hulking machines used for God knows what.

Most of the items still bolted to the deck were covered in dust and rust, left to decay with the passing of time. Ames had no idea how long this place had been abandoned, but he would wager it sat unused for more than a decade.

He had seen rundown buildings before. They were a hotbed for criminal activity no matter which hemisphere you were in. But what unnerved him most about this place was how quiet it was? His Audiums didn't pick up anything except the sound of his own breathing. Either the target wasn't there, or he was good at hiding.

Neither boded well for this mission.

Ames turned a corner and stepped into a large opening. Above him, the second floor sagged, a crumbling deathtrap. Below him chunks of rubble lay scattered amongst dust and grime.

Footprints.

He knelt to examine them. One set. Male. Fresh.

He wasn't alone.

Ames rolled as a lead piped slammed into the concrete floor where he had been a moment before. He planted his feet ready to counter, but no one was there.

"Peekaboo."

Ames canted his head enough to see a blur of motion before a fist connected to the side of his face. The impact drove him flailing forward. He caught himself on his hands and shoved upward, scattering back to the ready. He was gone.

"What the?"

"Hey big boy."

Ames twisted and charged, grabbing hold of whatever his hands fell on as he plowed towards the wall. He caught a glimpse of the masked man, his mouth curled in a grin beneath the thin veil of fabric. Their eyes locked, then poof he was gone, and Ames drove headfirst into the brick wall ahead.

It caved under his mass, and he collapsed onto the floor covered in dust.

"That's it," he spat as he charged his fists with electricity. "Let's see you do that again."

The man appeared across the room waving tauntingly. Ames stomped towards him ready to wring his neck and crush his skull.

"You seem to have anger issues; did anyone ever tell you that?" The man asked mockingly.

"You're about to have a breathing issue." Ames swung a mighty fist. It crackled with static electricity as it bore down on his target. The man merely sidestepped and drove a solid fist into Ames's midsection.

"You're going to have to do better than that."

Ames growled and sent his left fist in a backhand swing. The target ducked, two tapping him with quick jabs before Ames could swing all the way around. The second hit knocked the wind from his lungs.

Ames gasped and stumbled forward, catching himself on the wall. He cut his eyes to the other man, but he was no longer there.

"Show yourself," he choked.

The man reappeared a moment later in front of him, his arms crossed nonchalantly. "Had enough?"

Ames's eyes flashed with resentment.

The man stepped forward and unclasped the briefcases from Ames's legs and let them drop. He pointed at one. 'This one is the bomb, that one is the tracker. Know how I can tell?"

Ames peered at them questioningly but said nothing.

"The green dot on the hinge on the handle. Most people would see that unassuming color and think it was perfectly innocent, but you work for a man with a dark soul. His trickery has killed more people than you will ever know."

Ames clenched his jaw tighter and focused on regaining his breath. He watched the other man set the briefcases on the warehouse floor then step away.

"He's damaged more lives than you would want to admit."

"What do you know?" Ames spat.

The man sighed as he glanced back at Ames. "More than I want to admit."

Ames straightened up, glaring at his attacker. He balled his fists. "So, are you going to just take the money and run, or do you want to stick around and fight me like a man? No disappearing act, just fists and rage."

The man chortled. "Wow, you're a real piece of work, aren't you? You work for a nutcase Frankenstein wannabe and then challenge me to 'be a man'. That's classic, but I'll pass." He reached down and grabbed the case without the green dot near the handle. "I don't like my money to be too spicy." He shoved it back towards Ames with his foot. "See you around."

The man opened a portal and Ames's jaw dropped. He was escaping.

"Not so fast," Ames spat and darted towards the opening, stepping through into the nothingness. He spun as if he were caught in a whirlpool. The air around him was thick, but he could breathe. "This is impossible," he said before he was spat out. His large frame sprawled across the floor. When he came to a stop, he looked up at two barrels aiming at his head.

"That was stupid," a voice said from behind a mask. "You led him right to us." It was a woman.

"I did as I was told," the man from the warehouse replied.

"Who are you people?" Ames asked, ignoring the guns and the inherent danger.

"Who we are is of little consequence," his attacker replied. "The real question you should be asking is who are you?" He lowered the barrel and backed away. "Let him up."

The woman followed suit and gave Ames a wide berth. She held her weapon at the ready while the man stood lackadaisically by a large monitor.

Ames slowly rose to his feet. Puzzlement stretched across his face. There was more military tech in this one room than he'd had access to on any base he was stationed to. His first guess was these were government types, but their uniforms didn't match.

Mercenaries?

That didn't quite feel right either.

"My original question still stands," Ames said.

"Of course, it does," the man replied with an exasperated sigh. "How about I show you something that might put your focus on where it needs to be?"

"Like what?"

"Like the truth and why you're here?"

Ames clenched his fists. "Why should I believe anything you have to say?"

The man pushed a wheeled stool towards their guest and shrugged. "You shouldn't. But maybe we're not the ones lying to you. Don't take my word for it. See for yourself."

The man clicked a button on the keyboard and a video started playing.

Ames didn't want to watch their propaganda, but something about the timestamp and location made him fixate on the granulated satellite footage. There was no mistaking the Humvee being tracked by the feed. The Syrian valley was identifiable whether he was looking at it from above or at ground view. Within seconds he knew exactly what he was seeing.

"Where did you get this?"

"Keep watching."

Ames drew a breath and set his eyes back to the screen. He had read the report numerous times since the attack. If the timestamp on the screen was accurate, then in less than thirty-seconds everyone in the Humvee would be dead...except for him.

"It came from the northeast," the woman said, his voice void of its earlier irritation. "You'll see the flash in a few seconds."

Ames counted to three in his head and in the upper righthand corner the flash appeared. But what he saw wasn't a missile strike from an enemy combatant. The silhouette of the F-35 fighter was unmistakable.

"That's an American aircraft," he said through his teeth.

"It is, but it wasn't an American pilot." The man took a step forward with a file in his hand. "Suhad Amistar, no government affiliation, and a pilot for hire. He's a mercenary for the deep state."

Ames took the file but scoffed at what he heard. "You've read too many conspiracy theories." he looked at the file and most of the information on Suhad was missing. He was a ghost. "I'm assuming Suhad Amistar is an alias?"

"Yes," the woman replied. "But you might want to rethink what you consider a conspiracy theory. You're walking proof of our theory, and it's looking more factual by the minute."

Ames cut his eyes to her. "British SAS?"

She paused, then nodded. "I've tried to hide the accent."

He smirked. "You almost did." He dropped the file. "This doesn't prove anything. Whether Suhad shot us, or the Syrian military did, the outcome is the same. Two dead and my life relegated to being more machine than human. As I said, conspiracy theories."

The man cleared his throat. "The conspiracy isn't that someone else shot your Humvee. It's the why. It's who ordered it."

Ames glared at the screen, just realizing the play back was paused to seconds before the missile impacted. "And you know who ordered the strike?"

He nodded. "So do you."

Ames squared his shoulders. "Who?"

"David Graham."

The response elicited a snort from Ames. "Are you serious? That man rebuilt the tragedy that was my life. If not for him, I would be pissing in a bedpan and living in perpetual agonizing silence. You've got it wrong."

"That missile strike was a recruitment tool," the woman shot back. "He gave you the disease so he could sell you the cure. You were marked and a mission was planned to get you out in the open to execute it."

Ames wiped sweat from his brow and focused on breathing to lower his heart rate. This was ridiculous. *Why am I listening to this?* "What proof do you have?"

The man took another step forward and lifted his hand to his face. He paused, then pulled off his mask, revealing the pock marked scars on one side of his face from an incendiary device. "Because I was just like you and then I learned the truth."

Ames gawked at the man. There was something familiar about him, but he couldn't place him at first...then, "You're Jason Wills?"

"I am."

"We served in Somalia together...before the..."

"Before I was recruited by Graham?"

Ames didn't want to say yes, so he said nothing. From what he knew of Wills, the man was a hero. He was a former Green Beret and Congressional Medal of Honor recipient. He was awarded the medal posthumously, though the man standing before Ames was very much alive.

"This is a lot to take in...I..." Ames stopped short, his mind racing. The closer he looked at Wills, the more augmentations he recognized under the suit. "A part of me wants to believe you, but it's hard to accept."

"I know, I was standing where you are not that long ago. I wish I could say I was as calm as you are when I learned the truth, but I was a bit irate." Wills smirked at the woman before continuing. "We led you here for one reason," Wills said. "Graham isn't the man you think he is and as much as he's given to you, he's taken so much more."

"I don't know what to say," Ames muttered. He felt deflated, like his life was a lie.

If what they said was true, then his life *was* a lie.

"Give us a chance to make our case, then decide," Wills replied.

"Decide what?"

The woman placed a hand on his shoulder. He canted his head to meet her gaze. Bright green eyes bore into him without an ounce of aggression. For the first time in months, he looked at someone else and didn't feel like a test subject. "To decide whether you're going to help us stop him."

Ames glanced around the room. "There's only two of you? Graham has a lot of power. I don't know how you plan on standing up to someone like that."

A portal opened across the room and the lumbering mass of a war-torn man entered the room. "There's more of us than you think, Ames."

"Who are you?"

"I'm Michael Ryan," he said. "I'm the first victim of Graham's freak show, super soldier program. You might want to hear what we have to say."

"And if I don't?"

Ryan scoffed. "Listen anyway."

CHAPTER THREE

"Sir, we lost track of Ames."

Graham tightened his grip on the armrests of his chair as he glared at the monitor. Mere seconds ago, there was a blip overlay on the map, now there was nothing. "What about the briefcases?"

"We still have one, but the other disappeared from view when we lost Ames. They must be underground, but none of the blueprints we saw of the warehouse suggested there was a basement. The water table in that area is too high."

"That's because they aren't there," Graham said under his breath.

"What makes you say that sir?"

"We're dealing with a prior associate. He knows how we work, and he knows how to take advantage of our surveillance systems. It's unfortunate, but not a devastating blow...at least not yet." Graham typed in a command on his keypad and the monitor shifted to a satellite view of a different location hundreds of miles southwest of the warehouse.

"What is that blip?"

"That's the acoustic beacon I placed in the briefcase. It's antiquated technology, so I doubted that they would suspect it. It looks like I was right."

"Impressive, sir, but how did they get from Baltimore to Huntsville, Alabama so quickly?"

Graham drummed his fingers on the top of his desk. It was a nervous habit. He willed himself to stop before canting his head to his technician. "Do you know the number one source of leaked technology in the world today?"

The man gawked a moment with his mouth drooped. "I would say infiltrations of computer networks would be at the top of that list, sir. Why?"

A smirk formed on Graham's face. "Everyone thinks that technology is the culprit, but it's actually the human condition. Most leaks are the result of former employees stealing technology from an employer and giving it to a competitor. Our little friend is using my technology to evade us. But his cockiness has led them all to a trap."

"How so?"

"Take these coordinates from the acoustic beacon and send in an air strike. Level the place. I don't want any survivors. We'll send in a reclamation team to retrieve what's left."

The man stammered before saying, "What about Ames?"

Graham frowned. "He's compromised. We'll cut our loses and move on."

It was a heartless reaction, but this was how business worked. At Graham's level a human life was no different than a profit margin. Once the expense was too great, you let it go. The only real tragedy in Graham's mind was that he didn't have a chance to let his investment earn him any money.

"Are you sure?"

Graham cut his eyes at the technician. "Do it, or I'll find someone else who will."

"Yes, sir," the technician replied, and got to work.

"So let me get this straight, you two were recruited by Graham, and then separated yourselves based on information from her?" Ames gestured towards the female SAS agent whom he learned was Elizabeth Browning. The name sounded familiar, but after seeing her face, it didn't register. "This is all based on a file she discovered on Suhad, who is allegedly a gun for hire. Do you have a money trail, correspondence, or anything, because this is circumstantial at best?"

"I understand you're skeptical," Ryan said, "but believe me when I tell you that Graham isn't the man you think he is. I thought highly of him too...once." The older man looked like he'd seen the end of the world...twice, but Ames wanted to give him the benefit of the doubt. He was outgunned and outnumbered, if they really wanted to kill him, he'd have been dead already. But the story kept going in circles with nothing Ames was willing to throw his new life away for.

In short, he was getting tired of listening.

Ames exhaled. "I don't know why I'm still listening to this crap." He took a step back and let his hand fall slack near the grip of his weapon. Three sets of eyes watched unflinchingly. But in the breadth of a moment something struck him. "What is that sound? Did you detonate something?"

Ryan and Wills looked at each other, shaking their heads. "We didn't do anything," Will replied. "Why?"

Ames held up a finger to quiet the room. Over the months he'd grown used to his Audium implants and how they heightened his hearing. Though, it was still odd when others didn't hear the ping that felt like an ice pick in his ears. "I hear something. It's a pulse of some sort.". By the time his eyes set on the source, the others had jumped to the same conclusion.

"It's the briefcase," Wills spat. "Graham is tracking it."

"That means he has our location. We have to bail," Ryan barked. "Leave it behind and open a portal."

Beth ran past Ames and stood with her team as she used a device strapped to her wrist to open a doorway to God knows where. Ames watched as a doorway opened, but what was on the other side was a mystery.

Ryan shot a glance at Ames before stepping through. "Graham is about to level this place. You have about two minutes to get out of here unless you want to join us. I won't twist your arm, but you can guarantee that he will do anything it takes to get answers out of you now that he knows you were here with us. It's your call."

Ryan stepped through the portal, followed by Wills, then Beth. She hesitated, glancing back at Ames. "Whatever life you thought you had, it's over now."

"I know," Ames replied. Regret hung from the room like the death looming above. Two minutes was a conservative estimate. For all intents and purposes, they were on borrowed time.

"Are you coming?" she asked. Her eyes pleaded. It certainly wasn't the look of an enemy who wanted him dead.

Ames cut his eyes away from hers and looked down at the briefcase. It represented only one thing: betrayal.

"Yeah," he said, "I'm coming,". Ames drew a deep breath and ran after Beth through the portal. It closed just as a flash of light filled the area he'd been in moments before.

Ryan was right, Graham was willing to do anything. Ames couldn't help but question if that included having each of them ripped apart just so he could recruit them into his program. If it was true, then Graham was playing God.

That didn't sit right with Ames.

Not one bit.

Graham manipulated the drone hovering over the ruins of Rocket City. In the background rusted remnants of the early space age decayed unceremoniously. Once upon a time, this small city in northwestern Alabama had been a hotbed of activity for scientists. The man who gave humanity the Saturn V rocket spent years in the sweltering heat of this fading place.

Still, the gifts of our forefathers in science sagged pitifully in the glinting sunlight. Rust and decay were a part of life, but the legacy lived on.

"Sir, we've breached the bunker," a man said, pulling Graham from his daydreaming.

"Did you find anything?"

"Not yet, but there is much more underground than we thought. Someone cut miles of tunnels underneath the compound."

"Did the strike make it through?"

The man sighed; wiping sweat from his face with a wet cloth. "It appears to. We're sending in robots to survey the area on the other side of the debris field."

That's promising, Graham thought with a tight-lipped smile. "Keep me informed."

"Roger that."

Graham scooted away from his desk and rose from his chair. He stood by the window overlooking the sprawling metropolis of New D.C., a name befitting the new ideals of American supremacy. Much had changed in the twenty years since he started his ventures in government contracting. Money talked, and he was savvy with a dollar. He formed three corporations his first year, each of them earning millions in government contracts.

He thought he had made it then, but hindsight revealed that was only the beginning. The more he accomplished, the more people in powerful positions sought to do business with him. Business was a loose term as the deals struck behind closed doors seldom had anything to do with the output of his companies.

His eyes caught rising smoke in the distance. Another arson in the low-class sector of the city. It struck him how protests often turned into the people destroying their own communities as they raved for change. Their actions often resulted in empty promises and little else, but they never learned.

"Sheep," he muttered as the orange glow of flames sprouted against the horizon. Somewhere on the other side of the thick glass sirens howled. Dusk was the worst time of day for National Police. If it wasn't fires, it was murders. The simple-minded always found a way to destroy themselves.

Then again, so did the powerful.

Graham pulled his cell from his pocket and saw the notification from Secretary Sanders. "Fix this," he read it aloud. "What do you think I'm doing?" Graham replied to no one. Not every message required a response and for all he cared, Sanders could wait. An hour-by-hour update was cumbersome in the best of circumstances. Graham wasn't about to waste his time with nothing new to report.

"Sir, we've found something," Clark said.

Graham turned his attention back to his monitor. "What is it?"

The man held up pieces of hard plastic. The edges were singed and partially melted. "It appears to be parts of a briefcase."

"I'm not concerned with that. Did you find human remains?"

"Not yet," the man replied.

"Keep looking. I don't want a stone left unturned."

Graham cut away without waiting for a response. He hated waiting. He hated babysitting more. He paid handsomely for results, not for a play-by-play interpretation of what led to those results. The ends justify the means, he'd learned that in high school history, and it stuck with him ever since. By that standard anything could be justified.

He paced the room, hands in pockets and his mind on the past. Before he started his empire, he had nothing. His family came from money, but the selfish never bothered to give him a leg up in the game. "You have to earn it," his father said more times than he told his son, "I love you." Love wasn't profitable in the Graham home.

When his parents passed most of their estate was seized by the state. A lack of an updated will and a shady lawyer took their fortune and scattered it like dust in the wind. By the time everything settled, David Graham, heir to the Graham legacy had a modest home and a tiny stipend. The monthly checks hardly put food on the table and only lasted ten years.

It was a long, hard fall from grace, but an educational one.

A young Graham, with nothing to lose, went all in on revenge.

The lawyer would be the first to pay, then the state official whose judgement was paid for by the lawyer. It was a scheme, and one David was certain was planned before his parents died. It wasn't difficult to prove considering those who deemed themselves untouchable were usually the ones who did nothing to cover their tracks.

Their death was political, and intentional. His father's trusted lawyer, Carlos Morran, had taken a bribe and had fallen deep with powerful people. David discovered that the scheme had started innocently enough, just taking a little off the top for nearly a decade. It wasn't until someone with a conscience ran the numbers that anything was discovered. That accountant lost their life soon after his parents did.

If tying up loose ends was the second lesson of his life, then seizing opportunities was the third.

Those same powerful people who employed Morran to do their bidding were more than willing to work with someone as cunning and conniving as David. The heir got was coming to him, then he made his own legacy...in blood.

Those were better times, though. The walls were splintering, and he saw where his foundation had been laid on sand. He was too young and naïve to notice it then, but it was clear now.

His alliances had shifted and the powers that be saw it. One by one, they stripped him of his assets before he had the chance to use them against his growing number of enemies. Even Secretary Sanders shifted like a leaf on the wind, bending to outside influence.

"Has my time come?" he asked to no one.

He thought he knew the answer but couldn't bear to say it.

"Sir, we canvased the area and there are no signs of human remains."

"Of course, there isn't," he replied solemnly. "Have your men work through the night. Ensure you didn't miss anything, then report back to me in the morning."

There was a pause until Graham eyed the camera. "Yes, sir," the man answered. Clark's expression was forlorn. His eyes weary.

Graham closed the feed and pulled out his cell. He typed a response to Secretary Sanders and sent it. The Secretary would be upset, but that wasn't enough of a concern to lose sleep over. The real work to keep the peace would take place tonight, in the shadows of another gala. He used to look forward to the debauchery, but like all things, the allure faded.

He stepped to his desk and pressed the intercom, "Stephanie, could you send for my costume? I won't have time to run home before the festivities."

"Right away, sir," she replied. Her voice was jovial but forced. Anybody with half a brain could hear it through the tiny speaker, but Graham ignored it. She was paid well to work around the clock. If fetching his wardrobe was too much to ask, then she knew where the door was. Everyone who worked for Graham did.

They just didn't like what was on the other side.

CHAPTER FOUR

"Welcome to the Thunderdome," Wills said with a grin etched on his face. Ames hardly paid attention, instead focusing on the bare concrete walls of this underground...dungeon. It reminded him of the tunnels he'd vacated in Syria except for the stench of rat urine. He inhaled, taking in the soft aroma of scented candles in the distance.

"It smells like a candle shop down here," he said.

"That's Beth's contribution," Wills replied.

"Hey, I contribute much more than that," Beth retorted from the back of the group.

Wills turned and smirked at Ames. "Just not with cooking, ain't that right?"

Ames sensed a flurry of movement behind him, then a stone whizzed past his ear and struck Wills on the shoulder. "You might want to watch yourself, the next one will hit your hollow head."

Ames couldn't contain the smile itching at the corners of his mouth. This was the banter he'd enjoyed most about being part of a unit. For years, he and his men ripped each other apart in good fun. It passed the time and gave them something to focus on other than the misery of a looming attack.

He forgot how much he missed it.

"I need you to step inside," Ryan said, pulling Ames from his thoughts. The man was stopped outside of a barred door, and it took a moment to register that it was a cell.

"Are you serious? I came willingly," Ames shot back.

Ryan nodded. "I know. Don't take it personally, I just don't know if I can trust you yet."

Ames motioned at the narrow cell, a thin mat on the floor in front of a toilet and sink combo. "And I'm supposed to trust you?"

The smile on Wills's face faded as the tension grew thick. Ames's face turned flush as he measured up the domineering man standing before him. Ryan wasn't a spring chicken, but neither was he a crippled old man. He'd seen enough battles to be an efficient killer. There was always the chance that given their numbers, Ames wouldn't last a full minute if he decided not to cooperate.

But he wasn't about to suddenly be all right with stepping into a cage.

Not now. Not ever.

"You should have made that decision before following us through the portal," Ryan replied. His face was stone. His eyes cold and narrow.

"There was a strike. If I didn't then I'd be dead. Besides, you offered me the opportunity."

Wills took a step between them. "Ames, it's just temporary. Give us an opportunity to prove you can trust us."

"It's not temporary. It's undefined. I step into that cage and God only knows how long before I step out of it. If I step out of it."

"So, what do you suggest?" Ryan asked. His voice was low and grave. He stood unflinching.

"Let me be. I followed you here in good faith. Show the same to me."

"We showed good faith by allowing you the option to follow us. Don't test me now." Ryan took a heavy step forward. His shoulders squared as he glared at the younger man.

Ames eyed him warily, studying the other man, but discovering nothing he didn't already know. Ryan wasn't about to step down. This was his team. His compound. What other choice did Ames have?

None.

"Fine," Ames replied, hating the words as they left his lips. He stepped into the cell and pulled the door shut on his own. He stood, for the first time in years, behind bars. Three sets of eyes stared at him in silence. Then they broke away and left him alone to his thoughts.

There was only one place you could find a crooked politician flaunting his immorality, and that was behind the curtains of an Order gala. The debauchery contained within were as bipartisan as one could get, and Graham knew better than to judge their character by their words. Though there was something particularly odd seeing a senator on a leash with a ball gag while two naked men whipped him in the corner.

What authority does a man like that possess?

As much as he wants when he knows the right people, Graham thought as he bypassed the party and headed upstairs.

Men and women tugged at him, urging promiscuity through pouted lips and tiny pupils. Each of them was high on drugs, Portulaq if Graham had to guess. The synthetic chemical was known to induce split personality disorder when consumed in large quantities. Based on how these young people were acting, Graham doubted any of them knew who they were anymore.

Not that their captors wanted them to anyway.

"David, it's good to see you," Victor, the Master of Ceremonies said as he entered the candlelit room. He was more like the Master of Cronies, but Graham didn't say so out loud. Inside was a long oval table, a half-naked woman laid upon it covered with delicacies. Her flesh was paler than the light in the room should have warranted and despite being accustomed to this lifestyle, Graham couldn't bear to look at her.

Neither could the others he noticed as they all stood to the side of the room drinking absinth.

"Master, it's good to be here," Graham replied with a curt nod.

"I trust you know Jerry Swan?" The Master of Ceremonies introduced the young congressman from Iowa.

"Democrat?" Graham asked as he took the younger man's hand to shake it.

"You're familiar with my platform?" Jerry asked with a fake toothy smile. The disingenuous of his politeness raked like nails on a chalkboard. There was a stench to it wholly separate from the dead girl on the table.

"No, the blue tie gave you away, much like the republican senator downstairs being ridden like a horse. You guys are aware that more colors exist, right?"

"I uh..."

"David is just messing with you," Victor interjected. "He has a cruel sense of humor. How about you introduce yourself to the Canadian Prime Minister. Your stances on capital punishment are quite similar."

Graham exhaled as the Iowan stepped away awkwardly.

Victor then turned to Graham with stony eyes. "Why do you do that? Are you trying to draw negative attention?"

Graham shrugged. "I grow bored of the politics, Victor. I'm just here to show face to the few people I like and then disappear for another year."

Victor groaned as he pulled back his hood further revealing the weathered face of an old man. "You speak too openly, son. Careful, someone with their head not totally up someone else's ass might get the wrong impression."

Graham smirked. He and Victor had known each other for years.

Victor was part of the old guard, two generations in the Order and still breathing. He had done something right.

Or wrong.

"Tell me, who am I playing nice with this evening?"

Victor made a half turn and gestured with a node towards a man in a white suit. He stood out, not so much for wearing white, but his dark complexion and impressive beard.

"Looks like a sheik," Graham said.

"Just another billionaire playboy with a fetish. You know the type."

"Yeah, you're the type."

Victor chuckled lightly between sips of absinth. "Whatever you say. I am what I am. Good luck with your business deal. I have guests to entertain." The older man stepped away and swaggered to the dull thump of bass from downstairs.

Graham straightened his tie and walked over to meet the man in white. He turned to meet Graham's gaze as if he knew he was approaching.

"So, we finally meet," the man said with a thick Arab accent.

"We do. How can I be of service to you?"

"I'm looking for a new supplier for *playing*. Can you keep me well-stocked?"

Graham swallowed. He hated how easily this came to other people, toying with children in inappropriate ways. He hated himself more for having ever gotten involved in human trafficking to begin with. Arms and drugs were one thing. Peoples' lives were another, but he was in over his head. That was why he avoided these events as often as possible.

"I know a few guys," Graham replied.

"Guys, girls, it's all the same to me, but I like them exotic. Make sure they're exotic."

Bile rose in graham's throat. He swallowed it and resisted the urge to cut the man's throat. He was a predator. Graham saw it in his eyes and the way he kept licking his lip when someone *exotic* walked past, which essentially meant "non-Arab" to the billionaire.

"What kind of timeframe are you needing?"

"I leave the country in forty-eight hours. I would like to have concluded business by then, or at least have a treat for my journey." He smiled wickedly, and it took every fiber of Graham's being to smile back.

"It's easier if I meet you overseas. Less prying eyes," Graham said. He wasn't lying, but it wasn't the whole truth. He needed a reason to get out of the country for a while, his situation being what it was. "What name should I call you?"

"Chuck," the man replied.

It was a stupid alias. They always were.

The man retrieved a card from his pocket and handed it to Graham. "I'm leaving the country in forty-eight hours. Can you have my product ready and delivered here? There's a formal event I've been invited to. I can have a plus one."

Graham peered at the blank card before shoving it into his pocket. He knew enough not to ask. "Here's mine, in case you'd like to update your order." He handed the man one of his own.

Chuck took it and grasped Graham's hand. He stared at the ring for a moment. "That's impressive, and I own several stores in the Bazaar. Can I ask you where you got it?"

"My secretary picked it out for me," Graham replied, not wanting to get into it.

Chuck grinned. "She sounds...exotic."

"She isn't," Graham replied, trying to hide the snark. "I hire people to do a job. I'm not in the business of drawing too much attention to myself by employing someone good to look at." It was a lie, but Chuck didn't need to know.

Chuck's face shifted to a frown. "I'll be seeing you soon."

"Great."

The man left him alone and Graham retrieved the card from his pocket and angled it against a black light set on the table near him. The time and location were printed lightly, as was the cover for his visit. None of it matched what the Saudi mentioned. "A formal event my ass," he grumbled. "He's touring an aircraft carrier."

Graham shoved it back into his pocket and turned to walk away, but a hand grabbed his wrist. When he turned back his eyes met someone's he didn't expect.

"Vivian?"

"Hey," she said as she pulled the mask from her face. She moved her body close to his and smelled of alcohol and cigarettes. "What kind of scheme are you pulling off tonight?"

"Not much of a schemer anymore."

"Perhaps we can do something about that?" Lust bore at him through gorgeous green eyes.

Graham resisted the urge. It wasn't that he wasn't interested. It was that he knew what Vivian was about and the woman hanging on him now wasn't the same person mentally he knew before.

He hated what her decisions had done to her. He hated himself for not having the courage to stop it before she was too far gone.

"Tonight's not a good night for me." It was a lie thinly veiled in truth. No night was good to see the shell of a person you once...loved. He felt dirty for thinking that word but didn't know what else to call it.

She gave a pout and ran her hand across his chest. "Not even for old times?"

He shrugged. "It's not like that."

"Then what is it like?"

He didn't have an answer. That was a first.

Graham paused, his mind racing. It had been years since he had an anxiety attack. This felt similar, yet different. He looked down and her hand still holding onto his wrist and saw the syringe. She locked eyes with him then punctured the skin, injecting the drug.

"What are you doing to me?" His voice sounded foreign, as if he was underwater.

"Your master beckons. Don't make her wait," Vivian replied. Her voice oozed with sexual tension.

Graham's vision began to fade the faster his heart raced. Each poison-filled pump was a kick to the chest. It was all he could do to keep standing before the floor fell out from under him.

Then everything went black.

Ames didn't know how much time had passed since he stepped voluntarily into his cage. What he did know was that it was a decision he was growing to regret. There hadn't been a peep from the team that brought him to this place since they left him alone in the cell. Only the sound of an old sitcom playing in the background filled the empty halls of the underground facility. Canned laugh tracks drew his attention to the flickering lights at the end of the tunnel.

"That's it," he growled. Ames rose from his seat on the floor and stepped to the barred door. He griped the bars with both hands, receptors sent signals to his brain suggesting the metal was cold, though acknowledging it and feeling it were different sensations as far as his cybernetics were concerned.

Ames pressed his face against the bars to see if he could see anything. Under the weight, the door shifted. He eased back and let it slide open. "What the..."

He paused, second guessing what to do. He was free, but outside this cell was a labyrinth he didn't know how to escape from. Never mind the fact they were likely watching him.

Ames looked around for a security camera but found nothing. Several moments passed before he took a chance and stepped out of the cell.

He looked in both directions anticipating an alarm to trigger. With his ocular implant he would be able to hear the ping of a silent alarm, but aside from the television program, all was silent. At one end of the tunnel was where they entered through the portal. It was a dead end the best he could remember. On the left was the unknown. More prerecorded laughter came from that direction. It was like they were mocking him.

With no other options, he took his first step towards the unknown and hoped it wasn't a trap.

Ames expected to see someone sitting on the couch where the television played. Instead, he was met with a nearly empty room. There wasn't much inside aside from a couch, a television, and a small refrigerator humming softly in the corner.

Then there was the open door on the far side of the room taunting him. No light shone from the other side. It could be a test, but he was tired of waiting for someone to release him. They brought him here and it was time he got some answers.

Ames stepped into a narrow, dark hallway. Dim floor lighting reflected a green glow on the tiled floors. That glow crept halfway up the walls before fading into the shadows. He'd never been here before, but something about it felt familiar. The smell of wax on the tiled floors reminded him of Marine Corps boot camp on Parris Island.

He stopped at the end and faced a closed door. This was it; his only option moving forward. Ames clenched his fists and inhaled. He commanded his fear to settle as he slowly released his breath out and opened the door.

They were waiting for him.

CHAPTER FIVE

Graham woke with a start. His vision was blurry, and his wrists were bound to the armrests of a steel chair. The stench of bleach choked the air around him as he struggled to regain cognizance.

"Good morning, Sleeping Beauty," a voice said from the shadows. Graham didn't recognize the voice, but the gait of the man approaching was telling. The way he dragged one foot behind him like a dead tree limb sent a chill down Graham's spine. The stranger stepped into the light and revealed himself. "Someone tells me you lost another asset?"

"I'm working it," Graham replied. He resisted making eye contact with the man people in his circle only knew as "Zero". The burns and scars across the man's face were reminiscent of an over-the-top horror movie but staring at those eyes was like getting lost in Satan's gaze.

That almost would have been preferred.

"Working on it? My friend, you seem to be too well dressed for actively pursuing our weapons. Tell me, do you always lie when confronted with an uncomfortable truth?"

Graham swallowed, recognizing the metallic taste in his mouth from the concoction they had given him. "How long was I out?"

"Long enough," Zero replied. His voice was flat and unrevealing. If Graham was getting under his deformed skin, then he would likely never know.

He doubted the man was even human. No one who'd done what Zero was credited for could have a soul anymore.

"I have irons in the fire. There may be an update that I've missed because of this...ruse."

Zero straightened and paced under the hanging light. "Ruse? This is anything but, Mr. Graham. This is your reckoning."

"Reckoning? What have I done other than do as they've asked of me?" His voice was on the verge of going shrill. He knew what Zero's presence here was. The end of him if he didn't negotiate wisely.

"You have performed satisfactory until recently."

"Then ask that they give me a chance to correct my deviation. I only serve the Order. That's the deal. That's how it's always been."

Zero stopped and glared down at graham. Their eyes met for a fraction of a second. It was too long. "You serve yourself. That much has been known about you from day one. But you were a useful idiot, so they let you live. But now your usefulness is beginning to wane."

The marred man slid a blade from behind his back and examined it. Zero operated at a level beyond what most hitmen deemed sane. The typical hit was a one-and-done gunshot to the back of the head and leave the body to rot. Zero? He liked to make art with his kills.

Graham couldn't resist squirming. He'd seen what would happen and didn't want to feel what would undoubtably be a long night of agony. "Wait, give me a chance. I have the means to clear the deck. I just hadn't acted because I had hoped we could reclaim the soldiers before it came to this."

Zero paused. "Tell me and I'll forward your request to our masters."

Graham swallowed the bile rising in his throat. This monster had unbridled access to the upper echelon of the Order. He could do anything and everything with zero oversight; hence the moniker he was known by. Graham's life was in the hands of a mass murderer, but what choice did he have than to talk?

"The cybernetics respond to pulse magnetism. I have a weapon that operates at a precise frequency that renders them harmless. A soldier without arms and legs can hardly fight, right?" Graham hated himself for putting his cards on the table. Never would he have folded so easily.

But the alternative would have him filleted from gullet to gizzard, and that was the PG version.

Zero sheathed his blade and smirked. His deformed lips curled over yellowed teeth. "I'll relay this to our masters. Don't go anywhere until I return." Graham's heart nearly stopped at Zero's attempt at a joke. The emotionless killer making light of abducting and planning to kill another human being was beyond hellish.

Zero turned to leave the room and paused after opening the door. Yellow light burst into the room revealing the storage facility Graham was bound in. Tall, silver shelves rose around him filled with cookware and canned goods. Along one wall was stacks of ammo cases and giant storage cabinets.

How appropriate, he was in someone's home and that someone was a prepper.

"One last thing, Mr. Graham," Zero said, drawing his captive's attention. "I thought you might want to know that your friend Vivian has cooled from her earlier lust."

Graham looked at him questioningly before it clicked. "You killed her?"

Zero glanced back with a scarred, yet flat expression. "I did nothing, but her dealer aided in an overdose. Perhaps it's true what they say...drugs do kill."

He left the room and Graham sat in pitch darkness with news he didn't know how to process. He and Vivian were close once, but that felt like a lifetime ago.

Her dealings didn't match what Graham had been involved in and her recklessness was a liability. Dissolving their relationship had been a business move. He had been protecting himself more than her, but there was a since of mutual benefit by their parting.

Perhaps in a different life their relationship could have been something?

But that was the tragedy that no one talked about with life inside the Order. Everything that could have been would ultimately end in regret. Of course, people don't often tend to miss someone else until it's too late.

And then what?

That was the question Graham never sought to answer, and with the clock ticking towards his own demise, he might never know the answer.

———

"It's about time," Wills said sardonically as Ames entered. All three of them sat at a bar while Beth poured drinks. In the corner of the room a football game played on mute and the distinct smell of cigar smoke lingered in the air.

"You've been waiting for me?"

"You wanted us to trust you, and you wanted to trust us," Ryan replied, his eyes still glued to the game. "It's difficult to manage expectations, so I figured if you entered the cell willingly, then that was good enough faith for me. And if you weren't truly locked in that cage, then maybe you would be willing to trust us." he canted his head and stared at Ames. "Did it work?"

Ames shrugged. "It didn't hurt."

"That's good enough for now, I suppose. You want a drink?"

"Do you have anything dark?"

Ryan grinned as he looked at Beth. They spoke simultaneously, "Black Tooth Grin."

Beth got to pouring while Wills pulled a stool over for Ames.

"Do you like football?" Wills asked.

"Of course. Who doesn't?"

"That's not football," Beth quipped as she set the drink before Ames. "That's the wimpy American version of rugby."

"Ha! Spoken like a true Brit. Good thing we haven't cared about opinions from that side of the water in a few hundred years!" Wills spat mockingly.

Ames grinned. He recalled many times sitting with foreign military members and shooting the crap with one another. Each country had a rib to poke with the others, but the good guys always came together in a fight. Even if their ideas on sports and pop culture were ridiculous.

"Well, if we're done playing games, then maybe you can tell me what the plan is," Ames said.

The banter between present company died down and Ryan reluctantly switched off the television and faced Ames. "The plan is to take down Graham and the people he works for. As far as how we do that, well I'm all ears. It took three months of intel for us to discover you, so you can imagine how difficult it is to track his day-to-day routine without drawing attention to ourselves."

"Why would it take so long for you to discover me. I'm sure the attack made headlines."

"Yeah, front page for all of about six hours. In case you were wondering, you didn't make it," Wills said as he took another sip.

"Your whole team was reported as dead," Beth said. "I hate to say that it went under our radar because Graham usually operates differently. For some reason, he took more time to cover his tracks."

"When I got word about you, we had to devise a plan to lure you out. We can't breach Graham's compound, but we do have our ways of getting his attention."

"By threatening to release secret information?"

Ryan nodded. "We're all liabilities for him. We're the secret. All it takes is one of us exposing ourselves to the public and it would create a maelstrom of media attention he wouldn't be able to shake."

"Then why not shut him down that way?" Ames asked.

"Because that doesn't flush out the people pulling the strings," Beth answered. "Graham is a big target, but not *the* target."

"So, what do you want me for, or was all this a ruse?"

The other three straightened as they looked at Ames. He wished he could know what each was thinking, but the scowl on their faces said enough.

"First and foremost, we wanted to remove you from his control to better our odds. It might sound selfish but going toe to toe with a fellow super soldier isn't ideal. Second, we hoped you might have some insight you can share with us," Ryan answered.

"What makes you think I have any of that?"

"We were there same as you," Wills shot back. "The training was intense, but he pulled each of us under his wing at some point."

"He likes to gloat, to share his successes," Ryan interjected. "It might be his only weakness that we can exploit. At some point he told each of us about a piece of tech, or a location that could prove useful. Unfortunately, our personal intel is more than a year old. He covers his tracks well, so going to sniff those old leads won't prove as fruitful as intel coming straight from you."

Ames mulled it over. He should be angry. Graham set a trap for he and his team. Two men were dead, and Ames was erased from existence so Graham could turn him into a pet project. But for some reason disdain eluded him. He felt detached from his old life and thankful for the new one, as crazy as that sounded.

Still, he couldn't deny the fact that his best friend was killed in an attack with Graham's name on it. *What would Jackson do if he was in my boots?*

"He mentioned an annual party he was attending. There was a new client he expected to meet. Other than that, he didn't seem too thrilled about it," Ames said. "I don't know the location, but it should have taken place already."

Beth pulled a tablet from under the bar and set it on top. She typed furiously on the screen and shared her display on the large television in the corner. There was a satellite image of a compound within the walls of the capital.

"That's Le Crâne. It means 'the skull' in French. The gala was last night, but infiltrating that place is a nightmare. There's more security there than at the White House. Ryan was taken there before he defected."

Ames shot at glance at the older man and watched Ryan's jaw tighten. "What happened there?"

Ryan pulled his eyes from the screen and stared at Ames. "I saw the devil himself that night."

"Rise and shine, Buttercup."

Graham's eyes shot open as the door kicked open. He expected to see Zero, but instead his blurred eyes met a towering beast with hands bigger than Graham's head.

"Who are you?"

The beast stopped short, a dumb expression on his face before returning his attention to Graham. "They told me not to say. Just told me to let you go. But I get to kill you if you ask too many questions. That's one."

Graham wasn't about to ask how many questions would be too many. He doubted the man untying him knew either. He was simply playing the part they had given him. Graham knew the consequences for disobedience. He was sure this man did too.

His hands drooped forward as the man pulled away his restraints. They were numb to the touch as he kneaded them. He rose slowly from the chair, careful not to succumb to weariness and whatever concoction they had given him to knock him out. He still felt the effects of the drugs, mostly the fogginess in his head, but he was cognizant enough to not linger too long.

"Wait," the man said as Graham moved to walk away.

Graham turned to face him. Pleading eyes blinked at him and for a moment he felt sorry for the soul trapped in that monstrous body. The longer he stared, the more disfigurements he saw. His mind drifted to Frankenstein's monster. He was no better building his super soldiers, but at least they served a purpose. What was this man's calling to the Order, punching bag turned scary servant?

"Aren't you going to ask me which way the door is?"

"I don't want to ask too much of you," Graham replied, careful not to offend him.

"It's that way." He pointed to the right of the doorway. A gapped-tooth smile softened the terribleness of the beast.

"Thank you," Graham said. He hastened as he made his way for the exit. He had no idea where he was or how he would get home. But he knew two things: he had to find Ames, and he had to get out of the Order by any means necessary.

CHAPTER SIX

"Mr. Graham!" Stephanie shouted as he exited his personal elevator. "I've been trying to reach you."

He patted his pockets and frowned. "I seemed to have misplaced my cell. Is something wrong?" He continued towards his office, avoiding eye contact while fighting to hide the crippling fear looming over him. She didn't seem to notice.

"The team in Huntsville reported back. They didn't find anyone," she answered. There was a tinge of relief in her voice.

He chopped it up to her being a good person...or at least thinking she was. He wondered what her proximity to him did to taint her soul.

Misery loves company and somehow, he took comfort in the fact that he would ultimately drag her down with him. He shook the invasive thought from his mind and turned back to her. "Nothing at all?"

"No sir."

He sucked in a breath and uttered a silent curse. He was banking on them digging up Ames's remains and getting Zero off his back. Even if it was temporary. At least if Ames was dead, then Graham would be off the hook until he could recruit someone else. There were too many former recruits out in the wind and that didn't bode well for Graham's future.

"Have them search again. I want to be sure," Graham instructed.

"Sir, they've been at it for nearly forty-eight hours. There's nothing..."

Graham slammed his fist against his office door and took an aggressive step towards her. She shrunk back, a whimper puttering at her lips. "I said have them search again."

"Yes, sir," she muttered meekly.

Graham stared her down until she cowered away, tears streaming down her cheeks.

He watched her walk away, a small part of him ashamed of what he'd done, the other smiled wickedly. Graham stepped into his office and sighed at the shadow seated in the corner. "Does anyone know you're here?"

"Does anyone ever?"

"What do you want?" Graham asked as he took a seat at his desk. He shifted to turn on the lamp, but his visitor lifted a hand in warning. Graham settled back and steepled his fingers together, feigning nonchalance as his heart raced.

"I want to know what you're doing to get the Order off your back. Ames is in the wind, just like the others. I would say this program is a failure."

"You would say a lot of things. People fail you, it's the problem with humanity. Free will has its consequences. We choose our recruits based on criteria that makes them formidable. But it also makes them act outside the lines we want to confine them to."

"You use a lot of words to say nothing, David. The Order wants results and now their sending their meat puppet to threaten everything we've built—"

"I've built," Graham corrected.

Victor paused, then continued, "Their sending their meat puppet to trim the fat. That's going to lead them to you and then to me. You

53

might be the face, but you're not the heart of this business arrangement. And I, for one, want my heart to continue beating."

Graham smirked. "You act as if I don't."

"I act as if I don't know whether you're still the man you were...the man who got results."

"You're looking at him," Graham replied grimly.

Victor rose from his seat and leaned forward to meet Graham's gaze. It was like looking in a mirror. "Nice mask, but I wouldn't walk outside wearing it if I was you."

Victor scoffed at the remark. "Have you made your travel arrangements yet? I want my cut before Zero cuts you out."

Graham winced at the comment. Victor could be a real bastard at times, but that came with the territory. "I'll make them soon, but I don't think you need to worry about me being cut out. I have everything under control."

"We'll see," Victor replied. "We'll see."

Ames's jaw dropped. Before meeting Ryan, Ames suspected that anyone had the potential to lead a double life, but how the old soldier described Graham sent shivers down his spine.

"And you're certain it was him?"

Ryan sighed. "There was a lot going on, but our eyes met once he looked up from the young girl. His mouth was covered with blood, but there's no denying those eyes."

Ames cringed as he exchanged a look with Wills. "That story is all it took for me to walk away," he said after a breath. "Turned out that sinister freak targeted me like he did you. My life was exchanged to turn me into a super freak to help that man do the sick stuff Ryan was telling you about."

"And I was next in line to be his muscle...But I don't understand why you're going through such an effort to take on an organization that's larger than any of us could imagine. Why not just go after Graham and be done with it?"

Ryan shifted in his seat. "We come from a similar line of work. They recruit us with tall tales of preserving democracy and freeing the oppressed, but the actions we take are much darker than they ever put into words. Sure, we can take satisfaction in destroying a regime built on the death of innocence, but it's impossible not to see ourselves in our enemies. It's one thing to call a strike on the location of a terrorist cell...it's another to do so knowing there are women and children inside whose only crime was being forced into a marriage and being born into a cult. Where do we draw the line?"

"And you think by taking down the Order that it will give you redemption? That sounds like a personal crusade."

"Maybe it is, but we all know that no one else is lifting a finger to stop this evil from spreading. Maybe my life wasn't forfeit for nothing? Maybe my purpose was to be put back together so that others wouldn't be torn apart?" Ryan took another sip of his drink then sat it down.

Ames studied the man, trying to read any mark of deception he could from those cold, blue eyes. Ryan had seen something so horrific that Ames didn't want to imagine what else could be lurking behind the closed doors of the Order. "I thought I found my purpose when Graham called me to serve, but I unwittingly joined something I never would have if I'd known what was truly happening."

"It's a hard pill to swallow, I know," Ryan said. "But you can see why we're trying to bring down the whole organization?"

"Of course," Ames answered. "I'll do what I can to help."

"We appreciate that," Beth replied.

They stood in silence for a long time as the gears turned in Ames's head. Then a thought. "What about his secretary?"

"What about her?" Beth asked.

"I used to talk to her after my training. Graham always makes her stay late and one night I escorted her home. Maybe she can give us some intel?"

"Stephanie? She's in deep with Graham. I don't think she would risk her life like that," Ryan said.

"Maybe we can protect her?" Ames shot back.

"Or maybe she gets what's coming to her for being involved in his organization," Wills groaned. "She has to know what's up."

"Or she's blind to it?" Beth said.

Ryan rose and faced the group. "I guess there's only one way to find out." He eyed Ames and gave a curt nod. "Do you want to take lead on this?"

"Sure. I guess."

"Take Beth with you, just in case." Ryan addressed the Brit, "Track her for twelve hours before making contact. I don't want you to fall into a trap."

"I'm not leading you into a trap," Ames shot back, his voice tight.

"I know, but the Order has been a step ahead of us for months. They may have anticipated this move. Let's do our due diligence and not rush into it."

"Understood," Ames replied, settling back on his heels. His mind rushed with questions as to whether he was making the right decision. They weren't lying to him. The video of the airstrike proved that much. But Ryan's story, as compelling as it was, seemed too out of character for the Graham he knew. Was he really that kind of monster?

These people believed so. But belief wasn't always synonymous with truth. He felt it was best to be guarded with the struggle in his mind while he came to terms with everything.

As far as Ames was concerned, when it came to taking down Graham and the Order, he was along for the ride until Ryan and his team were proven wrong.

And for the sake of his sanity, he hoped to God they were.

Graham stepped out of his office, slowly closing the door to not alarm Stephanie. His aide sat dead faced, staring at nothing. She'd been like that a lot recently. He knew why but didn't want to say it out loud. He pushed it down like he did everything else.

"I took my anger out on you and I'm sorry," he said, barely rousing her from the distraction of her coping mechanism.

She canted her head to him, her eyes dilated. She was on the brink of sedation.

"How much did you take?"

She glanced down at her desk, to the tiny bag of dust. It only took a pinch and there was enough in that pouch to send her into eternity if she wasn't careful.

"May I?"

She nodded, the only change in expression was her quivering lips. Stephanie was behind that mask, somewhere, but out of touch with reality.

Graham took it, zipped it shut, and tucked it away. "Who gave this to you?"

Nothing.

He shook his head and paced the room while she sat statuesque. Graham's heart thrummed. Despite his efforts, his world was falling apart. It went beyond the super soldier program. The decay was everywhere. He saw it for what it was in her vacant stare.

He wasn't one for karma, but he believed that a reckoning was coming. Part of him craved it. The other part cowered in the shadows of his black soul.

"Will you come with me?" He extended his hand, and she took it. He led her away from her desk and towards a lounge room he reserved for his guests. Graham gingerly helped her lay on the leather chaise lounge then pulled off his jacket and placed it like a blanket over her. He hoped keeping her warm would help dissipate the effects of the drugs. He didn't think she had taken too much, but he couldn't be sure.

57

One thing was certain; now that she had started taking Portulaq, she would be caught in its snares. The only way to quit was to die.

"Another life ruined because of me," he muttered. Stephanie stirred but soon drifted off to sleep as he stood over her.

"You can blame yourself all you want, but how other people live their lives is on them."

Graham cut his eyes to his uninvited guest. Victor still wore the mask made in Graham's image. It would soon serve a purpose even his mentor knew nothing about, but he kept that to himself. "I thought you left."

"Not without ensuring you aren't about to do something stupid."

"Like what?" Graham asked. The only thing stupid was standing still too long and being an easy target for Zero. "I told you that I have business to attend to. My responsibilities don't change just because the Order wants to send a message to scare me. I've seen the worst of what they can do."

"I'd be careful if I were you. You're treading a slippery slope. Someone might think you want them to come after you."

Maybe I do. "Don't you have something else that's pressing?"

Victor smirked then pulled off the mask. "Be well brother. I don't want to lose a good thing."

You likely already have, Graham thought as the old man left the room. *And what isn't lost now will be soon.*

CHAPTER SEVEN

"I hate flying," Ames said as he crawled into the heli-pod. He took the rear seat while Beth assumed the controls in the front. He tapped his foot nervously as the engines sprang to life. Mechanical arms rotated outward as the propellers spun up. "Besides, this thing looks like a winged tic-tac."

"It's efficient," Beth replied as she went through her preflight checks.

"I'm sure it is." Ames kept his eyes on the horizon. In the distance purple clouds rolled, bringing with them a storm. It was the time of year when tornados were as frequent as bad traffic, and thanks to recent weather patterns, this area was a hotbed of twister activity. "How did you people get all this equipment anyway?"

"Money can buy you anything if you have enough of it," Beth replied. "Unfortunately, we don't have much of that, but we do have certain skillsets that makes acquiring such things a matter of motive."

"You stole it," he replied.

"Tactically acquired?" She looked in to the rearview and winked at Ames. "Or are we still calling it that?"

"We can call it whatever you want, but it still looks like a tic-tac."

Beth chortled. "Are you ready?"

"Sure."

Beth eased the heli-pod skyward and headed north, away from the rolling storm clouds, and straight into hell.

Stephanie woke with a start. She clutched the jacket draped over her as she blinked away the fuzziness in her eyes. Goosebumps freckled her skin as her teeth chattered.

"You're awake...finally," Graham said from across the room. She looked like he felt.

"How long was I out, sir?"

"Several hours. I was getting worried, so I attached a monitor to your arm while I watched over you."

She looked down at the device clasped to her arm and then back at him. "How cold is it in here? I'm freezing."

"You have a fever. I considered administering something for you, but I didn't want to act without your permission. Besides, I wasn't sure how it might react with the Portulaq."

Stephanie shied away. He saw shame on her face...and something else. Whatever it was, he knew questioning her wouldn't get him anywhere.

"Would you like a ride home?"

"Yes, sir," she answered. Her voice was strained.

Graham rose and reached out for her. She flinched, but then let him examine her face. "Your pupils are still dilated. Take these." He pulled out a pair of sunglasses and handed them to her. "I want you in top form tomorrow. We have pressing business."

"Yes, sir." She looked back at him, her green eyes a window of pain she fought to hide. He saw through it. "I'm sorry. I didn't mean to lose control. I only took a little bit."

"Shh," he whispered. He placed a reassuring hand on her shoulder as she looked up at him with wide eyes that he wouldn't soon forget. "Don't be sorry. Just go home and get some rest. I'll call the car around."

"Thank you," she replied, her voice cracking.

He stepped away, not wanting to look at her and lose his resolve. "You're welcome. Stay here. The car will be around shortly."

———

Ames led Beth to a narrow alley near Stephanie's apartment. The Brit pulled a small drone from her duffel and handed it to Ames while she retrieved a camera to mount onto it.

"How long of a battery does this thing have?" Ames asked as he affixed the camera to the mount. The whole assembly weighed less than two pounds and he wondered what a swarm of these drones could have accomplished on the battlefield.

"See the dark rectangles on the fuselage? Those are solar panels. Try not to smudge them with any fingerprints and we should be able to keep it flying all day." He repositioned his hold as a response and inspected it. It was clean.

Beth pulled the controller from the duffel and powered the unit on. Twin blades spun, lifting the drone from Ames's palm and sending it skyward with a quiet whir. Once the drone was above the building, Beth zoomed in on the apartment entrance and set the drone to hover mode.

"What time does she normally leave?"

"I usually saw her come to work between 8:30 and 8:45. It's a twenty-minute drive from here. Paul is her driver and should arrive to pick her up soon," Ames answered.

"Must be nice to have an employer send a car for you each day," Beth stated. "I guess it's a perk working for a monster?"

"I wouldn't call it a perk. I think it's because Graham likes to keep tabs on people. The car is monitored with recording equipment and a GPS beacon. He can track it to within ten feet and listen to any conversation in high-fidelity as if he were seated inside the cabin. If anything, it's a power move."

"Understood," Beth replied with an exhale. She manipulated the controls and zoomed in on a car rounding the corner. "I have a black limousine coming from the north side of the street."

"That's Paul. He'll turn around and have the passenger side door face the building."

Beth watched as the limo moved past the apartment. Less than a minute later it was back. The brakes screeched a little as it came to a stop and the rear passenger side door opened. Beth muttered under her breath as Stephanie stepped out of the limo.

"I thought you said she was being picked up?"

"She should be, why?"

Beth cut her eyes at Ames, "Because she's getting out of the limo."

Ames watched the screen. It was Stephanie, but there was something different about her. The otherwise confident woman appeared to look defeated and withdrawn. She was wearing a suit jacket that he could only assume was Graham's. "Something's off."

"I'll say."

Ames looked over to see Beth studying him. He knew what she was thinking. "I didn't lie to you. Any other day of the week and the schedule would have been the same. If she's being dropped off, then that means she was at the office all night. That means something was wrong."

"Like?"

Ames inhaled sharply. His mind raced with possibilities. "That's the million-dollar question. Maybe we should ask?"

"Ryan said to monitor her before confronting her," Beth shot back.

"Do you always listen to what he says?"

Beth gawked at him but said nothing. It was answer enough.

Ames entered the apartment complex from the rear, careful to be as inconspicuous as possible. This wasn't the roughest part of town, but it was chock full of people looking to make a quick buck by alerting the authorities of any irregularities. A nearly seven-foot tall, half-cybernetic super soldier would meet that classification.

"This is a bad idea," Beth said in his earpiece.

"What's bad about it? You saw her, she looked disheveled, not at all the way I'm used to seeing her."

"So that means not following an order so you can play the protector? How very chauvinistic of you," Beth replied indignantly.

"Stephanie is a friend, albeit a work friend, but a friend, nonetheless. I'm not reaching out due to some archaic sense of chivalry; I'm doing it because my friend looked like she needs help. Are you willing to let someone suffer to maintain an ideal that no one is really paying any attention to?"

"It was a joke, Ames. The only serious part of what I said was about defying Ryan's order."

"Oh." It was the only thing he could push past his teeth to say in response.

"Yeah, I don't play that activism card. Probably something you should know about me."

Ames smirked. "I don't either. Activism is just a word for people working hard at doing nothing. Most real change takes place behind closed doors. The ones that do it for sport are seeking something else."

"You should get on a soapbox and tell the world about it," Beth replied.

"I'll just talk to you about it since you brought it up."

"Let's not...I'm picking up movement on the other side of that wall to your left." Beth mumbled something under her breath that Ames couldn't make out. "Interference...Abort."

Ames stopped in his tracks and his eyes darted side to side, looking for an imminent threat. It came in the form of a double-barreled shotgun pressed against the back of his head.

"What's up, Snoopy?"

"Snoopy?"

"Yeah, you're snooping around where you don't belong, Lugnut."

"Are you trying to insult me?"

"I don't know. Is it wor..."

Ames spun around and drove the barrel of the shotgun out of the older man's hands and into the brick wall. It clamored to the ground a twisted mess. "No, it's not. Next time you pull a gun on someone, less talking, and more shooting."

"I..."

"Get out of here, now," Ames seethed.

The older man hobbled away, glancing back fearfully until he was out of sight.

"I must be losing my edge. I didn't hear him coming," Ames said.

"You said it, not me."

"Thanks for your support. What about the interference?"

"There's a static emanating from Stephanie's apartment. I think it's just a blocker, but it could be hiding something worse. This might not be a good idea."

Ames mulled it over. "I'm committed this far. I may as well see it through."

"Good luck and don't say I didn't; warn you," Beth replied.

"Noted." Ames moved slowly for the door. It was unlocked which didn't sit well with him. "Here goes nothing," he muttered to himself.

Stephanie lay crying in her bed when Ames slipped into her apartment. He walked gingerly on the carpeted floors, careful not to make a sound to startle her, or raise suspicion until he was sure they were alone. Once satisfied, he knocked lightly on her bedroom door before shoving it open.

Stephanie shot up, clutching a .9 mm close to her chest. Tear streaks ran down her face but did little to soften the anger in her eyes.

"Ames? What the hell! I nearly shot you."

He lifted his hands in surrender. "I was just checking on you," he said, treading lightly.

"*Nice one, bone head. You snuck inside a single woman's home? You should know better than that.*" Beth said through his earpiece. He ignored her.

"I'm sorry for barging in, I didn't know if you were alone."

"I thought you were dead," she replied as she let the barrel of her weapon droop. "Graham has been frantic since the warehouse strike."

"The one he called?"

"I don't know what you mean?" If she was lying, then she was good. "I was told things went south after you vanished. He said they found a beacon in one of the cases you took with you and that must be where they were hiding. You were nowhere to be found, so they called a strike. The ground crew was looking for survivors but found nothing."

"They won't find anything that isn't there," he replied, careful not to say too much in case anyone was listening in. "I don't mean to be rude, but you don't seem like yourself. Is everything all right?"

Stephanie shrugged as she looked away. She wiped at her face before saying, "I've been so stressed at work, I was just looking for an escape. I took something I shouldn't have."

"What?"

She cut her eyes at him, refusing to say it out loud.

She didn't have to.

He knew what it meant. She would be dependent on it to maintain any sense of normalcy until it took her life. He wanted to ask why, but that would only drive her anguish deeper. She was likely asking herself the same question.

"I'm sorry."

"Me too," she replied, regret heavy on her voice. She looked back at him, "I'm assuming you wanted something?"

He didn't want to change the subject, but she did it for him. Now he stood awkwardly, caught between her devastation and the inevitability of rocking her world a second time by asking her to turn on Graham. "I have some information that makes working for Graham problematic. I'm seeking information that might confirm what I've heard."

"What kind of information?"

Ames sighed. "The kind that makes me culpable for destroying innocent peoples' lives if I do nothing."

Her eyes widened. She knew something. "What are you looking for?"

"Graham has to have an impending business transaction coming up. If I can catch him in the act, then I'll stop him."

"You make it sound like you know for sure he's doing something wrong." Her hands clutched at the lapel of his jacket. Ames watched her rise out of bed and take a step towards the window. She peeked out of it before turning back to him. "Is it serious?"

"As a heart attack."

She frowned and dug her hands nervously into the jacket pockets. She came back with a black business card and handed it to Ames. "I found this on my way home. I don't think he intended me to find it."

He took it and eyed it. It was blank. He glanced back at her questioningly.

She then pulled a blacklight from her nightstand and shined it on the card revealing coordinates, a date, and time. "Someone thinks they're clever," she said sardonically.

Ames committed the information to memory and handed it back to her. "Pretend you didn't see it and return the jacket next time you see Graham." He took a step towards the door before turning back to her, "And this conversation never happened."

She smiled nervously. "What conversation," she replied. "Take care of yourself, I guess."

"You do the same," he replied as sirens sprang to life in the distance.

"Sounds like we're about to have company," she said.

"I met one of your neighbors," he replied. "It didn't go well."

"You better go, then. The Capital Police are in Graham's pockets," she warned.

He nodded. "Who isn't?"

She shrugged.

"Thank you." Ames said as he left her behind. He picked up the pace as the sirens drew closer. He had hoped things wouldn't be so dire for Stephanie, but he couldn't dwell on that now. He had to focus on stopping Graham however that might happen. Maybe with him out of the way, it would grant her the freedom to move on in peace.

It was a long shot, but it was all the hope she had, as sad as it was to admit.

"I should have done something sooner," he hissed as he climbed over the wall surrounding the property and ran through the parking lot. "It shouldn't have come to this."

CHAPTER EIGHT

Beth and Ames ran for the heli-pod as sirens rang and tires screeched outside Stephanie's apartment. Overhead, the whir of twin propellers droned.

"Do you think it was the old man?" Ames asked as they skidded to a stop behind an old warehouse. The brick structure was crumbling apart as grit rained down from the ambient vibrations of the approaching craft.

"I would assume so, but we can't rule out her apartment being bugged. Maybe if I had more time to scan it properly, we could be sure."

She didn't have to look at him for Ames to know it was a jab in his direction. He acted on his convictions, and he certainly wasn't military anymore. Ryan's authority began and ended where Ames allowed it. "We have the information we need. That's something."

"Unless it's compromised, then we have nothing," Beth shot back. The craft zoomed overhead and disappeared over the tops of the large pines growing wildly in the crumpled remains of a parking lot half a century past its prime. "Let's go."

They sprinted towards the cropping of trees and stayed hidden under the canopy as they made their way to the heli-pod. They found it as they left it, partially hidden under a tattered tarp. Ames ripped it off and let the gusts of wind claim it while Beth climbed into the seat and brought it to life. Ames jumped in moments before she started lift off.

He pulled on the headset to hear Beth reciting her preflight procedures while already airborne. He left her to it as he scanned the skies for their pursuers. He didn't have to look long.

"Seven-o'clock," he said.

Beth mumbled a curse and slammed the throttle. The craft jerked under the added torque and sent them eastward. G-forces sent a rush of blood to their extremities, and they grunted as they performed their Anti-G Straining Maneuver to keep conscious until the forces leveled out.

Once at an appropriate altitude, Beth began evasive maneuvers, dipping between dense clouds while allowing the onboard jammer to do the bulk of the work. "They can't shoot us if they can't see us," she said.

"But they still know we're here," Ames warned as he watched the RADAR. The enemy craft drew closer to their position. The readout provided airspeed and altitude information which placed their pursuers less than eight-hundred feet above them. It was too close for comfort given the limited visibility and the encroaching storm.

As the craft moved over them, the twin propellers partially dissipated their cloud cover.

Someone in the other cockpit noticed, and the banked craft sharply.

"They made us," Ames barked. He watched as the craft positioned itself to fire. At this range there was no way he could miss. "Evade!"

"There's no time," Beth shot back.

She cranked the heli-pod skyward and pointed the nose at their enemy. The heli-pod trembled under the strain. To Ames's shock, she engaged air-to-air weapons and spat fire from the 20 mm cannon.

Tracer rounds spewed wildly, zipping past the craft until Beth had the heli-pod under control. She fired off another round. The heli-pod convulsed as hellfire rained down on the combatant. Ames held his breath, refusing to blink as he watched blood splatter across the windscreen of the craft. The cabin filled with smoke while the craft hung limply for a fraction of a moment, listing precariously before dropping to the ground.

Ames watched it descend, disintegrating into a ball of fire in the rubble below.

Until that moment, he thought the war Ryan and his team waged was one of principle. He thought there was a way to go against the Order without the need to take human lives. But he just watched the first casualty combust, he knew there was no going back.

Whether he liked it or not, he had picked a side. He just hoped it was the right one.

***

Graham slammed his fist on his desk. "Get a RADAR lock on that craft," he seethed.

"They're jamming, sir. We can't get a lock on it."

Graham bared his teeth. "I want results, Captain, not excuses."

Muffled voices spoke away from the mic before a response, "We can track it via satellite and destroy it once it's landed."

"Not good enough. I want the people inside annihilated. The heli-pod itself is inconsequential." he watched the video feed, willing something to strike his enemy down.

"They disappeared in the clouds, sir."

"Then go after them."

"But..."

"But nothing. That's an order." Graham never let his lack of military authority prevent him from making calls. Besides, he funded half the military operations anyway. If money wasn't authority enough, then what was?

"Yes, sir," the Air Force Captain replied reluctantly. His hesitation was displayed on the screen as he slowly maneuvered the craft towards the dense clouds.

"Activate perimeter cams," Graham said. "I don't want to miss them."

The captain did as was ordered without a word. Eight small windows opened on the display giving a full perimeter view around, above, and below the craft. If the heli-pod was in the area, they would see it.

The craft rose above the clouds as the pilot scanned the area. As the prop wash dissipated the mist, the captain continued on an eastward heading until something came into view on display port six.

"There!" Graham barked.

The craft stopped on a dime and began to rotate to face the combatant. Graham waited expectantly. In mere seconds his worries would be over.

"I've got a lock," the captain said, but Graham wasn't listening. Instead, his focus was on the heli-pod rising from its previous position and the bark of fire spouting from its twin cannons.

Within seconds all displays went dark. There was radio silence. And graham knew he had lost once again.

"Sonofa..." He bit his tongue.

"I'm sorry, David," Secretary Sanders said over the com. "I thought it was a solid plan."

There weren't words for an adequate response to what Graham was feeling. There was only the immediate need for a cover story. "Training accident," he muttered.

"Of course," Sanders replied. "I'll discuss it with our public affairs office."

"Did we get a satellite lock on the craft?"

Words were exchanged on the other line before Sanders responded, "It was lost once the aircraft went down."

Of course, it was. "I'm compromised," Graham said after several moments of silence. Bile rose in his throat when saying it out loud, but he couldn't hide from it. "I need to wipe the slate clean."

There was a click on the com before Sanders spoke again, "I ended the conference call. It's just us."

Graham didn't care. He was carrying a burden that no one could ever realize, present company included. "She gave them the information. She betrayed me like I was nothing to her. I once commanded more respect...more fear than that."

"She'll be taken care of."

Those words meant too little to acknowledge. "Where do we go from here?"

"He expects a delivery. I say we give him one. If they show up, then that's his problem," Sanders replied. "Besides, you can always pretend to be someone else."

It wasn't a bad plan. If anything, it was satisfying to think that his misfortune could spread to someone much worse, and more deserving. By the time they figured out he was there, he would be long gone. "Make the arrangements. I have something I need to take care of."

"Anything I need to know about?"

"Not yet. I'll be in touch." Graham ended the connection and rose from his seat. His heart raced, reminding him of his recent bout with palpitations. He was supposed to limit the stress in his life, not compound it. He doubted he would live long enough for natural causes to be much of an issue. Still, he had to hope for a miracle. Or for someone to make it quick.

Mercy was for better men than him, though.

He reached to switch off the monitor. The inky blackness stared back at him, showing his grim reflection. It painted him as he saw himself. Deformed by darkness. His lips curled with rage as he gripped the side of the monitor, flinging it from the desk and sending it shattering to the floor.

He gawked at it as if someone else had done the damage.

It was always someone else.

That was the lie he believed for so long, but he couldn't stomach it any longer.

It was high time he acknowledged the truth. No matter how painful it was.

———

Ames slammed the heli-pod hatch and stomped away. His heart raced and bile periodically crept into his throat. He was a man comfortable with war, but it was different when the enemy wasn't in your own backyard.

"I'm sorry, I didn't have a choice," Beth said as she ran after him.

Ames lifted his hand to silence her before spitting rancid acid from his lips to get the taste out of his mouth. "I'm not angry. I'm just freaked out by the fact weapons of war were used by our own people against us. They didn't even try to identify us before they prepared to shoot."

Beth stood next to him but kept quiet as he purged himself once more. He wished she would look away.

"I guess they knew it was us?" Ames asked.

She nodded. "It wasn't our first rendezvous with Graham's military support. They'll pretend this was a tragic training mission...like last time."

He cut his eyes at her, "Last time?"

The SAS agent sighed and acknowledged, "Before we recruited Wills, we had a run in. It was a quick spat, over in a matter of seconds. We were ambushed and Ryan was trapped. A small detail of Marines closed in on him, so Ryan deployed a highly volatile concussion round. It damaged the surrounding structure and sent it crashing down. Two of the men were killed."

Ames frowned. He remembered reading about it. The details were precisely as she said, a concussion round started a chain reaction when the nearby structures caved in. The manufacturer was blamed for a bad batch of ordnance. He often wondered if they were just the easy scapegoat. Now he knew.

Ryan rushed out of the building with Wills hot on his heels. "What happened to surveilling the target before engaging?" The question shot from his lips oozed with an accusing tone.

Ames squared up to the older man, fists balled tightly. "I made a call and I'd do it again. I got the information you wanted."

"And how many lives did it cost?" Ryan snapped.

Ames wanted to answer, but something about the way Ryan posed the question unsettled him. "What did we miss?"

Ryan cracked his neck. His large shoulders rose and fell with each deep breath as he struggled to find the words.

Wills stepped in for him. "There was a raid on the apartment complex. After you shot down the craft, they leveled the building with everyone inside."

"What?" Ames asked. His knees buckled, nearly sending him to the ground. "Stephanie?"

"I'm sorry, man." Wills stepped closer and placed a hand on Ames's shoulder.

"I killed her." Ames choked on his words. There are casualties in every war, but what kind of evil would destroy that many lives?

"It's being framed as a training accident. The Air Force is burdening the responsibility, but we know better. Graham, or someone tied to him, made the call," Ryan said.

"What do we do, now?" Beth asked.

Ryan looked at her and answered, "If the information is solid, then we follow it. We take out anyone and everyone involved in this organization, but we do it my way. Surveillance first. Strike second."

Ames eyed the older man. Ryan all but put the blame on Ames. Maybe it was justified, but it hurt just the same. He wondered if the situation was reversed, if he would do the same. Likely so. "Fine. We'll do it your way," Ames said, and he meant every word.

CHAPTER NINE

"How soon?" Graham asked. He drummed his fingers on his desk expectantly. His mind raced in two places at once. At every turn his life was falling apart. Decisions were made for him that ripped what little heart he had to shreds. And now he was bedding with an enemy just to keep his head above water.

"Make it happen. I'll meet you there."

Graham ended the call and reclined back in his seat. Exhaustion sent another wave of trembling down his extremities. The last time he had anything resembling sleep he was strapped to a chair and on the verge of being killed. That was slightly more than a day ago but felt like it could have been much longer.

He sniffed himself and pulled back repulsively. "I need a hot shower and a year to sleep this off," he mumbled as he laboriously rose from his desk. He had set everything in motion to ensure his client's needs were met. Despite the short turnaround, he was able to meet the demands, as hideous as they were. "God knows we deserve what's coming to us," he said as he crossed the room, stopping to gawk at the weary man in the mirror. He looked like death warmed over. He wasn't far from feeling like it either.

Graham disappeared into a faux doorway leading to his personal quarters. He didn't have the energy to go home. Plus, he knew they would be waiting for him there. It was best to keep some distance. He was safer here. At least that's what he chose to believe. Anything was better than being on edge and waiting for Zero to arrive to finish the job as promised.

As near as Graham could tell, in less than twenty-four hours his fate would be known. If he succeeded in taking out his rogue soldiers, then perhaps the Order would forgive his missteps. If not, then it didn't matter who the trigger man was, the result would be the same.

There was something grimly satisfying in acknowledging that.

He pulled his clothes off and dropped them to the floor as he stepped into the walk-in shower. It was larger than some peoples' bedrooms, and twice as luxurious as most he'd seen in the homes of his contemporaries. Still, it dulled in comparison to what waited for him at home. But it would do.

Graham sat on the bench inside the shower and leaned against the stone-tiled wall, losing himself in the rush of hot water pouring over his aching body. "I could die here now and not care."

You should.

His eyes popped open and looked across the room, trying to see past the steamy glass of the shower walls. He saw no one, but he felt the presence that always accompanied the voices. That haunting feeling followed him everywhere he went. It was just one of dozens of burdens he could never rid himself of.

The voice was right, though. Dying here would save anyone else the effort, but he knew deep down that he still wouldn't find peace.

Ames sat on the other side of the room while the rest of the team stewed bitterly in their own little worlds. Wills sharpened a knife in the far corner, mumbling to himself between puffs of a cigar. Plumes of smoke wafted around him like snakes slithering towards the air vent above.

Beth sat at a table tapping on a tablet. Her lips were a constant frown as she researched the area Stephanie had shown Ames on the business card from Graham's jacket. It was their only lead, and they would follow it to certain doom if it meant avenging the innocent people in what was left of the smoking apartment complex.

Which brought Ames's attention to Ryan who stared at the news report on the television mounted to the wall. He had it on mute, but the closed captioning and images showed the destruction that Ames's arrogance had led to.

It was a miracle of God that anyone made their way out. Two unidentified survivors were being lauded in the most recent report, but the death toll was expected to be in the dozens. Ames's stomach churned, but there was nothing left to come back up. He was spent, emotionally and physically. So instead, he sat there and hated himself while the others preoccupied themselves with the next step in the mission.

It was wrong, but he couldn't dig himself out. Not yet.

A curse sprang from his lips as he rose and left the room. No one paid him any attention, not that he was seeking it any way.

Ames made his way to the tightly packed hangar space. The heli-pod was already folded up and parked in its spot. Massive crates of weapons and ammunition were stacked three high in uniform rows. Each was labeled by the contents inside. He didn't stop until he found the one with the big guns.

"M/A-297R," Wills said, drawing Ames's attention. "It gets the job done, but it isn't very personal."

"What's your point?"

Wills smirked, "Funny you should ask." He extended the blades built into his cybernetic arms. They protruded from his forearms and extended in a partial arc over his hand, coming to a sharp, glinting point. Wills moved it around and let the lighting above reflect at Ames who stood unamused. "It gets really personal when you can hear their last breath fade from their body. That's the easiest way to confirm your kill."

Ames clinched his jaw. He wasn't in the mood for exchanging bravado in the form of trade secrets. "Everyone in this building has confirmed kills. We share that just like we share our lives being torn apart by Graham and the Order."

"What about Beth?" Wills asked. "She's never said anything other than having discovered that Graham was behind the attacks that destroyed our lives."

Ames smirked. "You think you're so smart, but you missed the obvious," he said.

Wills stared back in puzzlement. "What's so obvious?"

"That I lost someone to Graham's role in the Order," Beth answered as she stepped into the hangar. "How did you know?"

Ames shrugged. "I can read people. Some carry their story on the outside. Others bury it inside. It's obvious you're the latter. You work with an intensity that made me think you had a personal connection to the mission. It goes further than wanting to do the right thing. You're seeking vengeance just like them."

"And what about you?" Beth asked. "Have you psychoanalyzed yourself yet?"

"Yeah. I'm an idiot who runs on pride. But I see where that leads. It affects more than me."

"So, what are you going to do about it?" Beth stood with her arms folded over her chest staring at Ames.

He looked back at the crate and ran a hand along the smooth, hard surface. "I think I'll take a few of these and lay waste to the people turning innocent lives into nightmares. Then, when all that's over, I'll bring the entire Order crashing down."

"That's big talk for a glory hog," Wills said.

Ames glanced back at him and said, "Good thing I'm not doing it alone."

The last time Ames stepped foot off a plane in the Middle East was for his final deployment with the Marine Corps. There was a time he thought he'd never see the brilliant haze of intense heat radiating off the ground surfaces again. It took time for his eyes to adjust past the steady fog. Optical illusion, or not, it was still distracting. Even in the city.

"Tell me again why we couldn't just teleport here?" Ames asked.

"The technology necessary to teleport this far haven't been developed yet. If we tried it then we would have plopped into the Atlantic Ocean and drowned," Beth answered as she went to fetch her luggage.

"I'm not a good swimmer," Wills replied as he lifted his metal arms. "I sink like a rock."

"Good to know,' Ames said as a man approached.

"Welcome to Dubai, Gentlemen," a Saudi man greeted them in perfect English. He shoved his dark sunglasses higher up his nose as he gave a toothy grin to the assembled team. "I trust your flight went well." There was a touch of an accent that gave Ames the impression he hadn't spent much of his life in his native land.

"And lady," Beth replied with a grin as she pulled her suitcase on wheels behind her. This was a military operation, but she packed like it was a vacation.

"Ah, Beth, so good to see you again my friend." They embraced while the men in the group shared glances with one another.

"How's your mother?" Beth asked.

"Happy to have me home again. Thank you for your generosity."

Beth looked to the guys and made introductions. "This is Abdel, Abe for short. He was a foreign national aiding the SAS for several years as an interpreter. I asked him to help in case we need it."

"I'm not sure an interpreter is necessary. Once we see money exchanged for people, it's pretty cut and dry from there," Wills replied.

"Yes, well my skillset goes beyond that of a typical interpreter," Abe replied. "I am a skilled marksman as well."

"Plus, he knows the area," Beth added.

"Sounds good to me," Ryan replied as he glared at his watch. "We have less than twenty-four hours before the meeting is to take place. We should get the lay of the land and make a plan sooner rather than later."

"I have aerial imaging to aid us, but that could change depending on which ships are in port," Beth said.

"I thought the meeting would be on land somewhere," Ames replied.

"I did too, but the coordinates were for a pier and when I checked the satellite imaging, I saw an aircraft carrier ported there, the *USS Intrepid*."

The ship was on its maiden voyage, so of course it would stop in every major port for a dignitary visit. It was good cover for a number of things. But it also made it difficult for the team to track their target given the added security. "So, what's our first step?" Ames asked.

Wills rubbed at his stomach. "Lunch?"

"Sure," Ryan replied. "Do you have any suggestions, Abe?"

Abe smiled. "Do you like Shawarmas?"

Ryan grinned. "Who doesn't?"

Graham entered the terminal through his private entrance. The smell of JP-8 brought back memories of the years he traveled abroad, jumping from country to country to do the bidding of the Order. Those were much better times than he often gave them credit for, though he hardly understood his purpose in their world at the time. He often wished he could cut himself off from those memories and the guilt they brought upon him. Though it would hardly make what he had to do any easier.

"Good morning, Mr. Graham. Is it just you flying with us today?" The stewardess was young and wore a smile full of life. "It's just me," he replied. He tried to return the pleasantry, but assumed she knew it was as fake as it felt.

Her expression never wavered. Instead, she simply scanned his passport and tagged his belongings. "The captain will board in fifteen minutes. Would you like me to help you with your luggage?"

"That's all right, I can manage," he said. He held a simple duffle with enough clothing to get him through an extended layover. His wealth provided him the means to have homes scattered around the globe, and where he was going was no exception. It was a matter of habit that he even brought the carry-on with him.

"Very well. You can board at your leisure," the young woman replied.

Graham nodded courteously and stepped past her towards his private plane. The Boeing 777X sat on the tarmac, ladder extended down to the red carpet the crew had rolled out for him. It was a massive aircraft for one man to take, but he was hardly the only passenger. He swallowed a knot forming in his throat and took the first step towards the entrance. He wouldn't have to lay eyes on the freight in the belly of the craft, but knowing it was there unsettled him.

"I wish I was anywhere but here," he said to no one.

Then he boarded.

Inside, the plane was adorned with dozens of photos depicting Graham with various world leaders. It was a veritable who's who and many of them were long out of power. He made his way to the center section of the plane where faux walls were constructed to provide a luxurious office space. He had no intention of working during the flight, but neither did he intend to sleep.

He opened the door and was greeted by a friendly smile. "I heard you had an inconvenient mole?" Victor said, making light of Graham's harrowing evening.

Graham stifled a sigh and took a seat across from the old man. He let his duffle drop to the floor as he reclined in the high-backed chair. "You could say that."

"Well, it all got sorted out in the end, so that's a good thing. I caught wind of your itinerary and thought you could use the company."

Graham kept his mouth shut. Victor shouldn't have had access to that information, yet here he was less than six feet away. It could have been Stephanie, but she wouldn't have given that information freely. Victor came by that knowledge some other way. *Maybe there's more than one person with loose lips*, Graham thought as the old man pulled a cigar from his pocket. Victor gestured with it and Graham nodded his consent, not that it would have mattered any way.

"Dubai huh? I haven't been there in years, not since that plane was hijacked."

"It never took off and the attempted hijackers were taken down without incident. I don't think that qualifies as an actual hijacking. Besides, they were refugees fleeing their country and became desperate when asked for their papers. It was more sad than tragic." Graham waved off a tendril of cigar smoke as Victor puffed on it. The older man noticed but made no effort to lessen the inconvenience.

"Yes, so sad how the situation resolved itself," Victor replied. His grin betrayed his words and Graham got the notion he knew more about the outcome than was reported. It was bait he wasn't going to take.

"Do you have plans for our trip, or just wanting to tag along?"

Victor kept puffing and rolling the cigar as he stared at the ceiling. "You know, I never was into babysitting." He cut his eyes at Graham and continued, "It's beneath me." Victor rose and looked down at the tycoon whose power was slipping by the minute. "My suggestion is don't be seen. Send someone in your stead to minimize your direct involvement. If I can't find you, then neither can he."

Graham stared up at the old man. He wished he was stunned, but his presence and warning were to be expected given the circumstances. "Thanks for the advice."

"Heed it, kid, and I'll see you on the other side."

Graham nodded. It was acknowledgement enough. He

watched Victor step out of the office, his smoky trail following him towards the exit, and Graham wondered if that might be their last goodbye.

———

Abe could have been a race car driver in another life. Ames gripped the handhold on the rear drivers' side door with a white knuckled grip as he made quick kilometer to miles-per-hour calculations. Sure, it wasn't just the going fast part, but the speedometer was pegged in less than desirable conditions. Sand washed over the highway in waves, obscuring the lines while Abe and other drivers of outlandishly expensive cars screamed towards the central hub of Dubai.

The city stretched well past its former borders, a token to the oil money former princes invested in to put their names in the history books. They were no more remembered than the dullest of American presidents, before and after the last Great War. But not for a lack of trying.

"Do we have to go this fast?" Ames asked as he leaned towards Wills. His eyes caught Abe's in the rear-view mirror, and he could have sworn the Arab man winked at him.

"What's the matter, still confined to the old ways in America, my friend?" Abe asked with a chesty laugh.

He wasn't wrong. America was conservative to change with speed limits only increasing to ninety miles-per-hour in the flatter lands of the Midwest. Most states still had laws requiring governors on motor vehicles to limit speeds. A sentiment that never made its way to other parts of the world.

"I just like to get where I'm going still breathing," Ames quipped.

Abe simply laughed and nudged the accelerator a bit. If he had a death wish, then he was certainly in the right line of work.

"This is a long drive for Shawarma," Ryan said, obviously hiding his nerves with a low, grunting voice.

"Only the best for my friends," Abe said. His tone shifted and hit Ames the wrong way. He shared a sideways glance with Ryan.

"What do you mean by that?" Ryan asked, leaning towards the driver with a clenched fist.

Beth shot a sideways glance at her friend. Abe removed his sunglasses and her eyes widened when he looked back at her. "What happened to you?"

He responded by gunning it. The car lurched, fishtailing to one side as it fought for traction on the sandy road.

"Abe, stop this," Beth warned. Her voice was strained.

Abe reached for the console and flipped a switch. A glass divider rose between the front and rear of the vehicle. Ryan leaped forward but was restrained by his seatbelt. By the time he unlatched it, the divider was up, leaving Abe alone with Beth.

All three men in the rear slammed their fists into the glass but couldn't crack it.

"What is this?" Ryan barked, but his words went unheard. Instead, a mist formed around them and choked them out.

It was a fast-acting agent. The others succumbed to it first, but Ames punched the glass several more times before it took him, and he slumped into a heap in the back seat.

———

The 777X took off from BWI airport for its first leg to London. Sunlight reflected off the surface of the North Atlantic blindingly, but Graham kept his gaze out the window with stoic stubbornness. It was one trait he knew he had inherited from his father. The rest was a mystery that death did not want revealed.

A younger Graham often wondered what it would be like to see his parents in the afterlife. Years had passed since then and he hoped beyond anything that all that welcomed him, and his kind was bitter, empty darkness.

He deserved worse.

They all did.

Graham pulled his cell from his jacket pocket and checked for messages. There were none which was unusual given the circumstances. "You would think with everything at stake, that someone would be hounding me for information," he grumbled.

A light knock at the door drew his attention to the young stewardess. "Mr. Graham," she said with a sweet enthusiasm as manicured as her makeup was. "Is there anything I can do to be of service to you?"

The innuendo was slight. The dullness in her eyes betrayed her tone and he could tell that she knew in her soul she was as much a slave as the caged people below decks. The only difference was that the stewardess was paid.

"I'm good for now," he answered.

Her brow furrowed as she gingerly stepped back. "Let me know if you change your mind," she replied.

"I will," he answered, trying to put her at ease with a smile. Instead, she scurried away like a scolded child.

Graham dropped into his seat and steepled his fingers under his chin. "We've cultivated a society that puts their worth with how desirable they are to others, only to be offended when someone doesn't take advantage of them," he said to no one as he pulled a keyboard tray from under the desk. He powered it on, and a monitor slowly rose from the tabletop. He typed in a few commands until he was in his personal account.

Graham opened the latest message from Secretary Sanders. It was a situational report on Stephanie's apartment complex. He combed through it looking for the survivors list. There were only three names, none of them familiar to him. He grit his teeth as he reviewed the document. Such a waste of life, and for what?

His pride?

No...*theirs*.

He switched the computer off in disgust. He had spent most of his adult life wallowing in the world of decayed morality and still couldn't find his way away from the stench. It was no wonder he was so miserable. He'd overstayed his welcome in this life and it was finally starting to show. Unfortunately, it only destroyed those around him and not those responsible for the disease they plagued on the Earth.

It was past time for that to change. People like Stephanie should not have been victims of his existence. She never deserved what happened to her. Neither had a lot of people.

"It should've been me," he declared. 'It should've been me."

CHAPTER TEN

Ames woke to a dimly lit room. His arms and legs were strapped to a gurney and tubes ran from machines into the thick veins in his neck. A metallic taste in his mouth Lingered from the knockout gas Abe had used against him.

His eyes darted to each side of the room, taking in his surroundings. Even with the cybernetic augmentations, his vision struggled to adjust. Just another effect of the gas.

"So glad to have you awake, Mr. Ames," a voice sounded from overhead speakers.

Ames followed the line of wiring going from the sound system to an overhead camera. It's blinking red light was a beacon that he was being watched. "I assume you're listening," he said indignantly.

"We are."

"What's the meaning of this?" A wave of nausea cramped his sides.

"To put it plainly, we detected foreign devices contained within your augmentations."

"You think I'm a spy," Ames replied.

"We think you're a danger to our operations, yes," the voice replied. It wasn't Abe, but that meant little to him in his current state. Ames pulled against his restraints before being overcome with exhaustion.

"My team has its own operation. My objective is to see it through. Whatever your team is doing here is irrelevant to me." Ames bit back the bitterness he felt being restrained. He would settle for peace if they released him. Otherwise, he wanted heads to roll.

"Who's to say our interests are not matched?"

"Apparently, you," he spat. "You're the one holding me prisoner."

"What of the foreign material in your augmentations?"

Ames glared at the camera, "I don't know what you're talking about."

"Is it a tracker?"

"It could be. Or it could be nothing. The only additions to my cybernetics to my knowledge are the charging devices on my wrists. But those are plainly evident if you paid any attention."

"The signal is coming from the devices in your ears," the voice replied.

"Seriously?" Ames tugged on his restraints but thought better of it. "They're hearing aids, Jerkwad. I lost my hearing in the explosion that took the rest of my body."

Silence followed before the door to the room opened to reveal the silhouette of a woman. She walked in slowly until the light revealed her features.

"What is this, Beth? I thought I was one of you?"

She reached up and released his restraints. "That's what I told them." She nodded her head towards a group of people standing beyond the threshold of the door. Most were armed while others stood leaning against the wall with their arms crossed. He saw Abe standing there with the sunglasses pushed up onto his forehead. His own cybernetic scanned over Ames with an infrared light.

"Am I everyone's enemy?"

Beth shrugged. "I guess it's hard to trust anything coming from a common enemy. I hope you won't hold it against them. They are our friends."

Ames glared at the Saudi team before glancing down at Beth. "I can't make any promises."

"Understood," Beth turned to the Saudis with an eyebrow raised, "Are we done here?"

The man next to Abe nodded. "I wish our reunion would have been under better circumstances, Beth." He turned to Abe and spoke in Arabic.

Ames watched as the men exchanged words, barely above a whisper, but the tinge of agitation coming from the senior man in the group was evident regardless of what language was being spoken.

Abe stepped into the room and pushed his hair out of his face. "I'm sorry. I had orders that anything out of the ordinary had to be cleared. I trust Beth, but I had to make the best decision for my people." It was a more sincere apology than most Ames had heard in his life, especially from someone who wore the uniform, past or present.

"Thanks," he said gruffly. "Where's the rest of the team? We have a short window."

"This way," Abe instructed as he led them from the room. Ames glanced down the hallway to see a group of Saudis eyeing him. They didn't trust him and no amount of influence from their SAS friend would change that. Still, they relented enough to let him go, so he couldn't hold that against them.

Abe led them to a lounge area with soft Arabic pop music playing over the speakers. Wills was dozed out on the couch and Ryan sat stoically; his eyes boring at Abe with as much indignation as Ames had felt when he woke up strapped to a gurney.

"Are we done here?" Ryan asked, his words echoing Ames's own.

"Yes, we can continue on your mission," Abe replied.

"I still haven't eaten that shawarma you promised me, so you better be buying," Wills said. His eyes were still closed, but a smirk spread on his lips.

"You can send me the bill," Abe replied, "But no promises on whether I'll pay for it."

Wills rose from the couch and walked up to Ames. He gestured at Abe and said, "This country has some of the richest tightwads I've ever met."

Ames's lips curled at the remark, but mostly to how low Abe's jaw dropped as a result. Just because they had to play nice didn't mean they couldn't play at all, and it was clear Wills and Ryan were just as ticked as he was. The day could only get more entertaining from here.

———

The 777X landed in London, stirring Graham from his slumber. He straightened in his seat and craned his neck to relieve the stiffness formed by slumping in the chair. As he straightened himself out, the stewardess rapped on the door and pushed it open.

"Mr. Graham, we're expecting an hour window before takeoff. Do you wish to disembark the aircraft?"

He shook his head. It was better to stay put then to get lost in the busy terminal. Besides, he had a familiar face, and this trip wasn't a public one. "I'll be fine here, thank you."

"Just so you're aware, we do have a party of two boarding. It was a last-minute change to the itinerary."

Graham's eyes narrowed. He'd made no such changes. "Can you remind me who the guests are? It seems to have slipped my mind," he said. It was weak as lies went, but she took the bait.

"Lev and Anya."

Graham frowned. "What do they want?" he asked, not meaning to say it out loud.

"I'm sorry?"

"I can't believe I forgot," he feigned repetition and rose from his seat. He took a dozen steps towards the door as she shifted to make room for him to exit. Graham stopped in front of her and glanced down at the small name tag on her vest lapel. "Sarah, do you know what time they are boarding?"

She read over the itinerary and looked up at him with emerald, green eyes. He wanted to get lost in them, but he couldn't get close to anyone. A stronger man would have chastised himself for the dangerous walk he put himself through. Love was a weakness that would be used against him. Even a plaything could be dangled like bait.

"About twenty minutes from now."

"Good. I'll be ready to greet them. I'll just take a few minutes to freshen up. Will you wait for me before allowing them to board?"

Sarah nodded. "Certainly, Mr. Graham."

He smiled. "Thank you."

Graham pushed past her and down the narrow passage of the 777X before entering a private cabin. He shifted one of the faux wooden panels to reveal a keypad and punched in his code. A moment later, the lock clicked and lowered a hidden compartment from the overhead. Graham reached inside and pulled a pistol from the compartment. He reached in a second time to retrieve a holster and clipped it to the back of his hip so his jacket would cover it.

Graham glanced at the time before counting the rounds in the primitive firearm. It was a revolver made of carbon fiber which held only six rounds, but it would have to be enough.

"I'm not going to sit here and wait for them to kill me," he muttered before wiping the beads of sweat from his brow with the forearm of his jacket. He holstered the weapon and took another look at the time. The second hand drifted closer to their boarding, and closer to their demise.

A chirp of his cell elicited a cry from his lips. He stifled it, cupping one hand over his mouth as the other fished for the cell in his pocket. Graham swallowed back the knot in his throat and spoke harshly, "What?"

"The clock is ticking. You don't want your usefulness to the Order to expire, do you?"

Graham cursed into the cell, his fear swirling with rage into a dissonant wail. But by the time his outcry was spent, the line was dead static. "Sonofa..."

A knock drove him closer to the edge and he snatched the door open in panic.

"Mr. Graham?" Sarah's eyes were wide and her face white like snow. It took a moment for his attention to pull away from her and to what put that fear into her. His eye caught a glint of reflection as the barrel of a gun lifted to meet his temple.

"May we have a word?" The female spoke with a sultry Russian accent, but the way she pressed the gun against his head was as far from sexy as he could imagine being with a woman of her...acumen.

"Is that what we're calling it?" Graham feigned bravado and it wasn't lost on anyone in his vicinity.

"We'll call it what we tell you. Put your hands up and step out," she ordered.

He did as she said and paused as the woman slipped behind him. The man forced Sarah to walk forward, and he ushered her into the office where he'd spent the flight. Once past the doorway, he shoved the young stewardess into a chair, forcing a yelp from her.

"You don't have to take it out on her. She has nothing to do with my business with you," Graham said.

The hulking man spun on his heels and slammed a meaty fist into the billionaire's nose. A flash of red formed in Graham's eyes before the gush of blood sprouted forth. His knees buckled, sending him to the deck. He held his face as the Russian stood over him.

"I was just saying..."

The man lifted Graham from the deck by his neck and held him high enough for the top of his head to touch the ceiling.

"I'll cut out your tongue if you say anything else," the man said.

Graham had only been in this position once before, and it was long before he had the money and means to defend himself properly.

The only thing he had going for him then was the arrogance of youth and enough rage for three men.

This time?

He reached instinctively to the gun in his belt and fired once at the woman. The point-blank blast took half her face off and cause the man to stammer in shock. Graham capitalized on it and fired a second round into the brute's neck as he drooped towards the ground. It wasn't where he aimed but the blood splatter across the bulkhead was evidence enough that there was no need for a secondary shot. The way the Russian fell like a tree with a dull thud cast a satisfying smile on Graham's face.

Sarah sat in muted horror when Graham looked to her. His heart raced as a mix of emotions swarmed inside of him. He should have been afraid, as any rational man would have been, but he had given himself over to that wicked part of himself he always tried to keep in check. He was tired of the fear. He was sick of being controlled. So, he did what they forced him to do.

This blood was on their hands, but they wouldn't see it that way.

His act of retaliation would serve as justification for the Order to come after him, but he no longer cared.

He welcomed it. He was forced into a corner and the only way out was to break free from their shadow. Luckily, he had a plan to do just that.

"Tell the captain it's time to go," Graham said.

Sarah stammered as she looked at the bodies. Blood oozed in every direction. "What about them?"

Graham looked down and shrugged heartlessly. "I have a schedule to keep. I want to be wheels up in ten minutes." He stepped out of the office and returned to his private quarters as his mind reeled from what had taken place. Both parts of his personality conflicted, but there was only one way to deal with what would come, and that was a show of strength.

They knew he was here, so they sent their people to kill him. In that moment he knew who the mole was.

He pulled his cell from his pocket and placed a call. "Your Russians failed, but mine won't. Stay out of my way."

He ended the call before Victor could respond. Graham's was the only last word that mattered, and it was high time *they* recognized the authority he demanded. If not now, then they soon would.

CHAPTER ELEVEN

Ames grit his teeth. The return drive with Abe behind the wheel was less than ideal, and even less so with a stomach full of greasy meat product swarming inside of him. It tasted good going down, but his acid reflux served as a warning that he had consumed too much. That or it was bad meat. The verdict was still out on that one.

"Slow it down," he griped. He tried to sound tough, an impossible feat when his stomach kept turning loops.

Abe ignored him, except for the glance in the rearview mirror. Ames's reflection in the mirrored finish of the driver's aviator sunglasses revealed that he looked just the way he felt...like crap. That realization merely served to increase Ames's agitation towards the Saudi.

"Beth, please," Ryan said on Ames's behalf.

She said nothing, but a simple look was encouragement enough for Abe to ease off the accelerator. It seemed that even the Arabs feared intense women with emblazed red hair. That or he just didn't like Americans.

She cut a glance back to Ryan. A soft, knowing smirk formed on her lips.

It would have been funny except for Ames's digestive distress souring every second of his existence. He held himself and said a silent prayer for an appropriate facility when they arrived at the pier. Worst case, he would have to let it go where the fish did.

Ames turned his nose up at the thought, but not too high. Desperate times called for desperate measures. At least this wasn't like the one time he ate something that didn't agree with him before a fourteen-hour convoy in Afghanistan. The only thing worse than that was the strike that killed his friends, leaving him a triple amputee and manipulated by a rich guy with a god complex.

"Were you able to retrieve the records for incoming ships?" Ryan asked, getting down to business despite the speedy swerving of their chauffer.

Beth canted her head towards him, glancing back with a sideways gaze, "We have suspicious vessels arriving within a six-hour window from Singapore, Russia, China, and Australia. There were a few ships from Italy and Portugal already docked close to our target. The USS *Intrepid* is sponsoring a dignitary visit tonight with officials from Britain, Germany, and Greece. We don't know whom may be involved with Graham, but with this many countries involved, it stands to reason that there may be a few."

"It takes balls to conduct this kind of business on a navy vessel," Wills said. "There's a lot of listening ears around."

"They use code for most of the illicit material they exchange. It's not like they will speak openly about trafficking people," Ryan replied. "But let's not assume that the carrier wasn't placed there due to the captain being part of Graham's organization."

That assumption made Ames's stomach turn worse than the shawarma. "Who could defend this scum?"

Everyone cut their eyes at him, and he looked away shamefully. He had no idea what he had been recruited into, but there wasn't a chance in hell he would have signed up had he known. He just wanted a sense of normalcy to return.

This truth revealed anything but normal.

"Point taken," he grumbled.

"We're here," Abe announced as he sped through a roundabout and skidded to a halt outside of a compound. On the other side of the wall rose the super structure and upper decks of the USS *Intrepid*. The side number beamed with iridescent radiance against the purple sky. They only had a few hours left to prepare and they still hadn't settled on who was doing what.

"What's the plan, Boss?" Wills asked as he kept his eyes outside the tinted windows of the car.

Ryan retrieved a notepad from his pocket and flipped it open. "Ames will board the carrier and collect intel. Your cybernetics will allow for heightened hearing, so you should be able to blend in with the onboard security force and monitor from a safe distance."

It made sense, though Ames hated the idea of going in alone.

"What about me?" Wills asked.

"You'll pilot the drone and keep an eye on ship movements leading up to the operation. We also need to know the layout of the hangar deck where the dinner is taking place."

Dinner, Ames thought? It sounded so casual. It also sounded like a disaster if he smelled something off while his stomach was churning.

"Beth and I will maintain radio communications. Abe will standby for the getaway if things go south."

"What could go south?" Wills replied with a smirk. It went ignored.

"How much information do you expect to glean from listening in?" Ames asked as he tried to put the plan together in his head. "Should I tag anyone with a tracker to follow them?"

"Wills will use the drones to track movements. We don't want to reveal our hand just yet. It isn't ideal, but it's what we have available to us. Once we know the next step in their plan, we can better coordinate our next move. Besides, facial recognition has come a long way. We should have plenty of information once we know who we're dealing with."

Ryan tucked the notepad back into his pocket and glanced around to meet the gaze of each member of the team. "This is our first of possibly many operations. We don't need to play heroics just yet. It's best to climb that mountain slowly."

"I'm no hero. I just want to make up for what part I've played in this mess," Wills grumbled.

"Likewise," Ryan replied. "Still, it's easy to act on emotion instead of following the plan. Let's make the right effort to get this done the way that affects the most change. Taking out one of these guys tonight, and revealing ourselves, will only make things worse. These people are replaceable. The Order is the primary target. Understood?"

Everyone acknowledged the plan with grunts and nods.

"Good. We'll come back later when it's time. Let's go, Abe."

Abe sent the car speeding forward and turned a sharp corner before speeding back to where they had come from. Ames watched through the sideview mirror as the carrier drew smaller. In a matter of hours true evil would be on the most advanced piece of American war machinery in the world. To know who had control of such things sent chills down his spine. He just hoped they could affect the change Ryan had spent years planning for.

Maybe then good would overcome evil?

Graham meticulously trimmed his nails as the 777X began its final descent. He lost himself in the swirling thoughts of the last few days. As much as he wanted to give up and let the Order claim him, the more he wanted to resist and bring the organization down with him.

Trying to reconcile those thoughts was the mental equivalent of holding two powerful magnets together with matching poles. Eventually, he would have to give up and let one side win.

Eventually.

He was still fumbling with the next step in his plan when the wheels touched down. Graham reached over to the window and raised the partition to see the towering skyline nearly blotting out the sunlight. A hundred years prior there was hardly anything but desert here. Now, every building was a monument to mankind's' resentment to staying on the ground.

That, or their feeble attempt at making themselves equal with God.

Once stopped, Graham left his quarters and stepped into the narrow passageway to exit. The Russian assassins' bodies were laid out, covered in sheets. Sarah's face was void of life as she robotically cleared a path for Graham to exit. She would have been dead if he hadn't acted, yet she refused to look him in the eye.

He didn't blame her. The kind of person it took to take another life wasn't the good kind. Even those who killed to protect had a darkness about them, whether they wanted to acknowledge it or not.

Instead, he stepped off without a word and made his way to the waiting car parked on the tarmac. His driver greeted him with a grin, but Graham was not in the mood to return it. He stopped the man from closing the door and said, "Tell the captain to ensure the cargo is ready to depart. The customer will use the plane to transport it. If he doesn't show up by morning, then the deal's off. He'll know what to do."

The driver nodded and closed the door, leaving Graham in the chilled back seat of the luxury vehicle. It was the best money could afford; like all his possessions, but he was as detached from them as he was to reality.

He drummed his fingers on his knee as he waited impatiently. His meeting would begin in little over an hour. The dignitary tour of the carrier was a stunning cover, but it required too much time in the open. He pulled his duffle open and retrieved the mask he'd packed. It was a custom fit and matched his skin color while adding enough features to markedly change his appearance. The last thing he needed was to be recognized by the common people on board.

He considered putting it on, but there was plenty of time to suffer the unbearable heat with the false skin. Instead, he placed it beside him and looked down at the eyeless monstrosity. "How fashionable to wear someone else's face," he mumbled as the driver's door slammed shut.

A moment later the car departed, leaving the dead and dying behind.

———

"Remind me again why sailors wear green?" Ames asked as he adjusted the uniform. It was a size too small, especially considering his massive arms, but he was grateful he didn't have to try and roll the sleeves up as a perfect roll would be impossible. Still, it was better than having to wear the cracker jack uniform with the bell bottoms. As a former Marine, he wouldn't be caught dead in that uniform.

"Because funding goes to waste if it isn't used for frivolous things like uniform upgrades and new office furniture. Heaven forbid they use it to build new living quarters or take care of their people," Wills answered bitterly.

It was a sentiment they all shared in some form or fashion. This mismanagement of government funding was easy to see if you opened your eyes just a little. This was doubly true for those in the enlisted ranks who suffered the most.

"But still, green? I know sailors envy *real men*, but this is a bit on the nose."

Ryan chuckled. "I guess someone at the top felt guilty about their career and wished they were a Marine. Is that the compliment you're fishing for?"

Ames smirked. "At least an old sailor like you is willing to admit it."

"We have ten minutes," Beth said in their earpieces from her perch a mile away.

Ames groaned as he donned the cover and did his best to obscure his cybernetic augmentations. It was practically impossible. "It's show time."

He stepped out of the trailer and headed up the pier towards the ship. The purple hues from the cityscape painted the sky, making the stars fade into the ether. There was a time long past where they would have provided the only light, but he doubted anyone could remember that far back.

The brow ran from Wheelhouse Three, ninety feet above the pier, at a steep incline. The parade of dignitaries had already formed in the sand box area and were moving through the security checkpoint. Ames climbed the brow and flashed an ID to a particularly disgruntled sailor who had the misfortune of visiting the Middle East during Dress Blues season. He would get no sympathy from a former Marine, but the misery on his face was telling.

"Permission granted," the watch stander said without a word from Ames.

"Well, that was easy," Ames said once he was past the quarterdeck.

"You should get a good view of who arrives from the sponson on the starboard side, one level above the quarterdeck you just entered," Beth said.

Ames found the nearest ladder well and climbed it two at a time. "Nothing says sponson above the doors," he replied. Instead, the tags had compartment numbers etched into the metal.

"Do any placards say 'exit' on them?" Wills asked.

"Yes, there's one."

"The sponson should lead outside the skin of the ship. Try that," Wills suggested.

Ames shrugged and pulled up on the hatch. The difference in pressure inside and outside of the ship met with a gust of wind. He closed his eyes as dust kicked up around him. The grit of sand pelted his face until he pushed through. Once outside, he had a bird's eye view of the dignitary line. But it was what he saw outside the perimeter that caught his eye.

"There's a limo pulling up now, just outside the gate," Ames said.

"That might be him," Beth replied.

"Or just another rich guy playing tourist," Wills said.

"In either case, get ready," Ryan warned. "We can't afford to make any mistakes."

Ames narrowed his eyes and watched. If Graham was coming, then this had to be him. He felt it in his bones.

What was left of them anyway.

Graham pulled the false flesh mask over his face, careful not to make his broken nose start bleeding again and exited the limo. The Dubai heat radiated from the ground, inching its way up his body invasively. He adjusted his suit and made his way for the entrance.

"Identification please," the guard said as he held a hand up to stop Graham. The sailor wore green camouflage with simple body armor. The M4A1 strapped to his chest angled towards the ground as he kept one hand on the grip and let his trigger finger rest along the guard. From the outside it looked lackadaisical, but Graham knew the guard needed only a fraction of a second to adjust and fire the weapon.

Graham pulled the falsified ID from his pocket and showed it. With hardly a look, the guard waved him aboard the compound.

Simple.

Graham made his way through the narrow scan field as the x-ray machines and metal detectors scanned his body. He knew better than to bring anything with him, but he wasn't completely defenseless. If his mask was the shield, then the pen in his pocket was the hammer. A simple click would activate a drone strike within minutes. He might not make it out, but neither would his enemies.

"Welcome to the USS *Intrepid*," a man said as he made it out of the scan field. Graham eyed the officer, the only distinguishing trait between him and the first guard was the silver bar adorning his uniform. The shiny stuff almost always meant they were important.

Or at least thought they were.

"Thank you," he replied, distorting his voice a bit. He stepped past the man and towards the crowd heading for the brow. There was a trail of a few dozen dignitaries boarding as he arrived. Each person was spaced several feet apart to keep the brow from shifting too much under the weight. Even with chains holding it in place, the current at the pier could still shift the enormous vessel ever so slightly. The last thing the Navy wanted was to send someone over the edge and create an international incident.

That was why Chuck had chosen this place to meet. If anything went south, then it would be a huge black eye to the nation. It was smart, but Graham was smarter.

He boarded last and disappeared in the crowd. He had already laid eyes on Chuck. The Saudi continued to scan the crowd, which drew Graham's attention to him. *Let him wait,* Graham mused. *No need to be in a hurry to satisfy someone like that.*

A voice boomed over the speaker system, and it took a moment for Graham to see the captain of the ship standing on a makeshift stage comprised of ordnance carts. The backsplash of the American flag hanging from the overhead screamed of posturing patriotism, but he was certain the non-cynical amongst the crowd were enamored by the display.

The captain spoke for a few minutes, his voice getting lost in the echoes. Not that Graham cared what was being said. If anything, he assumed this was the captain's way of stroking his own ego, to get recognition by a captive audience. Graham knew the type. He was practically surrounded by them anytime he was in the company of Secretary Sanders and the Joint Chiefs.

Once the captain stopped talking, the crowd converged towards a central location. Tables were spread in neat rows with over-the-top décor. Each table had a centerpiece with a wreath of red, white, and blue surrounding miniature flags of each country represented by this dignitary tour.

Of course, Old Glory was slightly larger. American ego purely intact.

Graham made his way to the table where his customer was seated. The man's face was stern, nearly panicked. Certainly not the cocksure version Graham had met at the Order's gala days prior.

"Finding anything *exotic* to meet your fancy?" Graham asked as he took his seat across from Chuck.

The man's eyes nearly bulged out of his head. "Mr.—"

"Falkner," Graham said with a nod. He brushed at his face to reveal the ring that Chuck had complimented at the party.

"I'm seeing much that meets my interest," Chuck answered.

"Good. Then this should be a fruitful night for both of us."

Chuck raised his glass and smiled wickedly. "Let us hope so."

Graham was glad he was wearing a mask to hide his face. It would be impossible not to show his disdain for the man seated before him. The only thing he had going for him was after tonight this would all be over, and he could try to forget he'd ever met Chuck. Then he could focus on his more pressing problem.

The Order.

CHAPTER TWELVE

Ames made his way to the hangar bay of the *USS Intrepid*. Large partitions were placed to create faux walls with giant curtains draped over for privacy. He moved about, slowing anywhere there was a gap to view the crowd. Dozens of guests flooded the weather deck, most in traditional garb, others in modern suits.

It took a few moments before his eye caught the man he'd seen exit the limo, but to his dismay it wasn't Graham.

"We have a problem," he said softly.

"What is it?" Beth asked.

"From a distance, that man looked like Graham, all the way down to his walk, but looking at his face that isn't him."

"Are you sure?" Ryan asked. His irritation oozed into Ames's earpiece as if they were standing right next to each other.

"Unless Graham grew bushy eyebrows and a mustache in just a few days, then yeah, I'm sure."

"Maybe he sent someone in his stead?" Wills replied.

"It's not out of the question," Beth said, "but he typically handles these deals himself."

"We were onto him before. Maybe he got skittish after his attack went south...twice," Ames said as he kept his eye on the stranger. The crowd was listening to the captain speak before they dispersed. The mass movement obscured the stranger and Ames swore under his breath.

"Maybe. Or he's wearing a disguise," Ryan shot back.

It was a long shot as far as Ames was concerned, but in either case, the stranger was a person of interest. "I'll keep an eye on him. I just need to change position for a better vantage point."

"Stay out of sight," Ryan warned.

"Not my first rodeo, pops," Ames grumbled as he moved to a new position. He was nearly on the other side of the hangar bay before he found his target again. Luckily, the man's back was too him. Ames strained to listen to what was being said, but there was too much ambient noise cutting in and out. He did, however, hear something that sparked his interest.

"Do you have my shipment?" The Arab man asked the stranger. The rest was muffled out, but it was a lead Ames wanted to follow.

"The man seated across from him is asking about a shipment," Ames whispered.

"What kind?" Ryan asked.

"Can't say. Too much interference."

"Are you near a wireless sound source?" Beth asked.

"I don't know, why?"

"Because if it is on then it could be amplifying the noise in the room making it difficult for you to pinpoint the source you're tracking."

"Oh, science huh?"

"Or just common sense," she rebutted.

Ames peered around the curtain at different angles and viewed the podium and stage from which the captain had spoken. There was a microphone that didn't appear to have any cords attached. He then looked behind the makeshift stage and saw a wheeled case with electronic equipment inside.

"Yeah, I think I see something," he said.

"Try and switch it off and see if that helps," Beth said.

"It's on the other side of the curtain," Ames replied.

"You're in a disguise, just make it quick and don't draw attention to yourself," Ryan shot back.

"Fine," Ames said and pulled enough of the curtain back for him to step through. He may have been in a uniform, but he certainly wasn't in one that matched what the sailors supporting the event were wearing. He moved with a purpose but avoided peering at the crowd in hopes he would blend in with the bustling environment.

He knelt in front of the equipment and tried to make heads or tails out of what he was seeing. It was mostly a series of boxes with LED lights scanning from green to red. It took a few moments for him to realize it peaked into the red as the crowd grew louder.

"This has to be it," he mumbled. His eyes followed along the front face of each box looking for a switch but found nothing. "I can't find a way to turn it off and I'm looking right at it."

"Did you check both sides of it?" Beth asked.

Ames didn't answer. Instead, he shifted to the back of the case and peered inside.

"Bingo." He flipped the switch at the top and a resulting pop as the system went down silenced the crowd. Ames froze where he was, praying to all that was Holy that no one would look his way.

It went unanswered.

"What are you doing, shipmate?" A scathing tone came from a sailor behind him.

"I was just turning this off," Ames answered, refusing to turn and acknowledge whoever had crept upon him.

"Why?"

"It was starting to give feedback. I didn't want it to get out of control and disturb the guests."

"Smart one," Beth whispered. He would have smiled at the compliment if he wasn't in the thick of being discovered. His only consolation was that he was out of view of the stranger standing in for Graham.

"Well, that didn't work out so well, did it? You could have just turned the amp down, not off," the sailor said as he stepped around. "You're not even in proper uniform. What division are you in?"

Ames wanted to say infantry, but not a squid on this ship would believe that. The closest thing they had was a tiny security force and he was willing to bet none of them had combat experience. At a loss for words he simply replied, "I'll leave now."

Ames moved to walk away, but the sailor wasn't having it. "I asked you a question, shipmate." the sailor moved to grab Ames's arm, but the former Marine shifted and yanked the sailor off his feet and onto the deck. It was instinctual, and a bit too much.

The gasp from the crowd was immediate.

Ames eyes darted up to meet the stranger's gaze. Without the sound system interfering with his cybernetics, he was able to hear what the man said clear as day. The stranger's lips moved in slow motion as the man spoke one simple word.

"Ames?"

Graham gripped the back of his chair as he watched his creation stare back at him. "Ames?"

The soldier gawked at him with confusion etched on his face like stone. The thin veil of the false skin mask was all that preserved Graham's identity, but he had never felt more exposed.

If Ames was here, then so were the others. Ames lacked the resources to get here on his own. That could only mean...

Graham canted his head towards Chuck, leaning towards the Arab with narrowed eyes. "That man knows why you're here. You need to leave, now!"

Chuck glanced at Ames, swallowed hard, and rose from his seat. "I need a distraction," Chuck said.

Graham slinked back, avoiding eye contact with Ames in hopes to not be made. "I have nothing to aide you. If I'm detected then your shipment will be lost," he warned. Graham kept an eye on Chuck, the man was shaking, likely he had never been involved in a deal that went south like this.

Chuck looked down and said, "Meet me at the Burj Khalifa tomorrow morning."

Graham nodded as he watched Chuck reach into his pocket and produce a pistol. How did he get that inside the compound, he wondered as Chuck fired point blank into the man seated next to him. The small caliber weapon didn't produce much more than a pop before the man slumped face first into the empty dinner ware before him. Blood oozed from the hole in the side of his head. Graham sat there staring as mass chaos ensued.

People ran for their lives as he watched the anonymous man bleed out needlessly. When he turned to see Ames, the soldier was gone. He hadn't seen him leave, but he was sure the former Marine bolted once the shot was fired.

Graham's future depended on it.

He rose and walked in the opposite direction as the crowd. He'd been part of enough ship christenings to know his way around. It helped to understand the tack-numbers displayed all over the bulkheads throughout the vessel.

Graham ascended three sets of stairs before making his way outside the skin of the ship. Across the pier was a smaller vessel with Portuguese markings, his escape route. He pulled a small penlight from his pocket and shone it at the bridge of the ship. Another light reflected at him, then flashed three times. A bang was followed by the sound of a grapple clinking against the guardrail along the catwalk in which he was standing.

Graham moved to it and climbed over the railing. He pulled off his jacket and wrapped it around the line, reenforcing his grip by double-wrapping his hands, he let himself go and ziplined towards the small ship.

Once aboard, he pulled off the mask and let it fall to the murky water below.

"Mr. Graham, welcome aboard the *Valoroso*," the man he assumed was the captain said with a thick accent. "Did everything go according to plan?"

Graham wiped the sweat from his face and groaned. "Not every plan is one you want to see succeed, Captain?"

"Heiter, sir," the captain answered.

"Captain Heiter," Graham continued, "But the outcome was as I expected. We leave at first light."

"Yes, sir. Should I see you to your quarters?"

"Please," Graham replied. Captain Heiter moved to exit the bridge, but Graham stopped short and looked at the carrier. Thousands of souls called it home. It was a marvel of American military strength.

But it was also evidence and would soon be swarmed by prying eyes.

He pulled the pen from his pocket and rubbed his thumb along the switch. "On second thought, Captain, we'll leave now."

———————

Three seconds was all it took.

Bang!

A momentary pause.

And then chaos ensued.

Ames struggled to keep an eye on the triggerman. The gangly Arab would have been easy to spot if not for wearing the same garb as sixty percent of the others gathered on the hangar deck. He jumped onto the makeshift stage and peered out over the crowd, but the human stampede was too much.

"I lost him," he grumbled.

"Any identifying marks we should look out for?" Beth asked.

"White attire, tall, scrawny, with a short, dark beard," Ames answered.

"That helps a lot," Ryan replied. His voice oozed with sarcasm.

"She asked. Should I pursue him?"

A momentary silence gave him pause, then a reply, "Is your cover broken?" Ryan asked.

"More or less," he answered. No one was challenging him anymore, but he'd been made by the stranger before the Arab murdered the man next to him.

Ryan groaned. "Go for it. Find him and tag him. Don't engage with the crowd. We don't want to hurt innocent people."

Ames wanted to tell him it was too late for that. He looked at the dead man slumped over the table. The pool of blood had spread out over half the tabletop and was oozing in tendrils over the edge. The smell of iron wafted heavily in the air with momentary gusts off the water. The smell only enhanced how disturbing of a scene it truly was to see the man shot in the head mere inches away. He felt sorry for whoever was going to have to clean it up.

Ames bolted for the exit. He followed the mass of people in search for the killer. He perched above them on the forward, starboard elevator and scanned the crowd. Most stumbled out into the sandbox in pairs, hastily making their way to safety. But a straggler caught his eye.

"Got him. He's walking just outside the crowd on the north side. He's by the row of dumpsters."

Ames continued watching as the man tossed something that looked like a wallet into the third dumpster.

"I see him," Beth said. "Painting him now. Wills, are you ready?"

"Yes, ma'am," Wills replied.

"I'm sending you the coordinates now."

Ames watched the man disappear around the corner of the building and swore under his breath.

"I have visuals and a RADAR lock," Wills replied. "If we hurry, then we can catch up to him."

"Abe, bring the car around," Ryan ordered.

Silence.

"Abe?"

Ames adjusted his earpiece in hopes he simply wasn't getting good reception. He shifted his position, tapping at his earpieces waiting for a response from the driver.

Nothing.

"Does anyone have visuals on Abe?" Ryan asked. It sounded like he was on the move as he breathed heavily into his mic. Their situation had gone from bad to worse and they were all sitting on their hands as the target fled. They needed to do something, but what?

Beth's voice cut through the silence, "I see Abe's car. Maybe his radio is off?"

"I can see it too," Wills replied. "But you're not going to like this."

"Why is that?" Ryan asked.

"Our target is running toward him."

"So, he was playing us as fools," Ames snapped. He ground his teeth and balled his fists tightly. He couldn't fight back the words on this tip of his tongue. "You can't trust anyone can you?"

"Oh no," Beth said under her breath. "Abe, look out!"

A familiar pop rang in the distance, just out of sight of Ames's purview. A scream from the crowd came next, followed by a shift in their stampede. "What was that?"

"Abe is down. Repeat, Abe is down. Wills, get a lock on the car. We can't lose him."

"I'm on it," Wills seethed. "And you better believe I'm not letting this guy get away."

CHAPTER THIRTEEN

Beth watched the car drive away. Her heart sank as the pool of blood formed around her friend. *He deserved better than that*, she thought. He was killed by a coward.

"Wills, do you have a lock?"

"Yes, ma'am," Wills replied, but I'm stuck in the compound. It's only a matter of time before he's out of range."

Beth's eyes darted around the perimeter until she found something useful to her. A sanitation truck. "I have an idea," she said as she made her way down the side of the building into the alley. The smell of whatever was still inside the tank hit her as she approached, but she held her breath and kept going. Beth climbed into the cab and thanked God the keys were still in it. She turned the ignition, and the truck sprang to life. She jerked the shifter into gear and floored the accelerator as hard as she could. The truck lurched, the torque of the back axle shifting it begrudgingly to the right before the tires caught traction. With a screech, and the smell of burning rubber, it took off in a semi-straight line.

"Beth, what are you doing?" Ryan barked into her earpiece. "You'll trigger an international incident."

"It's too late for that," she shot back, pulling the wheel sharply to the left to get onto the main thoroughfare. Abe's car swerved violently between lanes less than a hundred meters in front of her. "I have eyes on the target." She floored it, ignoring the unsettled movement of the truck in desperate need of an alignment. It took a second for it to register she'd stolen the truck from a repair facility.

I hope they have good insurance, she thought as she downshifted. The truck screamed between vehicles as she merged onto the highway headed for downtown Dubai. In front of her the gargantuan buildings rose like spires and disappeared in the low hanging clouds of the purple sky. The sandbox shone like a beacon behind her, but she ignored what was back there, failure, the death of her friend.

Maybe Ryan was right, and she was making a mistake, but she didn't care. Her mission changed when lives were lost before her eyes.

"Beth, the car is almost out of range," Wills warned.

"I have eyes on the vehicle," she said. "It's heading towards the city. I need to catch up before he takes an off ramp and I lose him."

"What about the other guy?" Ames asked. "What do we do about him?"

Beth ignored him. There was only one guy she was after and to hell with anyone else. This guy killed Abe. He was the priority.

"What other guy?" Ryan asked.

"Before the first gunshot I made eye contact with someone else...they knew my name."

That statement was enough to draw Beth's attention. "Did he leave the ship?"

"I don't know. What I do know is that he spoke to the killer before all hell broke loose."

"All right," Ryan said. Ames, stay on board and investigate the scene. I'll keep an eye down here. Wills, get transportation and catch up with Beth. I don't like us being separated, but we need to find the other guy. He may lead us to Graham."

"Roger that," Wills said.

"And Beth," Ryan continued, "Don't do anything stupid."

"Or what?"

The next string of words from Ryan's lips were scrambled by static.

Out of range.

"Figures," she said as she rolled her eyes and set her gaze on the runaway car. Beth knew what Ryan was getting at, but the only thing stupid on her mind was letting this guy get away and not settling the score.

Ames turned back to the body and approached the gathering crowd of sailors reporting to the emergency. Dozens of personnel secured the scene, but he wasn't concerned with the body. He was looking for something else. Someone else.

"This scene is secured," an armed sailor stated. "Unless you're part of medical or security personnel, then I suggest going somewhere else."

"I witnessed the murder," Ames declared. He didn't know if the sailor would bite on that information, though he thought it would be reckless for him not to. He had to have a chain of command to report this to.

"So did the cameras," the sailor shot back, indifferent.

Cameras?

Ames gawked at the overhead. The fire suppression system stood out most prominently. After that was rows of pipes marked for potable water and CHT. He didn't have to guess what that meant. Then his eyes fell upon the dark semi-spheres. *Out of sight, out of mind*, he thought. What better way to watch what was happening?

"Do you know where the feed is going?"

"Yeah, we monitor it in the precinct. Are you new here or something?"

"Something," Ames replied. "Where is that again?"

If the sailor rolled his eyes any harder, then his eyes would have spilled out of his head. Ames might be in a disguise uniform, but if he were still serving, he would chew this kid up and spit him out for lack of military bearing.

"3-49-0 ladder well," the sailor emphasized the word tack between each number as if he'd had to repeat himself a hundred times that day. "Head straight down until you see the blue door. Now, will you get out of here, the khakis are staring at us?"

Ames scoffed. "Yeah, man. Thanks."

He stepped away from the biggest event in recent naval history and made for the precinct. He'd been aboard enough ships to understand the numbers system, though he still thought it was annoying.

The ship was quiet for a vessel containing thousands of people. Sure, most were likely on liberty, but a quarter of the crew had to stay behind for duty. He expected to see more movement. Instead, he simply traipsed around unchallenged.

"Typical squids," he grumbled as he rounded the corner forward of the galley and found the ladder the guard had directed him too. The tiny placard above read 3-49-0. Beneath that it was gibberish.

Ames descended and stopped at the blue door. He knocked hard, expecting a solid steel door. But the hollow metal "non-type" door nearly buckled under the strain of his cybernetic strength.

"Holy crap!" A shout from inside preceded the door opening. A female sailor in a tactical green uniform stared at him like offendedly. "You trying to kill me? You scared me half to death."

"Sorry, I expected the door to be a bit more solid than that. I was wondering if you could help me?"

"With what?"

"I witnessed the shooting and I think I saw two people involved, but I only saw one of them exit the ship."

She swallowed and pulled the door open for him. "You think we need to call general quarters?"

Ames shrugged. "I don't know what we should do, but I was hoping we could see where he went using the security cameras?"

She nodded. "I know how to work them. Can you identify him?"

"Yeah, creepy guy in a suit worth more than my yearly salary," he replied.

"Should be simple, you're a seaman," she joked.

He smirked, looking at her rank. Two chevrons under a perched eagle. The sailors called them crows. He knew enough to acknowledge her rank, "It might be worth more than your salary, Petty Officer Greene."

She turned her nose up at the remark and said, "follow me, but don't touch anything."

Ames did as she said, and they moved deeper into the space. Banks of computers lined the walls, most of the screens blank. The others displayed a wallpaper of the ship's crest depicting the Fighting "I". It was faux pride, he was sure. Most sailors would have personalized their desktops if given the opportunity.

She stopped at a terminal and plopped down in the plush chair. "Pull up a stool, will you? I don't like people standing over me while I work."

Ames grabbed one from across the room and sat beside her. By the time he was settled, she had the feed up. The timestamp was minutes before the shot. He scanned the scene and then pointed, "right there."

She clicked over the image and zoomed in on the man. She then typed in commands and let the video play. It rolled with a halo effect surrounding the figure.

They watched as the shooter rose, said something inaudible, then fired. It happened just as Ames experienced it, only this time he watched the stranger who had said his name.

The crowd moved towards the brow, the stranger wove through the chaos and disappeared behind the curtain where Ames had been hiding before he had tried to turn off the pa system.

"Can you follow him?"

"I have to shift camera systems. Give me a minute."

Ames was growing impatient now. Not with her, but with the

fact he had let the man get away. The worst part was the threat to safety for others was on his head.

He just hoped he could find him before anyone else was killed.

Beth swerved the sanitation truck back into the right-hand lane. The target was three cars ahead, and traffic congestion ahead was making his driving more sporadic. "At this rate you're going to kill yourself or somebody else," she hissed, down shifting again to improve acceleration.

Other drivers seemed to draw the same conclusion as the cars directly behind the target began pulling over on the side of the highway, clearing the gap between her and revenge.

She seized it.

Beth accelerated, willing the truck towards the car. The headlights beamed inside, and she saw the killer's eyes through the rearview mirror. His knowing look was all she needed to justify what came next.

Beth slammed the front bumper of the sanitation truck into the rear end of the car. It swerved, tires screeching, but despite the killer's frantic motions with the steering wheel, it stayed on the highway.

"Let's try that again."

She pressed harder, this time aiming for the driver's side rear bumper. The truck drove into the car, pushing it towards the edge of the highway until the front right tire contacted the fluffy sand. It wasn't much, but it was enough to yank the wheel to the right and send the car tumbling.

Beth watched the car flip six times. The first shattered the glass. The second crunched the corners and deployed the life-saving foam. The third ripped off a wheel. The fourth darkened all but one headlight. The fifth sent it off the highway and deeper into the rising sand dunes on the side of the highway. And the sixth eased it to a smokey stop on its roof.

She pulled the truck over and stopped parallel to the accident. Without missing a beat, Beth jumped out of the truck and ran towards the car. When she reached it, she began ripping into the foam until she found the killer scrunched awkwardly against the roof. He was banged up, but not dead...yet.

"Who are you?"

He looked at her with a bloody grin. His purple, puffy eyes betrayed his cockiness. All she saw was his fear. "Chuck," he said as blood bubbles sprayed from his mouth and nostrils. He'd punctured a lung, or something.

"Who were you meeting?" Beth asked. He might have given a fake name for himself, but usually the vermin would rat on their friends.

"Wouldn't you like to know?"

She reached out and snatched another chunk of foam away, exposing more of him. She pulled her Glock and pressed it against his temple. "Death can be easy, or it can be hard. It's inevitable either way. Who were you meeting?"

He smiled, but the effort sent him into a coughing fit. He was choking on his own blood. He didn't have much time.

Beth pressed the barrel a little harder. He got the point.

"Graham. David Graham, the American billionaire," he answered. He wasn't smiling anymore. He looked like death was already taking hold.

"What for?"

He looked to her and narrowly closed one of his swollen eyes. A wink?

"What. For?" She centered the barrel onto his eye, pressing it into the socket. He was powerless to defend himself.

"He had a shipment for me."

"Of?"

"We only deal in the most exotic of commodities here," he replied.

"People?"

He nodded.

She could have shot him then, but a familiar voice filled her earpiece. "Beth, are you all right?" It was Wills.

"I'm good. Where are you?"

"Coming up on an accident. Traffic is backed up."

"When you reach the scene, that's where I'll be. But we have a bigger problem."

"What's that?"

Beth hesitated to say it out loud, but it was better to face the demon head-on. "The man Ames saw was Graham. He must have been in disguise."

"Oh, crap," Wills replied.

'Yeah. I'm out of range to tell them, but if he's still on the ship, then things could get a lot worse."

"I can relay that if you need me to."

"I'm good here. The killer isn't going anywhere."

"Roger that. I'll head back to the ship and tell them."

"I'll meet you there," she said.

Beth holstered her weapon and knelt at the driver's side door. She looked at Chuck, or whatever his real name was, and said, "I spent years tracking people like you down. You're one of the monsters under humanity's bed. But eventually, people no longer fear the monsters, and set out to destroy them. You're one of the lucky ones. You get to die by your own undoing. But your friends aren't long behind you."

She reached in and felt his pockets. There was a slight bulge near his heart, and she retrieved it.

"How quant, a little black book? I wonder, will I find this useful?"

He eyed her smugly. "What you find might kill you."

"Then I guess we'll meet again soon." Beth turned and walked for the truck, leaving Chuck to bleed out like he deserved.

"There he is," Ames said as he pointed at the screen. Petty Officer Greene manipulated the feed on the camera and zoomed in. "He's going towards an exit. What's out there?"

"The flight deck," she said with a shrug. "It's over a hundred feet above the waterline of the ship. I hope he doesn't intend to jump."

"Do you have security cameras for the flight deck?"

"There's a separate feed for that, but I do have access to it." She closed out one window and opened another on the computer, typed in her credentials, and scrolled back the feed to the proper time stamp. The video was grainy and pixilated. Not what one would expect from a world-class warship.

"There's movement there." Ames gestured to the starboard side where the faintest of shadows shifted.

The sailor zoomed in, manipulated the angle, and adjusted the contrast. What followed was a flash of brilliance to the man's right.

"What was that?"

"It looked like sparks," she answered. She made more adjustments and caught a glimmer of something protruding from the ship. Together they watched the man remove his jacket and wrap it around something. "What is that?"

Ames swallowed hard. "It's a zip line. He escaped." With those words the man leapt out of view of the camera. "We need to see where he's going."

"I'm on it," Petty Officer Greene said. Her fingers danced on the keyboard and a higher fidelity feed popped up. She made the necessary adjustments to see where their mystery man could have gone. Across the pier was two ships. A shipping barge, and a small frigate.

Ames stared at the shipping barge. The freight boxes were stacked two high in neat little rows. It likely was being used outside of what it was designed for. A typical move for those with ambitions higher than they could afford. He didn't see anything out of the ordinary. "Go to the frigate."

She scanned the small warship and they saw him climbing aboard the ship's bridge. "Got him." She looked up at Ames, her face two shades paler. "Does this constitute an act of war? We have to tell someone."

Ames nodded. She was right but explaining how she came about this information was going to be a slippery slope, especially if they found out he wasn't really a sailor aboard the *USS Intrepid*.

"Ames, do you read?" Wills said into his earpiece.

"I hear you, what's going on?"

There was static, then Wills answered, "Beth caught the killer, but found out that the man he spoke to wasn't some unknown target."

"Then who was it?"

"It was Graham."

Ames jaw went slack. His eyes darted to the Portuguese flag whipping wildly above the bridge of the frigate. He knew Graham was a man of means but having control of another nations' military craft didn't meet the scope of what Ames had expected. Who could?

He stepped away from the sailor and whispered, "Then we have a really big problem."

"What's that?" Ryan broke his silence.

Ames hesitated to say it. It was unbelievable. Then again, he'd learned to accept more than he would ever want to know about the man who had changed his life. "Graham is on a foreign military ship. And if my eyes aren't deceiving me, it looks like it's about to leave."

CHAPTER FOURTEEN

Ames looked to Petty Officer Greene and said, "I don't know who you need to notify, but I think this ship is about to be under attack."

"By who?" She asked, gawking at the screen. "Who is that?"

"Sound the alarm now." Ames sprinted towards the door as she keyed her security radio and made the call. Less than a minute later the General Quarters klaxon sounded, and Ames was on the third level working his way outside the skin of the ship. He shoved open the hatch and found the graplin hook cinched along the catwalk railing. The line stretched out towards the small frigate but dipped into the water as the ship shifted away from its pier.

Ames took in as many details as he could, but strangely could not find any identifying marks on the ship except for the hull number and the flag waving above the bridge. No other maritime flags were visible, and that small detail made him doubt whether he could trust the national origin. Flags were easy to get, even in the days of piracy, ships in the Caribbean would use false flags to lure their prey.

"I have eyes on the ship. The mooring lines are off and its drifting into the channel. They're definitely setting out for sea, even with the tide low."

"That's an unnecessary risk unless you're planning something," Ryan stated.

"Bingo. But what they're planning I don't know." The graplin line went slack and dropped towards the water. Ames grabbed it and hauled it up, hoping they could get something from it to help track the ship. "Do we still have a drone in the sky?"

"Negative, I had to let it go to catch up with Beth," Wills said. "I can get it running again in a few minutes. I just pulled up to the complex, but it's tighter than Fort Knox with security."

Ames swore under his breath. The threat wasn't in the sandbox, it was across the channel, and no one saw it but him.

"Is that it?" Ryan asked as he jumped down into the catwalk with Ames. Ryan was breathing heavy and the rage on his face was etched like stone as he glared at the departing vessel.

"Yeah, and Graham's on it. What should we do? Even if we tagged it with a drone, we can't follow it forever."

Ryan clenched his jaw. "We'll have to hope Beth has information for us to follow later. Our priority has to be saving the people on this ship."

Ames gave him a sideways glance. Ryan wasn't wrong, but it felt like he was dropping their primary mission for something else. The ship was already on the alert, what good could they do to help?

"Do you want me to commandeer a small boat and follow after them? I'm sure there's a small boat available on this carrier?"

"Not enough time." Ryan keyed his radio, "Wills, once you get the drone airborne, paint the frigate so we can get a satellite lock on it. We might lose visuals, but we can still track him digitally."

"Roger that," Wills replied. "Going up now."

Ryan moved to walk away but Ames stepped in front of him, holding a hand to his chest. "What's your game?"

"My what?"

"Your game? We have visuals on our target and you're letting him get away. The deck department can drop a boat in the water within a few minutes if given the order, but you shot that down and opted for satellite. Why?"

Ryan stared at him. If looks could kill, then Ames would be pushing up daisies. "Do you know what kind of fire power that ship has?"

Ames shrugged. "No."

"Neither do I. We have four people on this team and only three of us are here. Under the best of circumstances, we are undermanned to launch an attack on that ship. Additionally, this American aircraft carrier is an asset that will be destroyed to help cover that frigate's tracks. If we go with your plan, we'll lose twice. Now, get your hand off me before I send you to the bottom of this channel."

Ames eased up, taking a step back. He was speechless. Never mind the fact he just realized how wrong he was.

"Keep your eyes open. I suspect this night is going to get more exciting before it's over," Ryan said as he brushed past him. Ames watched Ryan march away, disappearing inside the ship and slamming the hatch shut. The old sailor dogged down the door and left Ames alone to stew.

The former Marine turned to face the frigate. It was picking up speed as the channel opened to the larger body of water. Within a few minutes, it would be gone, proving that Ryan had assessed the situation accurately. Ames had approached the situation with tunnel-vision, too blind to see what Ryan had just spelled out for him. It was a kick in the nuts and a bruise to his ego.

"Perhaps that's why he's leading this team," Ames said under his breath as he watched the sky in anticipation. He didn't know why, but he knew Ryan was likely clued into something he wasn't expecting himself. Ames just hoped it wasn't more than any of them could handle.

The *Valoroso* disembarked, easing quietly away from the American aircraft carrier as chaos ensued.

They were out of the channel now, and Graham watched from the bridge as helicopters appeared on scene. They hovered above the carrier deck, their search lights burning like miniature suns against the backdrop of the evening sky.

"How long until we're out of range?"

"Ten minutes?" The captain never spoke with any certainty. It was likely a result of being second guessed by leadership at the onset of his career, or perhaps he was just weak. In either case, it was what made him vulnerable to people like Graham. Too meek to say no, and too afraid to report his compromised position to the proper authorities.

"Make it quick." The view of the sandbox opened as the small ship drifted into the harbor. Local authorities were already on scene, but they wouldn't find Chuck. That man was too calm and collected to stand by as precious time ticked by. He had scattered like sand in a whirlwind as soon as he was off the ship.

That's precisely what Graham was doing, while forgoing any plan to stay true to his business dealings with the Arab. The people he left on the plane would eventually be turned over to the UAE authorities. They were as good as dead regardless of who collected them. It was a shame, and one Graham refused to acknowledge before setting off to this godforsaken country.

His life hung in the balance regardless of his business dealings. It was time he focused on self-correcting and getting the Order off his back. Zero would surely pursue him now that he had killed the Russians and failed to collect his lost super soldier. He would have to rely on outside help if he was going to get away.

"Ames," he growled. All of this was because he chose a man of weak resolve to be the future of his program. It was akin to building a castle in the sand. It was marvelous while it stood but would inevitably come crashing down with the first real gust of wind.

Captain Heiter stepped next to him and whispered, "We are out of range of the carrier, sir."

Graham gave him a sideways glance as he pulled the pen from his pocket. He fumbled with it a moment, eyeing the tiny switch that would deliver destruction to the USS Intrepid. He had second thoughts, a curse of fading power. In his prime he would have activated it with a smile on his face. Now, no one was smiling.

But only an idiot would stand by and do nothing. So, he did as he planned, depressed the switch, and waited for the fireworks.

It appeared as a twinkling light.

Then it grew bigger.

Ames sucked in a deep breath and barked, "Incoming!"

As if on his command, the ship's PDCs sprang to life as 20mm rounds screamed from their barrels in two-second bursts. Ames squinted as he watched the tracer rounds make impact. At first there appeared to be no sign at all, then the explosion happened.

The sound of the missile detonating overhead brought back a wave of tasteless memories to the forefront of his mind. In his mind's eye he saw the faces of his friends in that Humvee traversing the Syrian terrain. As fire rained from the sky, he saw those faces fade away, distorted by the flames he was thankful to not have seen in real life.

Nevertheless, their haunting memory remained, and between the thoughts and the smell of the raging fires, it was enough to drive him to puking over the railing.

Graham had nearly succeeded in killing him a second time in the same way. Hell, practically within the same year.

After blowing chunks over the railing, Ames wiped his mouth and looked off into the distance where the frigate had long since disappeared. He ground his teeth and clenched his fists. Murder was in his heart. It consumed his every thought. Graham was the boogie man in his closet and Ames was ready to open the door and release every bit of pent-up fear he had coursing through his body.

Ames's convictions wavered on many things. Most of them political, some personal. He felt it again as his blood pumped through his veins. He didn't believe in revenge killing, but he was willing to make an exception at that very moment. His heart rate accelerated and the throbbing in his head returned. It only took a few moments to put him back into the terror-stricken mindset he'd been in when he awoke in that German hospital, his body torn to pieces.

Knowing death was being delivered by the devil himself carved out enough dread in Ames's heart to send him reeling. He spat bile over the side and tried to get the taste out of his mouth when a voice broke the torment in his head.

"Did they get it?" Ryan asked into Ames's earpiece.

Ames sucked in a breath, steadied himself, and answered, "They did."

"Thank God," Ryan replied. "Now, we can start the manhunt."

Ames wanted to say it was too late. That they would never catch up to the frigate. But he couldn't bring those words to his lips without choking on the knot forming in his throat.

Ryan continued, "I received a message from Beth. She has the killer's black book. Better yet, she has his appointment schedule for what he was planning. There's no mention of Graham, but we could make an impact on the Order by taking out some of their heavy hitters. Regroup in the sandbox."

Ames didn't acknowledge. Then again, he didn't need to. He would do anything to get off that ship and get to work. He preferred to focus on Graham, but the prospect of taking out people just like him who preyed on innocent people would have to scratch that demented itch that craved vengeance.

He departed the ship without acknowledging the watch stander. He knew the protocol. He knew the sailor was simply doing their job. But he walked past without a second glance, his eyes focused on the rest of his group. Beth had stopped the killer, and he assumed they would see that as a win.

As for Ames, he felt like he had lost. Mostly because he was responsible for triggering the murder to take place. Had he not created a scene, then he never would have been made. He was reckless and it cost a life.

"This is on me," he said under his breath.

And the truth hurt.

The explosion sent a shockwave which rustled the waters under the frigate. Graham grasped a handrail to steady himself as burning shards fell from the sky.

"Their PDCs worked," the captain said as he took a swig from a bottle of wine.

Graham cut his eyes to the older man, then to the bottle. "Of course, it worked. I helped design the system. Once you eliminate human error, machines do all the heavy lifting."

"You expected this then?" Captain Heiter gestured as the mayhem burning in the dark waters around them.

"I did. Just as I expect you to take us the long way around to our destination. They'll be looking to the Suez for this ship."

"Mr. Graham, going around the horn will add several days to the trip. We may need to stop for fuel."

"And?" Graham's jaw was set, and his eyes narrowed at the old drunk. He knew the man had disobeyed orders to pull into Dubai. The ship was rogue, and a swift punishment was in order if the Portuguese government ever found him.

But that was Heiter's problem.

"It's nothing, sir," Captain Heiter answered.

"Good. Once we're in open waters I want to go full speed. Don't waste any time."

"I have a minimal crew on board," Captain Heiter said.

Graham glared at him. "What does that have to do with what I asked of you?"

"The crew needs to rest. Running the ship that hard requires more watch standers in the engine room. We don't have the personnel."

Graham wanted to shoot him on the spot. He felt the noose tightening on his own neck while this pathetic worm kept trying to slither out of his own trap. Everything was an excuse as to why not to do something and he was growing weary of listening. "I'll tell you what, you run the ship as you see fit, and when we're boarded by the pirates swarming those waters, I'll deliver you to them in pieces."

Captain Heiter swallowed hard, placed the half-empty wine bottle down, and advanced the throttle a bit. "Full speed it is, sir. We'll be in open waters soon."

Graham turned back to the carrier. Ames had joined Ryan's little team and they were onto him. Caught between the Order, and a few super soldiers of his own design, Graham had little wiggle room to come out of this alive. Still, he had to hold onto hope that his new alliances would keep their word.

His super soldiers weren't the only outfit roaming the globe. They were simply the only ones paid for by the Order. With their assets in the wind, the Order was desperate.

And for good reason.

They didn't want to know what would happen when their titans met their match.

CHAPTER FIFTEEN

"We have two major targets according to Chuck's little black book," Beth said. "There's an old Russian airbase in Siberia and an underground trafficking ring in West Berlin. The Germans have an appointment set for two days from now. There's nothing more than coordinates for the Russians. The question is how do we want to play this?"

Ryan rubbed at the stubble on his chin. He carried a weary expression, one of defeat, and it matched the way Ames felt. Especially when the older man looked to him. "What do you think, Ames? You deployed to Siberia before."

"It was a quick trip in the warmer months," Ames replied. "There's a mountain range just outside the perimeter of the base. We could drop down the mountainside using drones to avoid detection. I haven't used a wingsuit since I got these," he raised his arms, "but I don't think the weight would have too much bearing on the maneuverability in the wingsuit."

Ryan raised an eyebrow. "You want to drop in?"

Ames shrugged, "Better than walking up and knocking on the front door."

Ryan directed his next question at Wills, "What do you think?"

"I think we only have two drones that have that kind of load-bearing capability. If we go in, we go in at half our strength."

"Is it possible?"

The question made Ames's heart beat a little faster. "What are you getting at?"

Wills looked to Ames and said, "They want to split up and hit two targets at once. Is it possible? Yes. Is it without risk? No."

"Is it a risk you would take?" Beth asked.

Wills leaned back in his seat and grinned, "I'm down for anything, except for a wingsuit. I don't trust the wind coming off those mountains. If we do this, we go in on drones and drive right into their backyard."

She looked to Ames next, her expression asking the burning question without her needing to say it.

He glanced towards Wills before speaking, "It seems settled. Sounds like a blast."

―――――――

Preparedness was everything. In Ames's experience, it went beyond simple planning. It was ritualistic. It was the order in which he put on his socks and tied his boots. It was the order in which he situated his weapons.

It was the mindset he put himself into before he strapped himself into a self-guided flying machine aimed at an enemy base for which he knew very little.

But no amount of preparedness made up for the fact that it was the worst time of year for this sort of thing: dangling by a harness from the belly of a drone in negative zero-degree weather, screaming down the side of a snow-capped mountain, heading straight for enemy territory. Smarter men would have said no to this. Wiser men wouldn't have been in this situation to begin with.

"One hundred and twenty seconds," Wills said, his teeth chattering a staccato rhythm between his words. It only made Ames feel that much colder. In less than twenty-four hours they had gone from sweating profusely to becoming icicles. Acclimation be damned.

"Roger," Ames replied a moment later. He had to force himself to speak through the frigid wind beating down on him. He moved his visor down and scanned the terrain. The ground temperature was fifteen degrees warmer and much more hospitable than the icy torrent they were in now.

It was going to be a long two minutes.

"Weapons ready," Wills said.

Ames checked again for the umpteenth time. "Solid." The MT-20V was a modern marvel. Not only was it accurate, but it was also reliable. The problem was you needed cybernetic arms just to lift and fire it. Good thing for Ames and Wills, they had the necessary equipment.

"Sixty seconds."

"Come on, come on, come on," Ames willed time to move a little quicker. He prepped his grip on the release ring. It was a thirty-foot drop from the drone which was preprogrammed to fly in a tactical support pattern. Wills had full authority over the ordnance the drones carried. In lieu of backup, the drones would provide ground support if things got tight.

Again, smarter people wouldn't be doing this.

"Three. Two. One."

The two-man team released simultaneously, hitting the powdery snow less than twenty feet from one another and began the one-mile hike through a heavily wooded area towards the base. Once they arrived, they were met with the tallest wrought iron fence either of them had ever seen. The buzz of current pulsating through the bars made Ames's hairs stand on end and created static in his ocular implant.

Wills stepped in with a shorting rod, drove it into the ground, then released the free end into the base of the fence. Sparks shot out like fireworks on the fourth of July, before America was torn asunder by civil conflict. The sparks died out quickly and Wills looked to Ames, "So far so good."

Ames held his weapon at the ready while Wills sawed through sections of the fence. It wasn't iron, though. The steel was a dense alloy and stronger than the blade.

"This isn't working," Wills said under his breath.

"Let me try," Ames said as he stepped into position. He let his harness hold his weapon as he took hold of a bar in each hand and pulled them apart. It took every bit of effort he could muster to get the bars to budge. Once they did, he nearly ripped them off.

"I don't think this type of metal likes the cold," Wills said with a smirk as Ames tossed the broken pieces aside. "Two more and we can squeeze through."

Ames went back to work and opened a sufficiently sized hole for them to crawl into.

Wills led the way, ducking behind armored trucks and fuel tanks. Their briefing gave little to no information on the layout of the base, only that there were underground anomalies on the northern end. The expected tunnels leading to a larger compound under the mountain. What they might find was anyone's guess. Based on what they saw now, it would be a weapons cache.

But there was plenty of real estate to have those in the buildings along the perimeter. Underground would have to be the things they didn't want anyone to know about. The thought made Ames's skin crawl.

Wills motioned for them to hustle to another cover area. Ames supplied cover while Wills sprinted across. Then they reversed roles until Ames was behind Wills again. They continued this dance until they were three-quarters of the way to the first tunnel entrance.

That's when the lights came on.

A voice shouted into a loudspeaker. Wills looked to Ames, "My Russian is rusty, what is he saying?"

Ames shrugged, "Probably show yourselves before we blast you to kingdom come in the name of Mother Russia, if I had to guess."

Wills smirked at the joke. "Well, we can do as they say, but we both know they'll shoot at us anyway."

Ames rubbed one hand gingerly along the barrel of his weapon and said, "Good. We can return the favor."

Wills nodded. "Let's dance."

They both moved around the obstruction and faced the Russian soldiers. "Hey guys," Wills said. "Sorry, we no speaky the Russian, comprende?" He looked to Ames with a toothy grin.

"You're going to get us killed," Ames said.

"Maybe," Wills replied with a wink. "It's not like these guys know what we're saying."

"Put your guns down, Americans," the squad leader shouted.

"You were saying?" Ames shot back at Wills. The Russians closed in on them, weapons raised to the ready. Red dots covered both Americans like polka dot suits. "I hope you have something up your sleeve," Ames said, "Because I think one of these fools is about to fire at us."

Wills shifted ever so slightly, "be patient, it's coming."

Ames glanced up at the sky. A glint of light from one of the drones came into view. It accelerated towards them, descending from the clouds. A moment later, a flash and smoke.

Ames looked to Wills with a questioning look in his eye. Wills shook his head lightly, "Not yet."

A pause.

Then a nod.

Ames lifted his free hand and used his pointer finger and gestured towards the sky. "Don't look now guys, but I think the skies falling."

The missile hit the dirt with a thud, a split second later the earth erupted beneath the Russian soldiers like a firecracker in an anthill. The Russians screamed, mayhem ensued, and Ames followed Wills has he leapt into action.

The men sprinted towards the entrance of the first tunnel.

Gunfire erupted behind them, but most of the men were still screaming in agony from shrapnel wounds and burns.

"I hope you have more where that came from," Ames said as another squad of Russians poured out of the barracks several hundred yards away.

"I have a couple more, but I was more planning on using them to escape, not to get in," he replied.

There was a keypad for entry into the tunnel entrance. Wills looked at it for a moment and grew frustrated. There are more than a thousand possible combinations to get in, there's no way I can try them all before they're on us. We need to find another way in."

Ames looked around, but his eyes kept falling upon the dozens of soldiers running in their direction, rifles in hand. "The only thing I can think of is driving a truck into it," Ames suggested.

Will shrugged, "I'm not above that. Finesse went out the window when they turned the lights on."

As those words escaped his lips, a rumbling came from below. The entrance to the tunnel began to open on its own, and Ames looked at Wills as if he had said some magic word to elicit such a response. "What did you do?"

Wills look back at him, "Nothing, you?"

Ames shook his head no. But it wasn't long before they saw what was on the other side.

"Oh crap," Ames grumbled. "Run!"

The plane touched down in West Berlin while the birthday celebration in First Class grated on Ryan's nerves. He wore his scowl like a badge of honor and elicited more than a few sympathetic looks from the women in the group towards Beth, his "embattled wife".

"Everywhere we go it's the same thing," Beth whispered, "Why can't I be your sister, or a friend?"

"Everyone's a couple these days. Besides, you should take it as a compliment. I'm a stud," Ryan replied, his demeanor softening a touch as he glared back at the onlookers. Their eyes returned to their own business begrudgingly.

"Yeah, in your own head," Beth shot back. She would be lying if she said she hadn't thought about it. She and Ryan had been in many life and death situations together. She knew more about him than he did most of the time, and she did care for him, but she didn't know if that was a romantic entanglement or just being a decent human being.

It was hard to tell when your entire adult life was spent in kill or be killed mode. She preferred to look at herself as the den mother. Nurturing and caring, but more than willing to break a few bones when the wrong person slips in.

The remove seatbelt sign illuminated with an audible ding, stirring her from her thoughts, and provoking cheers from the partying crowd. She and Ryan let the rowdy group leave ahead of them, mostly so the stench of booze and air of belligerence didn't have to linger around them any longer than it had to. They were young once, but those days were lost in discarded calendars years ago.

Ryan rose and pulled their bags from the overheads. "Is the meeting setup with Han?"

"Of course," she replied. "He's even picking us up."

Ryan smirked, "You think of everything."

"That's why you hired me," she replied.

He looked away bashfully and it made her wonder if her previous thoughts may have had some founding in truth. Was there something between them that neither of them acknowledged?

Beth followed him off the plane and into the terminal. The good thing about arriving after midnight was that the crowds were smaller. The bad thing was that they tended to draw attention, largely due to Ryan's prosthetics. Even when covered by a jacket, there was something not quite right about his arms. They were too angular, bulky, and rigid. Plus, only a psycho wears gloves inside.

They made their way outside where Han waited for them in

what could only be described as a soccer mom van. Han looked like a tourist with his fanny pack and too large for his head sunglasses perched on top of his head. The camera dangling from its neck strap completed the ridiculous ensemble.

"That's your interpretation of incognito?" Ryan asked as he loaded the bags into the back of the van.

Han smirked, "I'm here for pleasure. Besides, this car may look innocent enough, but it's masterfully crafted to be a death machine."

Ryan raised an eyebrow, "With your driving, I'm sure it is."

Beth laughed while Han lifted his hands in feigned surrender. "Our football is better than yours."

Ryan closed the rear door and looked down at his German friend. They had known each other nearly as long as he and Beth had. The German had saved his life at least three times, but a fourth was still under debate. They had decided to let the upcoming World Cup settle that argument for them.

Based on current stats Han was winning.

"You have me there," Ryan replied as he brought Han in for a hug.

"So, what's the plan?"

Ryan shrugged. "Sleep and then get to this location by two-o'clock local time." He handed a piece of paper to Han.

Han looked it over and typed it into a GPS on his cell. "That's downtown in an industrial complex."

"Yeah, not exactly the scummy places you think about when you discuss human trafficking."

Han shook his head. "War used to be simple, like sports, but with killing."

"It's probably always been like this, we just weren't paying attention," Beth replied.

Han cut his eyes to her and nodded. "The truth has a way of wrecking our beliefs. Patriotism really is skin deep."

"If that," Ryan replied. "You want to help clean up the streets around here?"

Han looked up at the brooding American. "I'll do what I can, but it isn't much." He lifted his left pant leg and revealed a device on his ankle. "They got to me early."

"Do they know you're here?" Beth asked.

Han nodded softly, a pained expression on his face. "My government has been after me a long time. I figured I would give them just cause to come after me. Take the van and I'll catch up to you when I can."

"How much time do we have?" Ryan asked.

Han glanced down at his watch. "A few minutes. The van is inconspicuous enough for you to get out of here. I have a motorcycle for my grand escape. I'll head in the opposite direction. Weapons are in the floor storage under the middle seat."

"Thank you," Beth said, a hint of sorrow clutched her words, dragging them down with the weight of regret. She knew how he felt. Her own government had abandoned her too, before labeling her a war criminal. There was no going back for either of them.

"I'll get you a beer next time I see you," Ryan said, taking his friend's hand.

"As long as it's not that pale goat piss you always drink," Han said with a snicker. "You two best get out of here. I can smell them getting closer."

Ryan and Beth loaded into the van and took off, leaving Han behind. They watched in the side mirrors as the German waved goodbye, then darted off into the shadows.

CHAPTER SIXTEEN

An armored personnel carrier raced from the tunnel, shooting sparks as it skidded in a tight circle as the driver directed the vehicle towards Wills and Ames. It took a moment for Ames to notice the sag of the rear leaf spring. Either the personnel carrier was poorly maintained, or whatever they were hauling was massive.

The latter rang true when the panels opened.

A pained, animalistic roar erupted from the back of the personnel carrier. Two behemoths rose to their full heights, nearly ten feet of corded muscle and mutilated fury.

"What the hell is that?" Ames muttered. He took a cautious step back while Wills gawked at it.

The beast nearest them roared again and whipped a tendril protruding from his arms out towards the men. Wills ducked the attack as he jutted to the right. He pulled the trigger and sent a blast that merely deflected off the monstrosity.

"He has some kind of armor built into his skin," Wills said. "I've never seen this before."

A blood curdling scream rose, and the beast whipped again. This time the tendril wrapped around Wills's torso, squeezed tightly, and sent enough electricity into the man to make the hairs on the back of Ames's neck stand on end.

The monster dropped Wills with a dull thud and eyed his next target.

"I don't think so, Scooter," Ames spat. He took aim and fired, keeping the trigger depressed as a torrent of tungsten steel munitions pummeled the monster from the depths. It cut and run away, whipping its tendrils madly like a defiant toddler. It wailed, slammed into the personnel carrier, flipping it like it weighed nothing, and glared back at Ames.

He looked at the useless weapon in his hands, then looked to Wills. Steam rose from his teammate's mouth in shallow puffs. He was alive, but unable to fight. Ames had to act. He had to do something, or they were both dead.

Ames looked to the squad of Russians as they stood by, cheering on the onslaught the monsters brought with them. The soldiers didn't need to worry, their battle was one-sided, and practically over.

He looked around for a sign of something he could use, and found it, a fuel truck.

Ames sprinted towards the truck and climbed in. He whispered a quick prayer as the keys fell into his hands from their perch in the sun visor. He turned it in the ignition and gunned it. The fuel truck screamed towards the monster in third gear. Four thousand RPMs of whining diesel engine careened towards the deadliest thing Ames had ever seen.

Then he hit it center mast.

The beast roared along with the spinning read tires. The gas pedal was on the floor while Ames held the steering wheel with a white-knuckled grip. The truck lurched and grabbed, seeking traction and losing it almost as quickly. A moment later the beast lifted the truck over its head, spewing hot saliva as it roared in Ames's face from only a few feet away.

He looked the devil in its eyes, pulled his sidearm from its holster, and emptied the magazine in his enemy's face. Flesh tore away in chunks. The monster flinched and blinked with each shot, but kept the truck raised like a sack of flour.

Even after finding the monster's weak spot there was no winning.

There was only the breaking of bones if the beast ever got his hands on Ames.

How do you defeat an enemy that you can't kill?

That was the question that was about to get Ames killed.

"Ames!" Wilson shouted over the roar of the beast.

Ames looked away from the snarling monster to Wills as he lay on the ground. He had his hand on his weapon, barely lifting it as he watched the chaos. "Get out of the truck," he called.

Ames understood what Wills was planning and placed his hand on the door handle. He jiggled it, expecting it to fling open, but it wouldn't budge. He adjusted his grip on the handle and put his shoulder into it to force it open. Nothing.

The beast roared again, then smashed the fuel truck back to the earth. He beat his fists against his chest, howling before he slammed his massive forearms into the body, crushing the front end of the truck like it was papier-mâché. The beast began ripping shards of steel from the fuel truck, tearing it apart piece by piece to get to his target.

Ames lay on the seat and kicked the door with the cybernetic leg. He once pressed two tons with his prosthetic leg, but as he frantically tried to escape, he couldn't seem to muster the necessary strength.

"Calm and collected," he reminded himself. "Focus." He went at it again, using both legs while holding himself steady with the back of the seat and the steering wheel for leverage. He kicked with everything he had, blasting the door off its hinges. Ames wasted no time leaving from the truck and sprinting away from the monster as fast as his legs could move him.

The gunshot made his ears ring, then the explosion happened, the force of it catching and sending him face first into the ground. He rolled over with a groan, looking over his shoulder as flames reached for the sky. The beast lay in a mutilated heap. Large pieces of shrapnel protruded from his chest cavity smoking like a furnace.

"That's one of them," Ames said as his eyes darted from side to side, "But where's the other one?"

"I don't understand your thinking," Sanders said over the video conference. The man looked weary, dark circles under his eyes, hair unkempt. He looked like Graham felt.

"I'm thinking both sides converge against one another," Graham replied. "Ryan and his new recruits are looking for something to fight, I suggest we give it to them. The Order wants to retaliate against me because they believe I lost the super soldiers. They'll have them. Win/win."

Sanders shook his head, looked off camera a moment, and said, "It doesn't work that way. It never does."

"Is someone there?" Graham asked.

"There's a bit of a ruckus outside my office. I saw movement, but I don't know what's going on."

Graham hesitated. The Secretary of Defense was a guarded position. Any movement outside of his office should have been his own people. Unless... "Have they reached out to you?"

Sanders's jaw slackened. "I received a call."

"From?"

"Not a friend," Sanders replied. "I upped the number of guards after you left."

Graham swore under his breath. He had everything under control, but there was nothing he could do in the middle of the ocean. They wanted him away, this was their plan and he fell into their trap. "You need to get out of there. Go somewhere safe."

"Where?"

That was the question, wasn't it? "Get on a plane and decide in the air. No itinerary will make it difficult for them to track you."

Sanders stammered a moment before replying, "I have responsibilities here."

Graham scoffed in disgust, "You have a role to play. Your location
isn't as important as the fact that you remain breathing."

A slamming sound on the other side of Sanders's door drew the
secretary's attention away from Graham. A moment later light
poured into the room and Graham got a better look at how weary his
old friend looked.

"What's happening there?" Graham asked through his teeth.

Two pops followed, and two pinpoints of blood trickled down
Sanders's chest. Graham watched the light fade from his friend's
eyes, watched his skin turn gray as a shadow crept over him.

The monitor shifted, revealing a dark figure. It bent down to gaze
into the camera. His face was marred and disgusting. He looked like
Halloween in the eyes of a small child.

"Tick tock, Graham. Time's up. You die."

"He had nothing to do with this," Graham shouted. He bit each
word, forcing the syllables to disconnect with emphasis.

"Neither did I." Zero said, showing his jagged teeth in a wicked
smile. "This is all on you."

Sleep alluded her the way it always did before a mission. Beth tossed
and turned, trying to find that one comfortable spot where she could
doze off more than a few moments at a time. Her mind raced, not just
with the pending mission, but the sudden loss of Abe, and the dire
straits Han was in with the German government.

It seemed everyone she was once associated with was either dead
or one the run.

A far cry from being heralded heroes less than a dozen years ago,
before worldwide events turned critical.

That was when common people woke up to the fact that a
shadow government was in place and that all wars were merely a

means to launder money and power to the next echelon of authority. It was sick and she would have no part in it.

Most of her friends felt the same way, abandoning their posts, their commissions, their lives. There weren't many left. And men like Ryan were hard to come by, the ones battle-hardened, but still longing for peace if they endured just one more fight.

She envied him that. It was better than the hopelessness of yet another mission, another opportunity to die without affecting real change.

Some people said it was a game, if that was true, then she never wanted to find out that the lives torn apart were for the entertainment of someone else.

Ryan snored on the other side of the room. His hulking frame caused the bed to sag, and Beth wondered how long before it would snap. It would be funny, but he was so far out of it that she doubted he would notice.

Beth rolled over again and peered out the narrow slit in the curtain out at the West Berlin skyline. All cities were too big now. The overflow of humanity into giant pockets created a pressure cooker for people's nerves. There was nowhere to go to escape the rat race.

Except underground like she and Ryan had done. They had means that very few others did, aside from the rich. They carved out their own niche and lived off the unmarked bills left behind by their home countries alphabet agencies. It was far from an honest living; except they were being true to themselves.

That had to count for something.

At least, she hoped it did. She hoped to never find out otherwise. That might be more than she could bear.

While the smoke billowed from the beast's corpse above, Wills and Ames descended into the tunnel. Their fight with the monster left them both shaking but determined to investigate what the darkness below contained. "I've never been afraid of the dark," Wills said under his breath, "but I think this is the most unnerving place I've ever been."

"Likewise," Ames replied. This was far from his first tunnel, but the ones he had investigated in the Middle East were used for the enemy to traverse unseen. After the two monstrosities exited the tunnel, their power beyond anything he had ever seen, Ames didn't want to think what else could be down there.

They came to an obstruction on the floor of the tunnel. It was partially obscured by shadow from the dimly lit space. What they did see looked mangled and messy.

"What is that?" Wills asked as he switched on his flashlight. The LED beam fell upon a pair of twisted legs ripped from the torso of an unlucky Russian soldier.

"I think we found where the other one went," Ames said, struggling to keep his trepidation from showing in his voice.

"It seems like they can't control the monsters they made," Wills replied indignantly. He stepped over the remains and kept trudging along. Ames followed, tightening his grip on his weapon in case he needed to use it even though it seemed useless against the other one.

They came to an opening in the tunnel, with a large door partially hanging from its hinges. Whatever had opened it, had ripped it. It didn't take much thinking to know who had done it, but it left the question as to what lay ahead?

"He went in there, so do we go after them?" Ames asked.

"I don't want to, but I don't know that we have much of a choice," Wills replied.

The pair of men stepped into the gaping hole where the door used to hang and shone their flashlights into the depths. There were young men and women chained in rows. Scattered amongst them, dead Russians lay in bloody heaps, targets of the monster's rage.

"If I didn't know any better," Ames said, "I would say I think he's on our side."

Wills shifted the beam of his flashlight across the far wall, stopping with a gasp as the beam fell upon the beast. It cowered in the corner next to a malnourished woman. His massive hand clutched onto hers. Both sat trembling with fear and rage.

"Ma'am, do you speak English?" Wills asked, keeping his tone even as he tried not to disturb the deadly beast on the other side of the room.

"Yes," she replied with a thick, Asian accent. "I do know some English."

"Are you all right?"

"I'm cold and hungry and afraid," she replied. "But my brother protected me."

Ames's jaw dropped as he peered at his partner "Did she just say her brother?" Wills nodded. "Ma'am," Ames said, "did you say that he's your brother."

She looked at him with tear filled eyes. Sorrow darkened the lines in her face but softened when she looked at him. "Yes. He is my brother."

CHAPTER SEVENTEEN

West Berlin sprang to life as the sun rose over the horizon. Traffic outside the hotel turned a quiet street into a madhouse and Beth was thankful they were staying near the rendezvous point. She just hoped word hadn't spread that Chuck was dead.

"They'll find out soon enough," she muttered as she sipped her coffee and looked out over the balcony.

Ryan stepped out of the bathroom, his hair dripping from the shower. His t-shirt clung to his body awkwardly until he freed it up by tugging it down around his waistline. He looked at her with feigned irritation, "No towels. Two stars."

Beth laughed. "Did you look under the sink?"

His scowl faded into a look of confusion. He turned back and opened the cabinet to see a stack of fluffy white towels. "Stupid occupant. One star," he groaned as he closed it back and pulled his toothbrush from his overnight bag.

Beth grinned and turned back to the city below. She watched the cars speed up and slow down manically. She wondered why they wasted so much energy stomping the gas and slamming on the brakes instead of going slow and consistent. It was this kind of erratic behavior that made her hate driving in cities.

"Two hours until show time. Are you ready?" Ryan asked as he came up behind her and looked over her shoulder. "Hopefully this will die down a little by then."

"Hmm, I'm always ready, but this is just the calm before the storm," she replied. "What about you?"

"Same. I just want to get it done and over with. I hate waiting."

Beth nodded in agreement. This was the hard part. Waiting to do something. Everyone always assumed the worst part of their duty was getting shot at. Though uncomfortable, there was something about bullets flying that was more palatable than the waiting game. Perhaps it was the rush of adrenaline that gave a little dopamine hit to that sick and twisted part of her brain, she wondered?

"Do you ever wonder where we'll go when all this is over?" Beth asked.

Ryan looked down at her, his eyebrows lifted, "You and I, or us in general?"

She hadn't meant it that way, but back peddling would only make it worse. "Where do you see yourself when this is done?"

Ryan let out a sigh. He did it every time he had something he was holding back. "I hope to be on a large plot of land as far away from society as I can get. I would prefer a river or lake, but at this point, there's not many places left that are untouched by the *disasterships* running this world."

He had coined that phrase when she first met him years ago. He seldom used it anymore and she wondered what prompted it this time. She turned to face him. His eyes were deep and penetrating. The kind of blue that matched the sky on a cloudless winter day. "So, not New York?"

He scoffed. "Yeah, that's a big no for me. What about you?"

Beth shrugged. "I don't mind a few people, but the buzz of a big city makes it hard for me to sleep. I might just set out on a boat to nowhere, pull in when I need supplies, and set off again."

"You want to live on a boat?"

"Maybe, I don't know. That's assuming we ever get to the end of whatever game this is." She stared back over West Berlin, her eyes narrowing on the parking garage a few blocks away. Somewhere their targets were preparing to meet someone for nefarious purposes on the third level, aisle F.

They would meet someone all right, but it wouldn't be the encounter they were hoping for.

———

Graham paced the cabin. He made barely five strides before having to turn and face the other direction, but there was no other way to release the pent-up energy coursing through his body. He wanted to blow up on somebody, anybody.

That was when the klaxon sounded.

He made his way to the bridge to see the oncoming vessels. Somali pirates armed to the gills with rocket launchers and AKs. A properly manned warship would blast them out of the water, but this was hardly well manned. "I told you full speed, Captain," Graham said biting each word.

"We are full speed, sir. They just have better boats." He handed Graham the binoculars and continued, "Those are special forces boats. Twin engines with over five-hundred horsepower each. There's not a ship of this size that can outrun them."

"What options do we have?"

Captain Heiter shrugged. "Keep going in a zig-zag pattern? Make it hard for them to board. Eventually they'll launch rockets at us, but depending on where they land, it might not be fatal to the hull."

Graham rolled his eyes. Neither option was one he was willing to buy off on. "What weapons do we have?"

The captain pointed to .50 caliber mounts on each side of the ship. Thick steel plating served as shields on each side of the mounts.

They were partially covered in rust like the other parts of the ship, but anything was better than nothing.

"Any warheads?" Graham asked.

Captain Heiter shook his head. "We were scheduled for a yard period, we offloaded most of what was useful. We do have some flares that could burn through the thin hulls of those boats, but they aren't very accurate. You would have to have the boats right up on you to hit them."

Graham bit his lip. He wanted to spew vitriol and put his hands on the incompetent captain standing before him. It was no wonder why the drunkard was compromised. Excuse after excuse and zero good ideas. Still, he was a useful idiot to have around. Even if that meant handing him over to the pirates.

"Get your men on the .50 cals. Wait until they're close enough and unleash hell. Do whatever you can to keep them off this ship because you know what they'll do once onboard."

The captain swallowed hard. His wide eyes accentuated how pale his face became at the thought of the coming slaughter. It would be slow and painful. It would send a message to anyone who crossed the Somali pirates. Their heads would literally be on pikes like trophies.

"Yes, sir," Captain Heiter said, and made the order across the ship's coms.

Graham turned to face the oncoming vessels. Two of them bore down on the frigate with intense speed. They were close enough he could hear the high-pitched whine of the engines. They were close enough he could hear their screaming jeers.

They were too close for comfort.

Ames approached cautiously. He kept his hands in front of him, palms open, as unthreatening as he could manage. He knelt before the woman and the monster, trying to piece together how something so savage could have been a person.

Pain looked back at him through large brown eyes. Its face was covered by tufts of hair. The skin was scarred and mutilated. He looked down at the tendrils as they lay like snakes on the concrete floor, slithering about as they protruded from his inner forearms. Blood seeped from where they exited his body, the skin and veins dark as if they were slowly decaying on their host.

"How old is he?" Ames asked.

"He was seventeen when we were taken. I think it's been about ten years. What year is it?"

Ames swallowed the knot in his throat and answered. "2047. Where are you from?"

"Singapore."

He looked around. Wills was in the background removing the chains from the others, whispering directions and comforting words. The soldier's face was as pale as a sheet. No horrors of war could have prepared them for what they saw.

"Who was the other man they did this to?"

The woman shook her head. "I never met him before the transition. This is the first time I've seen Adriel in years."

"Are you..." Ames couldn't finish the question before she glared up at him and turned the beast's arm outward to reveal a tattoo on his wrist. It matched one on hers. Ames nodded. "All right, do you trust that it's safe for us to leave here with him? There's so many people we're trying to rescue."

Adriel roared, but it sounded more like a deep whimper. He understood, which meant Ames could communicate with him.

"It's safe," she replied, her voice breaking. "He doesn't want to hurt anyone."

Ames wanted to believe her, but the disembodied legs they had found in the tunnel suggested otherwise.

Adriel reached out and placed a heavy hand on Ames's shoulder. Ames stopped breathing, holding it as he tried not to react to the fear screaming in his head for him to run. "No. Hurt." The words were strained but understandable.

"No hurt," Ames said back, eliciting a nod from him. Ames looked to the woman, "There's dozens of solders outside waiting for us. Once we emerge, there's going to be gunfire. I don't want to scare you, but it's going to be hard to get everyone out of here safely. We lost the element of surprise."

She wiped a tear from her eye and nodded. Her stoic expression hid the worry from her face and Ames was impressed by how well she was holding it together. She had lost so much of her life, but was still compassionate, holding to her brother's hand despite his outward appearance.

She looked to him and spoke in Malay. He grunted, nodded, whimpered, but never moved aggressively. She spoke calmly, directly before turning her eyes back to Ames. "He will help you."

Ames struggled to find the words. He knew Adriel was more than capable but asking him to be the brutal monster they made him to be seemed unconscionable. But what choice did they have? "Let me discuss it with my associate," he said before removing her chains and helping her to stand. "What's your name?"

"Tian," she said. "You?"

He held her hand and answered, "Roderick Ames."

"Thank you, Roderick Ames, for helping us." It was the first time he'd heard those words from someone on a mission like this. For the first time in his adult life, he saw what he was doing in the light of good. His impact on another human life wasn't always to end it, but to provide hope.

That was what he always wanted but never achieved.

He looked at Adriel and saw past the monster the Russians had created. They were the same, only the tortures of war were more visible on the young man. Despite all Ames had been through, most of his scars were internal from the conflict of who he'd become.

This was his life's purpose.

Ames turned to Wills, "We have backup."

Wills looked up from his controller and his eyes fell on Adriel. There was a knowing expression in his eyes before he spoke. "I've lost control of the drones; we're going to have to fight our way out without knowing their positioning."

"Is it the tunnels?" Ames asked.

He nodded, "Probably. I'll keep an eye on it. If he's going to help, then we need a plan. There's too many people and most of them are too weak to run."

Ames turned to Adriel. "Do you understand that we need to fight, but also protect these people?"

Adriel nodded with a grunt.

"We don't know where the enemy is up there, but we're sure they're waiting for us. We can't go up without drawing attention to ourselves."

Adriel continued nodding. "I. Go."

Wills stepped up beside Ames, the color in his cheeks returning to normal. "It's our only option."

Ames wanted to disagree, to not send an innocent kid who didn't deserve this into conflict, but Wills was right. As soon as they emerged, the gunfire would begin, and the Russians had the superior position. Maybe if they could reestablish their connection with the drones, they stood a better chance.

"Are you sure you're willing to do this?" Ames asked.

Adriel answered, "I. Go."

Ames let out a stale breath and replied, "Then it's settled. Adriel will lead us out. God willing, it'll be enough."

———

Beth and Ryan pulled into the parking garage in Han's van. Their German friend had provided enough small arms to get the job done, but that was providing that their targets were taken by the element of surprise. If the scumbags they were after had better weapons, then it would be an uphill battle. Not that the prospect of working for a

154

victory wasn't any fun.

She parked the van two aisles away from the drop location and killed the headlights. The windows and windshield were tinted dark enough to obscure them from view and the scrambler installed in the van would provide enough static in the surveillance cameras to prevent their presence from being detected. All they had to do was wait for the other party to show and take them out.

Easy.

"Hurry up and wait," Beth said as she pulled off her seatbelt. She checked her Glock and holstered it.

Ryan replied with a dissatisfied grunt. It took years for her to understand that it was his way of responding while his mind was elsewhere. It took longer for him to confide in her that in those moments he was praying. Beth hadn't grown up in a religious household, and neither did he, but somewhere along the way Ryan had found faith and clutched onto it with a death grip.

She envied him that. Beth, on the other hand, focused her attention on what she could control. Favor from the Almighty felt elusive. Having faith in anything was hard for someone with control issues and a history of being let down. Even if she wanted to believe, she didn't know if she could go all in like Ryan.

He cleared his throat and looked over to her. "I have a good feeling about this."

She cut her eyes at him, "Really? Why?"

Ryan shrugged, "I checked the news and no word on Han being arrested, so that's good news. Maybe it'll work out for us too."

"Those aren't the same kinds of things," Beth replied. "He's running from a pansy government that wouldn't know what to do with him if they had him. We're dealing with human traffickers."

"The government is probably involved in that too," he said.

"Good point." Those words were followed by a white box truck pulling into the space designated for the drop. There was no branding or identifying marks on it. Even the emblems for the manufacturer had been removed. "That's interesting. No markings and right on time."

"Speak of the devil," Ryan said as he pulled his weapon from its holster.

"And the devil shows up," Beth replied. She followed his lead, pulled her weapon, and looked at him. "I think he's expecting company."

Ryan grinned and grasped the door handle. "Then maybe it's time for us to say hi." he pulled open the door and stepped out gingerly. He let the door ease shut while Beth killed the dome light before the men in the truck could see them.

He gestured with one hand where he intended to go and she watched, holding her breath for his signal.

In the quiet calm before the storm, she hoped Ryan's prayer was enough to cover for both of them.

CHAPTER EIGHTEEN

Adriel erupted from the tunnels with a roar. Ames and Wills followed with their weapons drawn. Within two heartbeats, the Russians started firing. Ames assumed a position behind the crumpled remains of the fuel truck and returned fire. Wills sprung up behind him, using his controller to regain access to the drones.

Ames targeted a squad of Russians assembled at the top of one of the buildings as they fired down at Adriel as he lashed out at the troops on the ground. Adriel swiped a massive tendril and cut four men in half with a single blow. He beat his closed fists against his chest and howled in anger.

"I've got it," Will said. "I have a birds eye view of their locations. There's a twelve-man team to the north trying to flank us, but I have something up my sleeve for them."

Ames smiled at the news but was too busy to say anything. He was focused on laying down suppression fire to give Adriel a chance to take out more of the soldiers so they could evacuate the prisoners.

Moments later an explosion erupted from the north. Wills rooted, and slapped Ames on the back as he moved from his position and took another several yards away. Ames saw elation in his partner's face. There was a certain joy about winning, even though they were laying waste to human lives.

Not that the enemy wouldn't do the same to them.

Adriel charged another squad. Each foot fall sounded like a tree falling to the ground, and the dull thud made the hairs on the back of Ames's neck stand up. The young man turned monster delivered death and destruction in a wave of violence unlike any Ames had ever seen.

"Thank God you're on our side," Ames whispered. His joy was brought low when a motion behind him drew his attention. He moved to turn, with the barrel of a rifle pressed against his cheek forcefully.

"Lower your weapon," the Russian shouted.

Ames did as he was in instructed, wondering how far the man was willing to take it. "Take it easy," Ames said with a smirk.

"What are you smiling at, American?" The Russian asked indignantly. "I'm going to splatter your brains out and burn your corpse."

"That sounds dirty," Ames said. He made a quarter turn to the left and sized up the soldier.

"I said don't move."

Ames eyed the men with a raised eyebrow. Sweat ran down his face and his index finger trembled on the trigger guard. His expression screamed that he didn't want to shoot, but he didn't want to die either. Little did he know, the choice wasn't up to him. "Or what?" Ames said through his teeth.

The Russian took a deep breath then shoved the barrel harder into Ames's face. That was all it took. In a flash, Ames slammed his arm against the Russians weapon, flinging it from the man's grip. The Russian looked back at him with his jaw slack. Ames charged the bracelets on his wrists and sent a kinetic blast from both arms with enough force to fling the man into the gate surrounding the base.

Ames watched the crumpled body fly away only to sag to the ground like a discarded wad of cloth. It appeared the force had broken the man's neck. He might still be alive, but Ames didn't care to find out. Sympathy was for people who didn't prey on innocent women and children, for people who didn't mutilate kids and turn them into monsters.

Instead, Ames returned his focus on what mattered, lifted his weapon, and continued laying down suppressive fire.

———

The Somalis fired the first shot. An RPG exploded just below the bridge, well above the waterline. It was a scare tactic and the expression on the captain's face suggested it was working.

"Are you going to do something?" Graham hissed.

Captain Heiter stammered, clutching at his chest as he searched for the words to get him out of this.

None were necessary. Graham gritted his teeth and shoved the drunkard out of the way, taking the helm. He shouted over the com, "Put every bullet you have into those boats!"

His order was answered with a flurry of .50 caliber rounds pulsing in unison. The report of gunfire echoed off the water creating a cacophony of noise at first unsettling, then deadening into a drone as Graham's ears rang. He'd never been in a firefight like this, but he fell into his new position as if he was born for it.

He snatched up the binoculars and watched the damage being dealt.

One of the boats maneuvered out of the way, leaving the other in the line of fire. The man who'd fired first was riddled with bullets with enough force to rip his arm off his torso. Several more rounds sunk into his body, convulsing him until shaky, lifeless legs no longer supported his weight. The splatter of his remains hitting the deck spewed over the men next to him.

"That ought to persuade them that this was a bad idea," Graham said. He keyed the com again, "Keep it going. Kill all of them."

Two gunners focused on the boat directly behind them. The dead man lay in a puddle of blood and mutilated meat. Through his binoculars Graham could hardly tell the remains were human. The driver cut the boat hard left, sending a wave towards the frigate before tucking tail and running. They were giving up and it brought a satisfying curl to Graham's lips.

Movement caught his eye as the second boat tried to flank them, firing from their own weapons mounts. Bullets flashed against the steel hull unceremoniously. The rusted shields on the frigate's weapons mounts did their job dutifully and protected his men as they adjusted aim and returned fire.

.50 caliber rounds tore through the hull of the approaching vessel, splintering it down the middle. The Somalis frantically tried to plug the holes while more were put into the boat by the Portuguese sailors. It was a futile effort, but one that preoccupied them with saving themselves rather than continuing their attack.

Graham marveled by how efficient the men were at delivering violence. They channeled their primal nature and unleashed hell with deadly intent. He shouted with elation while the cowardly captain rocked himself in the corner of the bridge.

Captain Heiter had failed his men and everyone on board knew it. Having someone else take the lead in the heat of battle was evidence enough that the captain was too weak to lead. How that would play out would be interesting, but Graham decided it was best to leave it to the men to decide.

For now, he watched the fireworks, and smiled as piracy received justice.

Ryan exited the van first, moving behind a pillar to keep a lookout on what was happening with the box truck. He waved for Beth to come to him a few seconds later. She moved out, careful not to let the van door slam.

Ryan took the next position several yards away. They had the box truck between them and only a few dozen yards ahead in the dimly lit parking garage. Three men had exited the vehicle armed with M4s strapped over their shoulders. They spoke in German, erupting in laughter every so often. It made Beth's stomach turn to know they were enjoying themselves while doing such evil things.

It would be over soon.

Beth had laid out the plan, they just needed to ensure there was no one else at the drop point.

"You boys looking for someone?" Ryan asked. Beth flinched, her eyes darting over to Ryan. This wasn't the plan, so she adapted and kept her position as he closed in. Ryan's weapon was raised and pointed at the man closest to him. They turned to face him with confused expressions on their faces. It took a moment for them to recognize the barrel zeroing in on them.

One of the men shifted. A large guy with the forehead of two men reached for his weapon. "Don't move," Beth ordered, springing from her position behind a pillar. He stopped but didn't lower his hand. He stared blankly at her. He was clearly the muscle and not the brains. "Put your hand down or I'll shoot."

He lowered it slowly while his friends exchanged glances.

It was a Mexican standoff. Three against two, but the three men occupied the same space. Hitting one would potentially strike another. They're lack of movement suggested they recognized they were in a desperate position.

Beth and Ryan had them dead to rights.

"Who are you?" One of the men asked with a thick accent. He was dressed nicer than the other two. The leader? Maybe. He was at least the one they looked to as their spokesman.

"I'll asked the questions," Ryan spat. "Who do you work for?"

The Germans looked at each other before the man responded, "We work for your mother, all night long." His jab elicited a laugh from his pals.

"Ah, a funny guy. You like to laugh?" Ryan said as he took three steps forward. "I like to laugh too. How about I tell you a joke now?" He grabbed a fire extinguisher with on hand, ripped it off the wall, and threw it like a football into the jokester's chest. The blow sent the man back, his chest caved in as he collapsed to the ground.

His friends looked on in horror.

Ryan took another step forward, cracked his neck, and said, "Who's next?"

The shorter German took a pop shot and scrambled for a door. His dumb looking friend jumped behind their truck before Beth fired her first shot. She swore under her breath and glared at Ryan. This wasn't how they planned it.

"Go after the other guy, I'll take care of big dummy," he said as he rushed the truck like a football player doing linebacker drills and slammed the box truck into the cement wall, crushing the German.

"We need one of them alive to get information," Beth said. Her heart raced and she hadn't done anything yet. Her fears were realized when Ryan broke their plan. He was on a rampage. His past came back to haunt him and all he wanted to do was kill the people that hurt him. These men weren't those people, but they were certainly close enough.

"Then don't kill your guy." Ryan said as he stomped towards the truck and pulled it back off the wall. The German was slumped on the floor, his body sagging like a wet cloth. Vacant eyes stared straight ahead, unblinking.

Beth sucked in a deep breath and bolted for the third man. She burst through the door and took the steps down two at a time. Once on the ground level she looked in both directions and saw a blur of motion cut left between some buildings.

"I hate running," she hissed before taking off after the third guy. She ran like her life depended on it. She ran like his life depended on it. Ryan had given into his darker nature. Blind rage had taken hold and threatened their mission. She would have to do whatever it took to save what she could and hope that they got the answers they were after.

If not, innocent people would die, and Ryan would blame himself.

Ames ran as hard as he legs would move as the Russians fired rockets and mortars from a well defended position. Somewhere in the distance Adriel roared as he mauled a squad of soldiers, but the enemy had regrouped and strategized to divide them. Without cover fire from Ames and Wills, Adriel was vulnerable, though not unstoppable.

At least not yet.

It was a solid plan, except now Ames was pissed and ready to rip heads off. This fight was no longer about surviving; it was about revenge. Just a glimpse of what they had done to those innocent people was enough to send anyone over the edge.

He would kill all the men responsible if it saved one of the victims they found in the tunnels. He couldn't let it go. Not yet.

Ames leaped up the tower and punched through the brick and stone to create handholds to climb with. The Russians fired wildly with small arms. Most missed, but a few bullets bounced harmlessly from his cybernetic arms as he shielded his face and torso. He warded them off with a kinetic blast from his bracelets and continued climbing as rubble and debris spilled over him like running water.

Wills joined him in his pursuit. The blades extended from his arms aided his climbing as he sprinted up the tower, screaming profanities before diving into the madness.

By the time Ames joined him, the Russians were laid out, spilling blood and guts out over the stone floor. The smell of iron and gun powder were heavy in the smoky air as Ames huffed and puffed from his climb. "You could have saved some for me," Ames said.

Wills shot a glare at his partner and a flash of anger poured from his soul through his eyes. He was overcome by the war in his head, the one that survivors never return from. Ames recognized it, felt its snares on his own mind. He wanted to fight it, but it was a losing battle. It always was.

"Less talking and more shooting," Wills said as he took up a weapon and searched the terrain for more Russians. He fired rockets at them, hissing expletives with each shot.

Ames nodded and assumed a position next to Wills to help lay to waste anything in uniform that moved. Gone was the satisfaction of doing the right thing and in its place was the hollow numbness that came when he turned his mind off to quiet his fears. He gave into the mindless killing with surgical precision.

He gave into what he was created to be.

CHAPTER NINETEEN

Two sailors led their former captain to the bow in chains. Graham watched them berate the old drunkard, tossing objects at him, screaming indignantly at his betrayal of their trust. He deserved what was coming. This was war and he had turned his back on his duty to protect the crew.

"Do you have anything to say, sir?" A sailor with the name Anacleto stitched onto his uniform asked as he approached Graham. They saw the American as their captain now, but he had no ambition to lead them beyond ensuring they got out of that attack alive.

"No. As I've said, this is your ship to lead. You should choose one of your own to take the helm," Graham replied.

"None of us has the proper training," Anacleto replied.

Graham leaned in to respond, "Neither do I." He stared the man dead in the eye and willed the young sailor to seize the opportunity presented to him.

"What shall we do with him?" Anacleto gestured towards the former captain.

Graham shrugged. "You're in international waters. What law is there to rule you?"

Anacleto looked back at the assembled men circling their former captain. There was bloodlust in their eyes and Graham wanted nothing more than for them to scratch that itch.

"We can toss him overboard?"

"You can do whatever you deem necessary, *Captain*," Graham replied, his inflection stirring something in the Portuguese sailor's eyes. There was a reason Anacleto had come to speak to him; he was a natural leader. The rest of the crew would let him take control. They would follow his orders, and his lack of confidence would have to take a back seat to doing the right thing.

"Yes, sir," Anacleto replied before turning back to the assembled men. He stepped up to the bow, his shoulders squared as he looked down at the whimpering coward shackled to the deck.

"Attention to tribunal," Anacleto shouted. The sailors popped tall, all except the former captain. There wasn't enough slack in the chain for him to stand.

"Captain Heiter, you are accused of dereliction of your duties. How do you plead?"

"Innocent," Heiter said. His voice was shrill and brittle. He looked like an overgrown child who just broke the cookie jar.

"Did you take control of the vessel to lead us in life-saving maneuvers?"

"No."

"Were you drunk on duty?"

"Yes."

"Did you prepare the ship for the coming attack?"

"I sounded the klaxon."

"Did you order the crew to their appropriate stations?"

The disgraced captain stammered, a muted "no" falling deafly from his lips. His shoulders slumped in shame. His spirit broken.

"Then you are guilty," Anacleto said. "Toss him over the side."

Heiter's eyes darted up from the deck and stared the new leader down. "I was there when your son was born. I helped you when you couldn't put food on the table. I—"

Anacleto stepped away, ignoring the pleas for mercy. He walked to Graham and wiped a tear from his cheek. "I don't know that this is right."

"You would be dead if he stayed in charge. Now, you can return home and say he forced you to take the ship. You will not be at fault."

"How can you be so sure?" Anacleto asked.

Heiter screamed as the men tugged him to the side of the ship. The chains clanked and rattled against the deck before they hurled him headlong over the rails, his screams cut short by the resounding splash of seawater. All this, and Anacleto never looked back, his eyes locked with Graham's.

"I've seen this sort of thing before. Your government will see you as a hero."

Anacleto smiled, accepting the encouragement like a child. "What are your orders now, sir?"

Graham gave a sideways glance to the ripple of water as the ship passed the point where Heiter was thrown over. The chains would send him to the bottom. The world would never see his face again. "Continue to Lisbon. I have plans to meet people there and I don't want to miss it."

"Yes, sir," Anacleto replied and stepped away, leaving Graham with his thoughts.

The American stared at the fading ripples as they were overcome by the choppy waves. Somewhere in the depths oxygen was depleted from Heiter's lungs. He would suck in mouthfuls of warm, dark water until he drowned. There would be nothing but pain until his heart stopped beating.

Maybe he didn't deserve what he received, but it was too late now. Graham succeeded in turning his men against him. The only witness to what had transpired was dead. No one on board knew the true nature of their mission in Dubai. For them, Graham was a refugee seeking asylum. Once in Portuguese waters, their services would no longer be needed.

Their blind ambition would be their ruin.

A smile curled Graham's lip. It was only a matter of time before he had what he needed to defeat the Order at their own game. Then the war would truly begin.

Beth slowed her gait as she approached the alley the man had run down. She held onto her Glock with two hands as she turned the corner, leveling it as she aimed down the dark path. Dumpsters lined the sides and trash was strewn along the ground. She took a bold step into the narrow path and forced herself to breathe slowly, to focus her senses.

The deeper she moved into the alley, the darker it became. The tall buildings further shunned the light from the overcast sky. Her eyes had barely begun to adjust to the difference in lighting when she heard movement to her left.

It started as a blur before her vision focused on the man stampeding towards her. He used his M4 like a bar as he pummeled into her, drawing her off her feet and then slammed her against the brick wall behind her. The Glock fell uselessly to the ground as both hands instinctively came to the M4 pressed against her chest and easing towards her throat.

Menacing blue eyes bore into hers and the man bared his teeth like an animal. "I'm going to kill you, but first how about a little fun?" He stuck out his tongue and moved in on her.

Beth grimaced under the strain of his weight and her revulsion of him coming in to lick her. Her hands may have been occupied, but her legs weren't. A moment later she found her target as she kneed him in the balls. It wasn't hard enough to cause damage, but it was enough to drive him back and that was all she needed.

The man held himself a moment before shaking it off and springing towards her, his M4 held up like a bat. He swung it mightily, but she jutted out of the way as it came crashing down into the brick wall, bending the barrel in the process.

"What's the matter, too scared to shoot?" Beth spat as she rubbed at her neck. It was already swelling. "I heard that happens a lot with men your age."

"Cheap shot, whore. I'm going to make you pay." He dropped the gun and pulled a bowie knife from behind his back. "I'm going to stick you so good."

"Right," Beth replied sardonically. She pulled off her leather jacket and wrapped it around her left arm to use as a guard. "I'm not even sure you know how to use it."

The man drove towards her, stabbing wildly like he was in a fencing competition. She avoided the blade, stepped to the side and cracked him in the ribs with a jab. He let out a satisfying groan but recovered his footing and squared back up on her. "Lucky shot."

She ignored his taunt. Instead, she took small steps backwards to increase the distance between them. She watched his footing, calculating his next move. He switched hands clumsily. Amateur.

Beth turned, putting her left arm out. An easy target for someone who didn't know what they were doing.

He went for it, slashing with his weak hand. The knife glanced the padded leather around her arm, deflecting his reach past where her body had been a moment before. She closed the gap, headbutting him in the face while wrapping her free arm around his. She used his momentum against him, placing her foot on his thigh and wrenching his arm up, bending the elbow in the wrong direction.

The man cried out when it snapped, dropping the knife in the process.

Beth snatched it up before it hit the ground and slashed. One swoop cut through his clothing and tore into the flesh of his chest. He stumbled back, clutching the wound with his good arm while the other dangled uselessly at his side.

He panted, out of breath and trembling. "They'll kill you if they find you," he spat. Gone was his confidence, but there was enough hatred and resentment to continue his bravado.

Beth took a step forward, holding the knife so the dull edge was towards her forearm. "Who are they?"

He spat in her direction. "I'll die before I tell you."

Her lip curled. "You'll die regardless. You may as well make it quick."

"Go to hell."

"You first," she spat.

He took a wild swing and she ducked as he stumbled forward. She shot up, lashing out with the blade, stabbing into his right thigh and dug in. The blade continued up his leg as she stood, fileting his flesh and severing his artery. By time he realized what had happened, a pool of blood puddled beneath him.

He had minutes left to live.

The man collapsed to his knees. Wide eyes stared at her with panic and fear. He was broken. Dying. He sought mercy from her, but he would get nothing without answering her questions.

"Who are they?"

The man's lips quivered. His eyes hopelessly searched hers. "The Order," he answered.

"That's not enough. I know about the organization. I need to know who you were meeting."

He stared blankly. His time was running out and he would soon go into shock.

Beth placed the blade to his throat and stared down at him, emotionless. "I can end your suffering, or I can prolong it. It's up to you."

"Please?"

"Answer me."

"His name is Kaiser. He's with the government."

"What's his game?" Beth asked, searching his eyes for more. They always had more to say with the right persuasion.

"He sells people. Whatever they want, science, sex, drugs, whatever."

Sex and drugs made sense, but something caught her attention. "What kind of science? What are you talking about?"

"Some governments test on humans. I think it's a weapons program or something."

"What else do you know?"

"Nothing. That's it, I swear."

His eyes pleaded with her to save him, but it was too late for that. He was already lost. "I believe you," she said, then swiped the blade across his throat and let his heart do the rest.

The fighting was over, and smoke billowed over the horizon. Ames's ears rung, a piercing screech like an icepick in his skull, but he was alive. He walked over the terrain, lifeless bodies littering as far as his eyes could see. There was nothing left to kill, yet a strange sadness settled over him. Melancholy.

"The survivors are coming up," Wills said. "We need to find some kind of transportation to get them out of here before the cavalry comes."

Ames nodded as he scanned for something they could work with. The base was two hours from anywhere by land, but a strike team could deploy via air and be on location within half an hour. They had spent more than that fighting, so the clock ticked maddeningly away.

A hangar in the distance looked hopeful, so Ames jogged in that direction. His senses were on high alert even without the bullets flying. Wills's drones showed nothing with a pulse hiding for a surprise attack, but Ames trusted technology as much as he did a wild animal.

He pulled the rusted doors opened, straining under the weight despite his cybernetic augmentations doing most of the work. Whatever they were hiding at a base like this, they didn't want found. And whatever was behind door number one they wanted to protect just as much. Once the light shone in his jaw dropped.

A massive, multi-axle, all-terrain vehicle stood stoically. Perched on top of the vessel was a cannon not unlike those on an Abrahm's tank. Smaller barrels protruded from the sides and twin tracks on the rear were suspended in case the vehicle encountered harsh environments.

It was a Marine's wet dream come to life and his heart raced looking at it.

"I have something," Ames said into his com.

"What is it?"

Ames smirked, "Our way out of here, I think."

"You find a bus or something?"

Ames scoffed, "Yeah, something."

"Hop in and bring it over. I'm counting refugees right now," Wills replied.

Ames stepped up to the vehicle and pulled open the door. It opened and the satisfying new car smell hit his nostrils like a fond memory. He climbed up the step rails and entered the vehicle. The cab was separated from the back by a small hatch. He shoved it open to reveal a spacious cabin, but little seating. It reminded him of the Humvee his squad used in Syria, the Behemoth.

The Humvee was long gone, may as well reuse the name, he thought as he pulled open the hatch. He entered and looked around, trying to determine how many people could fit when Wills said, "We have twenty-three refugees, plus the big guy."

Ames counted out spaces and visualized them as rows. He left the back of the vehicle to be relegated to Adriel." "It'll be tight, but we can accommodate them."

"Good. We need to hurry; I think I hear aircraft approaching."

Ames hadn't noticed over the ringing in his ears, but as he held his breath and focused, the familiar frequency of a twin jet engine loomed closer. He leapt into action, jumped behind the wheel and thrust the Behemoth to life.

He put it in gear and pulled out of the hangar. The engine roared as he accelerated, and it handled like a sports car. Within seconds he was parked outside the tunnel. Ames climbed out and opened the rear doors to help the refugees in.

Wills led them out, pointing them to the vehicle as the people scurried fearfully out of the darkness. Most held their hands up to their faces to shield them from the blinding sunlight. Others simply held onto the person in front of them while looking downward with their eyes closed.

In the light the horrors they experienced came to realization. Every single one of them was covered in bruises and scars. They were malnourished, their cheeks sunken in and their eyes void of light.

"Monsters," Ames said through gritted teeth.

Once everyone was in the vehicle Ames looked to Wills. "You drive and I'll play gunner."

Wills nodded and took off for the cab while Ames climbed up top and made way for the cannon. He opened the lid and climbed in, racked the chamber open and smiled to see it was loaded. "God bless the Russians," he said before keying his com. "I'm in, let's go."

The Behemoth lurched forward, spun wildly for the gate, and sped away before Ames could locate the approaching aircraft. He had no idea what kind of rounds were in the cannon, but he was more than sure he was about to down his first aircraft using their own firepower.

The vehicle slammed through the gate and careened down a rocky path along the foot of the mountain. The aircraft came into view and began its descent, rolling ever so slightly as it fought the heavy wind coming off the mountain.

"Come on, baby, daddy wants to play," Ames said through his teeth as he positioned the cannon. He counted down as he calculated altitude and speed of the craft. He would have to hit the plane on its smallest side in a vehicle grappling for traction on rough terrain.

He'd been in worse situations.

Ames pulled the trigger and the cannon spewed fire. Tungsten rounds spat from the barrel and knocked chunks out of the fuselage of the aircraft. One went straight down the intake and erupted in a fireball out the back of the jet. It lurched and stalled, rolled right until it inverted, then careened out of the sky into the mountainside in a spectacular explosion.

Ames watched the smoke rise to the sky and grinned.

"I got them," he said.

"Good, but you might want to see what's coming from the other direction."

Ames swallowed his elation and canted his head towards the direction they were heading. Three helicopters hovered a few miles ahead. "Well, that ain't good."

"No kidding. I hope you're not out of ammo."

Ames looked down. He had plenty of rounds but putting them where they needed to go without getting blasted off the rock was another story.

"Stop the vehicle," Ames said.

"What? Why?"

"Just do it. I have an idea."

The vehicle came to a skittering halt at the bottom of a divot in the road. Ames could barely see the tops of the whirring blades. "When I say go, head straight for the one in the middle. I'll fire, then cut into the woods and down the hill."

"What? That's suicide," Wills barked back. He had a point, but if they did nothing then them and twenty-four other souls were about to be barbeque.

"Just do it. Trust me."

A long pause followed, then Wills answered, "You better be right."

Ames agreed but didn't say it out loud. Instead, he sighted in the cannon on the horizon and muttered a silent prayer.

He sucked in a deep breath then gave the order. "Now!"

CHAPTER TWENTY

Tires screeched to a grinding halt as Beth exited the alley. She pulled on her jacket and climbed into the passenger side of the van. "You get anything?" Ryan asked as he shoved it into drive and took off. A back-drop of sirens rang in the distance.

"Under Secretary Kaiser is part of the human trafficking ring. They were going to meet him, but that won't be happening now."

Ryan nodded. His lips tight over his teeth. "I'm sorry about what happened back there. I lost control a bit."

"I noticed," she replied flatly. Beth kept her eyes on the sides of the road and away from his gaze. She was fortunate enough to get information but that was only because the target fled. Had he stuck around to fight, then he would have been killed before saying anything. "You almost cost us a lead," she said finally.

Ryan tensed, gripped the steering wheel tighter and cleared his throat. "I know. I'm sorry."

"I know you are," she replied. "Let's just use the information we have and move forward. I'll take the lead on this."

"All right."

It was enough of a response to settle the argument neither of them wanted to have. They both carried baggage from their past. You could call it PTSD, or any other acronym, but it didn't change the fact that they had endured trauma and experienced life differently ever since. The fight in the parking garage was just as much a battle in his mind as it was in the physical world.

The same was true in the alley for her, she just didn't let herself lose control the way he did, as much as she wanted to.

Beth pulled a tablet out of her bag and searched for information on Under Secretary Kaiser. He had offices all over the country, but the one that interested her the most was the one in West Berlin. They were only five kilometers away.

She pulled the up address, put it into the GPS, and said, "This should be interesting."

The GPS chimed and the AI voice said, "Turn left in five-hundred meters."

"Let's hope so," Ryan replied, then made the turn and floored it.

Minutes later he slowed the van to a stop in front of a government building. A series of flags waved above the building, the German flag was centered and taller than the rest as they whipped in the stiff breeze. The stone veneer of the building gave it a stoic appearance when situated next to the muted bricks of nearby businesses. It was as inviting as a dentist's chair.

"You want me to come in with you?" Ryan asked.

Beth cut her eyes to him, "I think I can handle it."

He nodded knowingly and part of her felt bad about it, but she couldn't trust he wasn't still worked up and wanting to let his inner monster out. This wasn't the time or place for that. They needed finesse.

She entered the building and made her way towards reception. A young, soft male receptionist organized files on the desk. He was dressed in a three-piece suit and his nails were acrylics painted in a gloss base coat. She reminded him of the perfectly manicured metrosexual vampires she'd seen in movies growing up. Hardly scary, but secretly deadly.

"How can I help you?" He asked as she stepped up.

Beth flashed a smile and said, "I would like to arrange a meeting with Under Secretary Kaiser."

"Regarding?"

She swallowed, stalling for time, then said, "I'm looking to make a sizable donation and would like to discuss with him which charities he would recommend. I would list him as a contributor."

The man looked at her like he was looking past her, then reached for a brochure and pushed it across the flat top of the desk. "This contains all of Under Secretary Kaiser's causes. Feel free to choose which one best matches your own."

Beth hesitated to take it. Despite the man's previously warm expression, there was a flash of coldness in his eyes. A chill ran down her spine, but she kept pressing, "I would really rather discuss the topic with him if I may."

"You may not."

"Why not?"

"Because he is unavailable. Under Secretary Kaiser is away on business."

Interesting. "When do you expect him back?"

The receptionist looked to the clock on the wall as if there was a secret message hidden there then said, "I don't know. His plane leaves for Lisbon in an hour. He didn't tell me more than that. If you please, I have work to do."

"Of course," Beth replied and stepped back.

"By the way, I think you have blood on your shirt. It's obscenely inappropriate for someone to want to meet a man of Under Secretary Kaiser's caliber and expect to conduct business dressed in such a way." His snooty tone made her wish Ryan had come inside. The scrawny priss of a man might have held his tongue.

She looked down and the streak of blood. The splatter pattern matched what happens when blood spews from the jugular. "It must have happened when I cut the tongue out of the last guy who spoke to me that way," she said.

He eyed her, unshaken by her comment. "Ma'am, I'm in politics, you have to try harder to impress or scare me. Whichever it is you're trying to do. Again, I have work to do."

Beth scoffed. She didn't know which she was going for either, but the way he shot her down impressed her more than she wanted to admit. She was just glad that she got some information on where the Under Secretary was heading. He had a head start but knowing where he was going was enough of a lead to get eyes on him when he landed.

She climbed into the van and looked to Ryan, "Airport. Now."

"Yes, ma'am," he said and took off.

The Behemoth charged forward, crested the top of the hill like a ramp as Ames fired a tungsten bolt through the windscreen of the center helicopter hovering menacingly above the mountain. He hardly had the chance to see it fall from the sky before Wills cut a hard left and drove into the dense wooded area.

The push bar on the front of the vehicle smashed through the thin stalks of trees like they weren't even there. Overhead, the helicopters whirred to life and began blasting cannon fire wildly. They hit nothing of importance but crept closer as they turned. It was only a matter of time.

Ames took aim at one of them, scarcely seeing through the foliage. He squeezed the trigger, sending a blast skyward. The top of a great pine splintered, taking the brunt of the force and deflecting the round away from the approaching enemy.

"I can't see them," he said.

"If you can't see them then they can't see us."

"Fair point, but I can't shoot them either," Ames replied.

"Do you want to shoot them, or do you want to stay covered long enough to get away?" Wills asked, his breathing heavy.

"Both," Ames replied, knowing the argument for either would get them nowhere. He had to make do with what he had; plenty of rounds and at least the smidge of an idea where they were above the canopy of trees. "I'll do what I can," he continued.

"Likewise," Wills replied and sent the vehicle down an embankment. Below them a rushing river ran southward and above the tree line opened to reveal pristine skies. The vehicle cut right and leaned into the turn as the tires skidded in the mud. The engine screamed a high-pitched whine as it accelerated.

Ames moved the cannon barrel to point in the direction of the approaching craft. Once one came into view, he let it rip, blasting the round through the side window and out the top. Two of the four blades shattered off, flinging outward into the trees, decapitating the tops of the lofty pines. The fuselage slumped in the air for a moment, the rear set of blades holding it aloft enough for the craft to descend slowly.

But not slow enough. The helicopter crashed to the ground in a marvelous spectacle of fiery theatrics.

"Two down. One to go," Ames shouted.

"Good, but we have another problem," Wills said.

Ames cut his eyes ahead and the sudden drop they were speeding towards. Behind them, the third helicopter soared through the billowing flames of their wingman. The shot was lined up perfectly for the kill. Ames saw his reflection in the windscreen as it zoomed closer. He fired, but the cannon didn't respond. "Oh, no."

"What's oh, no?" Wills asked.

Ames glared down at the weapon. Red fluid sprayed from a hose and soaked his pant leg. "The hydraulics are shot. I can't fire."

Wills spewed expletives and jerked the controls to send the vehicle back into the woods. The helicopter flew past. Then ascended above the trees out of view.

"You got any good ideas?" Ames asked.

"Fix the gun," Wills shot back.

"Right," Ames replied as he eyed the leaking line. He fiddled with it a moment to find the disconnect. He popped it off and let the check valve built into the quick disconnect stop the leak. He crawled out of the mount through the bottom and searched for a spare.

The refugees looked at him with trepidation in their eyes. The rescue mission was as damaging to their psyche as their imprisonment. He just hoped they could make it through this and give them a new life. But in order to do that, he needed firepower.

"I need one of these," he shouted as he held the line up and let it dangle like a dead snake.

Voices murmured unintelligibly for several seconds before one of the young men raised a hand. He spoke in a language Ames didn't understand, but the kid gestured towards a line plugged into the bulkhead. It was a match.

"Thank you," Ames said as he rushed towards it and pulled it from whatever system it was powering. The hydraulic line was a little short, but it would have to work. Ames made his way back to the cannon and plugged it in. The next round chambered automatically. "Thank you, Lord," he said under his breath.

The helicopter hovered nearby, to the left of their position. Ames went to move the cannon, but it wouldn't budge. He let out an exasperated sigh and confessed, "I have good news and bad news."

"Spill it," Wills urged.

"I can fire the cannon again, but I can't aim it."

"What? Why?"

"I took a line from down below and I think it powered the servos that move the cannon. It's pointed directly behind us at about a fifteen-degree incline."

"Well, what do you expect me to do with that information?"

Ames racked his brain for a solution, but the only one glaringly obvious enough to work was practically suicide. "You could park us out in the open and I can aim it manually."

"Are you stupid or crazy?" Wills shot back.

"Maybe a little bit of both, but we don't have many options. They'll find us eventually."

Silence followed, then a flurry of profanities as the vehicle turned back towards the open air around the river. "If you get me killed, I'm going to be so pissed," Wills said.

"Me too," Ames said. "Me too."

The West Berlin Airport bustled with activity. The flight manifest showed hundreds of flights in and out of the international hub, but Beth's eyes searched for a specific one; the 11:35 am flight to Lisbon, Portugal.

"Terminal 47," she said into her com. "Are you sure you can make it there today?" She hustled towards the terminal halfway around the airport form her current location.

"I should be good to go. It's been a while since I piloted one of these, but it's like riding a bike, right?"

Beth smiled. The thought of Ryan's hulking frame inside of a single engine Cessna was comical. But it was necessary. There was no way he would pass through an inspection to get on a traditional flight. Even with proof his prosthetics weren't weapons, he simply wouldn't fit in the standard seating of a passenger plane.

"I think if you can get it off the ground, then you'll do just fine," Beth replied. She moved quickly through the metal detectors and grabbed what few belongings she had with her; a small carry on with mobile device, money, and binoculars. A general lack of weapons would help get her on the plane, but her mission would be relegated strictly to surveillance until Ryan arrived with the goodies.

"I'll need to make a fuel stop, but I shouldn't be too far behind you. I'll meet you at Colombo?"

"Yes." The mall was a safe bet. Tourists clamored to places like that, and considering it was the largest shopping center in the western part of Europe, it was a magnet for people who wanted to go unnoticed.

An announcement sounded above, first in German, then in English, "Now boarding flight 687 for Lisbon at Terminal 47."

"That's me, I need to board," Beth said.

"See you in Portugal," Ryan replied. "Fly safe."

"You too." Beth switched off her com and showed her ticket to the stewardess. The woman flashed a fake smile and welcomed her aboard. Beth had a seat in coach which allowed her to board last and walked through first class and business class to see the others on the flight. She had enough of an idea what Under Secretary Kaiser looked like that when she saw him, she nearly laughed. He had the same softness his receptionist did, with an edge of flamboyance in his mannerisms. He laughed heartily with someone seated across from him and that gave enough of a distraction to warrant what she would do next.

Years in combat boots gave Beth a steady stance, so forcing herself to fall was about as unnatural as breathing underwater, but she faked it well enough. Placing one foot on top of the other, she let herself sprawl out and land against the Under Secretary...hard.

Maybe too hard.

Kaiser cried out in a shrill, tinny voice. The following commotion nearly ripped Beth away from him before she had the opportunity to plant the tracking device onto the back of his jacket.

"I'm sorry. I'm sorry," Beth said, trying to slur her speech. "New feet!" She laughed like she was barking up a tree. It reminded her how other Brits used to poke fun at Americans as they sat around drinking and telling stupid jokes about each other's militaries.

"Please take your seat, ma'am," a flight steward said as he helped her up.

Under Secretary Kaiser gawked at her with a superiority complex expression painted on his face as thick as his makeup. Ironically, he was literally looking down his nose while craning his neck to look up at her. She pretended not to notice as she stepped away, trying to give the impression she was intoxicated until she was out of view of her target.

Thankfully the hard part was done, and all that was left was pinging the device and making sure she could track him once they landed. She plopped into her seat and pulled out her mobile device for a quick check. "Bingo," she whispered. "See you in Lisbon."

CHAPTER TWENTY-ONE

The frigate made it to Lisbon and set anchor. This wasn't a port call, nor was it a return home for the crew. It was a business transaction and Graham was getting impatient for it to begin.

The sun was high in the sky, its luminance reflecting like millions of crystals over the choppy waters of the bay. The stench of dead animal filled the area, much stronger than the fishy smell of other ports. The fact the local fishermen used dead land animals for their crab pots was a contributor to the smell, but not the sole reason.

There had been speculation for years that the bay was the final resting place for people who defied their government. A few bloated bodies washed up on the shore, but any ties to foul play were never reported. There was no proof of government involvement either, but no one searched for proof when speaking about a compelling conspiracy theory. You just need enough plausibility to get the other person to think it might happen.

Graham knew the truth; at least part of it. It was worse than the conspiracists thought and he would leave it at that.

"Who are we meeting with, sir?" Anacleto said as he approached Graham on the bow.

Graham kept his eyes on the sky, watching the planes come approach for landing at the nearby airport. "I have a few business associates coming over the next several hours. Some of our business dealings have had unexpected interruptions. Nothing for you to concern yourself about."

"Yes, sir. I only asked to see what resources might need to be made available to you. We have a limited crew, as you are aware."

"Yes, I am aware. A small craft to move visitors from the pier to the ship is all that's required at this time. They'll contact me when they're ready."

"Yes, sir," Anacleto replied and ushered away. He was a good man, willing to do what he was asked, but he was scared. The part he played in the killing of their former captain was weighing on him. He would break eventually, but by then Graham would be through with him.

The Behemoth rampaged over the terrain, zig zagging through the trees and out into the open. Ames climbed out over the top of the vehicle and manually positioned the cannon to a suitable angle while the helicopter circled back.

"Go slower, give them time to catch up," Ames said as he climbed back into the gunner's seat.

"I feel like a sitting duck here," Wills replied.

"They're coming back around. Probably two miles out."

The vehicle screeched and shuttered to a stop, giving Ames a solid platform to ready his shot. He couldn't see the helicopter, but they couldn't see him either over the tree line. It was the perfect position but imperfect situation. The craft had to come in at just the right angle, unless...

"Cut the wheel to one side and move about five degrees," Ames said.

"What? Why?"

"Just do it. I want to see if we can aim manually."

The vehicle lurched, then settled. It wasn't a smooth transition, but it worked. Ames focused on the sound and zeroed in on the helicopter's relative location. "Go back in the opposite direction about ten degrees."

Wills did as he was instructed, grumbling under his breath the whole time.

Once the vehicle settled again the blades whirred into view. It was a deadeye shot. Ames gripped the handle, let out a breath, then fired.

The round exploded forth from the cannon and struck the helicopter's forward gearbox, ripping the front blades clean off the craft. The nose dipped but continued its forward trajectory as gravity dragged it towards the dirt...right in their direction.

"Gun it!" Ames shouted.

Wills put it in gear and slammed the Behemoth into motion. It dug in as four axles worth of tires spun in the mud. "I'm not getting any traction."

Ames jumped out of the gunner seat and climbed down from the vehicle. It was too big and heavy to push, and the terrain was too slimy to get traction anyway. His good idea was about to get them killed. Then he noticed the tracks.

"Is there a setting to engage the tracks?"

A pause, then Wills shouted back, "Yeah." the tracks dropped into position and Wills hit the gas, sending the vehicle forward.

Ames looked back at the approaching helicopter and ran for the trees, sprinting with everything he had left.

The earth trembled under his feet. Then a wave of heat washed over him and the familiar scent of JP8 wafted around his nose. He kept running, expecting a series of secondary explosions to occur at any moment.

He wasn't disappointed.

The trees on the edge of the tree line shook wildly as a fireball bloomed over the horizon. Fires engulfed the treetops like giant torches. He kept moving, not knowing where he was going except that it was away from the encroaching death.

Ames made it to the main road, panting like an Olympic runner, before he fell to his knees in the muck and mud.

"I hate Russia," he spat between breaths.

"Even Russians hates Russia, why else would they live in these conditions?" Wills shot back. "What's your location?"

"The road," Ames replied.

"I'll be there in a few," Wills said.

Ames nodded, too out of breath to speak. A couple of minutes later the Behemoth tore out of the woods and onto the sloppy trail leading down the mountain. Wills brought it to a stop next to Ames and looked down at him from the cab.

"I like this piece of machinery. You think they'll let me keep it?"

Ames shrugged. "There's no one left alive here to tell you no. So, why not?"

Wills smiled. "Climb in and let's get out of here."

Ames rose from the ground and walked around to the other side. The cab of the Behemoth was warm and inviting. It was the only thing about this trip that had been.

He glanced to the back of the vehicle to see the refugees sitting quietly. They were dirty and full of fear, but they were alive. Wills and Ames had seen to that. It was the most rewarding thing he had done in longer than he could remember.

"Will this thing get us to town?" Ames asked.

Wills glanced at the fuel display. "It says it has a two-hundred-kilometer range on this tank. I think it'll be close, but we'll make it." He put the Behemoth in gear and continued down the mountain.

Ames leaned back into the seat and settled into the jostling rhythm of the vehicle. The fight was over, at least for now, until they had orders for the next step.

"We make a good team," Ames said, pulling Wills attention to him. "I think we're doing the right thing.

"I think you're right. Welcome to the team."

Ames smirked at the response. It was the first time he felt like he belonged since he was a Marine. He'd found his crew, as unusual as they were. Under ordinary circumstances things might have been different, but he didn't believe in coincidences. They were called to come together. He just hoped they had what it took to make a real difference.

He glanced back at the people they had just liberated and saw the glimmer of hope in their eyes. That was the real difference he had committed his life to achieving before it went off the rails. Graham may have recruited him to be a monster in his machine, but Ames was committed to bringing the Order's house of cards down.

Maybe this was the first step in making that happen, but it was an effective one. He turned back to face the road and smiled at their victory.

The plane touched down in Lisbon before the first drops of rain fell. The overcast sky loomed with impending doom as purple clouds rolled in. Beth stepped off the plane and onto the tarmac. The passengers from first class were let off the plane a solid ten minutes before the rest, but according to the tracker on Under Secretary Kaiser, he was no more than a few football fields away.

Beth moved swiftly through the terminal and out into the parking lot. She hailed a cab and said "Colombo, por favor," as she strapped on her seatbelt.

The driver nodded and pulled away from the airport. Beth watched the screen hoping beyond anything that the distance between them wouldn't be a problem. It hadn't been before but testing a product and using it in an actual mission almost always yielded different results.

Under Secretary Kaiser stayed put for the entire drive, and bored, Beth fell into a rhythm of looking at her device and out the window. New construction was sprinkled in with the old country style, but nearly every surface was covered in graffiti. Most of it was political, some of it a peculiar mix of a turf war mimicking what happened in London after the crash in 2026.

Either way it was an eyesore and a perversion of what the Portuguese people were previously known for. This place was once a lovely getaway for honeymooners. Now it was an easy place to get lost permanently if one wasn't careful. How it continued to maintain such a large tourism industry was mindboggling.

The cab rolled to a stop at the north entrance of the Colombo and the driver handed a tablet back to Beth to scan for payment. She swiped her palm over the tempered glass and handed it back to him with a smile and thank you before exiting the vehicle.

The mall was sprawling with activity. It was a beacon in a decaying city where every resource was used to beautify two square miles of landscape. There were no graffiti, or homeless, or protests in the street here. It was hallowed ground for the only legitimate money maker the city could depend on. And "policia" was everywhere.

"That's new," Beth grumbled. She expected a bit of security, but armed, and armored police outside of a shopping center was a bit much.

She made her way to the entrance and kept her head down. It was easy to pay attention to redheads, but enough local women got their color from bottles that she was confident she would blend in as long as she didn't make a big presence. Her biggest distractor was how pale she was, not her hair color.

Inside, the mall wasn't how she remembered it years prior. Every third or fourth store was barred closed. The lights were off, and no one was home. If this was the first floor, then she could only imagine how dead the upper floors would be.

Beth found the small coffee shop she and Ryan had agreed to meet at. They knew the owners, though the couple never worked at the location anymore. Mostly due to old age, but there were other factors too heartbreaking to think about while planning the next phase of the plan.

She lay out a paper map she'd taken from the plane and spread it over the table. She scrolled her finger across it, finding the airport, then Colombo, to establish where she was in relation to Under Secretary Kaiser. She pulled out her device and pinged the tracker. "Still there? What are you doing?" Beth asked to herself when the barista arrived.

"Can I help you?" The barista asked in perfect English.

Beth looked up to see a woman smiling back at her. A pin on her apron showed an old representation of the American flag. Possibly an exchange student, or an expat, Beth thought as she glanced over to the menu over the counter. Her eyes settled on something good enough to keep the girl from waiting or getting in the way of her planning.

"I'll take a caramel mocha frappe," Beth said.

"Whipped cream?"

"Please," Beth replied.

The barista handed over her own tablet and Beth scanned for payment. She didn't bother looking at the price, she hated trying to work out the conversion in her head. Growing up using Quid, but having an account using Dollars, and then converting to Euro was a surefire way to get a headache.

Once more alone, Beth glanced over the map and committed some of the landmarks to memory. The surveillance view on her device was scaled differently, the orientation not quite right when compared to the foldable map. Along the border of the city was the bay and her thoughts drifted to Dubai.

"Sonofa..." Beth trailed off.

Ames had mentioned a small ship with a foreign flag waving on the mast above the bridge. He had described the markings in some detail before they split to do their own missions. Could that ship be coming here? If so, was Under Secretary Kaiser implicated with whatever was to happen on that ship?

Beth bit at her bottom lip and racked her brain. "How could I have not seen this coming?"

"Is this seat taken?"

Beth looked up to see Ryan smiling down at her. He had an over-sized trench coat draped over him like a cape to help hide his pros-thetics. His hair was wet and half-clinging to his face.

It had finally started raining.

"I think I know where our Under Secretary is going," Beth said matter-of-factly.

Ryan took the seat across from her and glanced down at the map. "Hopefully, he's coming here so I don't have to go out in that rain again," he joked.

Beth ignored it and pointed at the bay. "The ship from Dubai could be heading here. It's possible Kaiser is meeting our friend from the *Intrepid*."

Ryan nodded, taking it in. "I wouldn't discount that. Where is he now?"

Beth pulled out the device and opened the app again. "Still at the airport."

"Still?"

The question hit a nerve. Beth pinged the tracker again. It hadn't moved from the GPS coordinates since she pinged it the first time coming off the plane. No one was ever that still. "I think we have a problem."

"What's that?" Ryan asked.

"I think he may have found the tracker and dumped it."

CHAPTER TWENTY-TWO

The airfield on the Siberian border was covered in sheets of ice when the Behemoth plowed through the border fencing. Wills had called for a transport large enough to accommodate the passengers, and they half-expected an archaic C-130. Instead, they had two Ospreys, their twin propellers spinning in protest to the frigid temperature.

"That's our salvation right there," Wills said as he put the Behemoth in park near the rear cargo holds. The doors were drawn down, guarded by active-duty Marines who probably wished they were anywhere but here.

Ames followed Wills as he climbed out of the cab and approached their superior. "We can't thank you enough for this."

Gunnery Sergeant Shade nodded curtly and shouted over the sound of the props turning. "This is off the books, so tell Ryan he owes me big."

Wills clapped the man on the shoulder in acknowledgment. "Once we get the rats out, we can make a real difference. So, how do you want to do this?"

The Gunny shrugged. "I have two transports; we can load them however you like."

"We have a bit of an issue," Wills said. Even knowing the issue, Ames heart pumped a little harder. This wasn't an easy evac under the best of circumstances. Wills did the best he could to explain, but it wasn't until the Marine saw it for himself that concern was chiseled into his stone demeanor.

"How did they do this to another human being?" The Gunny asked. His jaw clenched with righteous anger.

"We want to take him and his sister separately. Ames and I will go with that transport. The others can go wherever you deem safest," Wills said.

"We can take them to Fairbanks. The Air Force can put them up and get this sorted out," Gunny Shade said. "Where do you need to go?"

Wills looked to the Marine and asked, "How far into Europe can you get us? Ryan and Beth are in Germany."

Gunny Shade brushed his hand over his face as he considered the repercussions. The amount of fuel spent and the hours away from home base had to be reported somehow. There was no doubt a bean counter somewhere would see the discrepancies. Despite that, he said, "Germany it is, but not an inch further."

Wills nodded his thanks and turned to Ames, "Let's get them boarded up before we waste any more time."

Ames moved to the rear of the Behemoth and helped the refugees out. None of them were dressed for these conditions, and they clutched onto themselves, teeth chattering so hard they nearly broke. As good as Ames felt about their deeds, the harder it was to think of a time he wouldn't be haunted by what he'd seen. This was beyond inhumane. This was just short of genocide. It could have been just that if anyone knew how many people lost their lives over the course of these mad science experiments.

Ames watched the last few refugees file out of the rear of the vehicle and load onto the first Osprey. Wills stood with Tian and Adriel. They had blankets draped over them but stayed outside to observe. Tian still clutched her brother's hand.

Once the first Osprey was loaded, it took off, disappearing into the clouds settling over the horizon. It was their turn to strap in and Ames found himself seated next to Adriel, separated only by the aisle between their seats. The young man barely fit inside the plane, but sat calmly, his gaze outside the cargo ramp until it finally shut.

Ames wanted to reach out and tell him everything would be all right. The truth was much different. If any government set eyes on him, they would want to seize him and do tests. They would likely torture him further trying to replicate the misdeeds done by the Russians.

That was no way to live.

"What do you have planned?" Ames asked as he turned to Wills.

"I don't think it's a good idea to separate them. I also don't like his odds if he's let loose. People would treat him like Frankenstein's monster."

"I was thinking the same thing," Ames replied. "But what choice do we have?"

Wills shrugged off the question as he pulled a cigar from his pocket. "I wish I had answers. I wish I had enough words to give them hope. But I'm just a guy damaged by the system trying to hold myself together." He held the cigar up and continued, "My father sent me this cigar when my brother was born. I was already in the military, and my brother was a late in life, born to a different mother situation. Before I got home to see him there was another protest. People set fires and bombs were planted in the streets. He died before I got a chance to celebrate his life."

Ames trembled under the weight of that story. Everyone had someone who was lost to the evils of society. The rebirth of their current democracy was a demonic thing brought to life by a monstrous idea they once called the Great Reset. It was supposed to level the playing field.

Instead, it leveled cities.

No one talked about the worst of it, the innocent lives lost. They only talked about those they called domestic terrorists clamoring for dear life to the ideals they were born into. In any other time, they would have been called patriots. In the end, freedom wasn't free and fighting for it cost more than they could afford.

Patriotism turned into a dirty word until it was reclaimed and rebranded to stand for something with no real definition. That's why everything was so bleak. No one knew what side they were on.

"However you want to play this, I've got your back," Ames said after a long silence.

Wills looked back to his partner and tucked the cigar back into his pocket. "Thanks."

The first vessel was tied to the back of the frigate before the first raindrops fell. The choppy waters churned beneath the camel chained to the ship that the small craft tied onto. It was supposed to provide an even platform for people to traverse, but it was like walking in a bouncy house full of kids cracked out on sugar.

Graham smiled as he watched his first two guests arrive.

Under Secretary Kaiser was as stylish as ever. His suit looked as it if it could be painted on. His hair a coif of perfectly manicured mess. It was hard to tell if he woke up like that, or if he spent an hour getting it right.

The other guest was the opposite of the Under Secretary. Doctor Nikolay Timur was a Russian military scientist assigned to more weapons projects than he could count. Somehow, he kept it all together, though it had an effect on his haggard appearance. "Perhaps all geniuses look like they roll out of bed and haven't showered in three weeks," Graham muttered to the new captain of the *Valoroso*.

Anacleto man smiled. "He does look a mess. Should we provide him quarters to clean up?"

"No need to be rude, but he will be staying with us for a time. Let's hope he makes good use of his time and utilizes the facilities properly."

"What is that the men are dragging on behind him?" Anacleto asked.

The large crate looked like a military grade coffin. There was a refrigeration tank installed and steam rose off the surface as the chilled air inside caused condensation on the much warmer outside. Condensation dripped as he rolled across the platform.

"That's what I asked him to bring to me. Protection."

"This needs to be refrigerated as soon as possible," Doctor Timur pleaded. He was a ball of nerves, his fists balled up and shoved deeply into his jacket pockets. His glasses were smudged from his constant fiddling with them and the closer he got to the ship the clearer it was that the buttons on his shirt were misaligned.

He looked like he could be a crazy man living in the streets if not for the military funding.

"Under Secretary Kaiser. Doctor Timur. Welcome to the *Valoroso*," Graham said with a fake, painted on smile. He was happy to see them, but not that happy. He was more eager than anything. What they had to offer made them useful to him. Nothing else.

"I had plans, David. I don't have much time for your cryptic messages," Under Secretary Kaiser replied. It sounded as much like a teenage girl whining as it did a grown man speaking. The dichotomy of his status was laughable. All the while, the doctor simply looked around confused, agitated.

"Cryptic?" Graham said. "The world is caving in on us and you think I was just being cryptic? I wish that were the case."

"Then what is this?" Kaiser asked.

"An opportunity. Anacleto, will you see our guest to their quarters? I'm expecting a few more guests to arrive before the announcement. Until then, relax and get comfortable." Graham stepped away and walked up the ladder to the bridge. Rain was heavy in the air, the stench of rot coming off the water was unbearable. Or maybe it was Doctor Timur's arrival. In either case, he preferred to be alone to prepare his statement.

War was coming and these men brought with them a sense of

protection. Having the Order's golden child on board would prevent them from blasting the frigate to kingdom come. And the weapon the Russians provided would keep anyone unwanted from infiltrating the ship.

All that was left was to take the seat of power and usurp the Order. Afterward, all its wealth would be handed over willingly in a new alliance.

America's sovereignty was lost with Sanders dead. Now it was the old world's turn to perish as the sun rose on a new leader. They had crossed the wrong man and they would pay dearly for it.

Beth ran into the airport, leaping over border tape as she made her way through the corridors to where the beacon chimed. She was on the other side of a clear window looking in at the empty room. There, draped over the arm of a two-seated chair was the discarded jacket Under Secretary Kaiser had worn on the plane.

"It's here, but he's not," she said. She wanted to kick herself for being cocky enough to let the tech do her job for her. She knew better than that. At least she thought she did.

"Do you want to check the surveillance video?" Ryan asked from the rental car.

"I don't know what we might find other than the fact he left here," Beth replied.

"You may as well look. We have a window of opportunity, maybe you'll find something useful."

Beth bit her lip and turned a half-circle before spotting the security office. She dug in her pocket for the fake Interpol identification she kept with her and knocked. A man two times bigger than he needed to be opened the door before sagging back down into his chair.

"Si?"

She flashed the identification and asked for access. He shoved the chair out of her way using his feet and situated himself in the far corner of the room. If only everything in life was so simple.

Beth typed in the commands she was searching for and scanned the video feed leading out of the airport terminal. She began her search minutes before she left and continued to search until she spotted her target.

Under Secretary Kaiser had changed clothes, but there was no denying it was him. His hair was distinguishable, as was the tightly trimmed beard he sported. He was the opposite of rugged. But something else caught her eye, another person she didn't recognize from the flight. A wild-haired man in glasses who didn't seem to belong in the company of a politician.

"Who are you?" Beth muttered under her breath.

It was enough to stir a response from Ryan, "What do you have?"

"I don't know, but I think they have been called away to a summit of sorts." She screen-grabbed the image and printed it before continuing the feed. Both men entered a van, and a large crate was loaded in afterward. Drugs? Money? It was hard to tell, but she did get a good look at the van and the identifying marks. She noted it down and turned to the security guard. "Gracias."

He nodded with indifference and went back to leaning his head against the wall.

Beth left the room and jogged back to the car with the image tucked under her jacket to keep it out of the rain. She handed it over to Ryan and asked, "Have you seen him before?"

Ryan glared at it intently for several seconds before shaking his head. "I don't think so. He doesn't look German, though."

"My thoughts exactly. I want to go to the bay and see if the van is there. I have the information written down."

Ryan put the car in gear and eased it out of the parking lot. "So, you're thinking a summit? For what?"

Beth shrugged. "Graham is a power player. He is probably vying for more authority in the Order; trying to gain prominence."

"Rank up," Ryan grumbled.

"Yeah."

"This is getting out of control. There's too many moving parts to this mess."

Beth agreed but didn't say so. She focused on what was in front of her and wished to God things weren't as bad as she thought they were.

Ryan made it across town to the piers in less than half an hour. The rain caused a bit of congestion in the traffic, but not enough to hinder their progress. Most of the issues were going in the opposing lane. He drove the car slowly down the piers while Beth surveilled the bay with binoculars.

Most of the vessels tied to the pier were sailboats and smaller fishing vessels. Further away from land, in the deeper water, were the yachts. But in the distance was the familiar grey of military warships anchored nearly a mile away. There were five ships total, each similar in size and style. The mist of rain made it difficult to make out the finer details, but it called for a closer look.

"Do we know anyone with a boat?" Beth asked.

"The Navy?" Ryan shot back with a smile.

"Nice try, but I'm serious. Do any of those look like the ship Ames mentioned?" She handed off the binoculars and pointed where to look.

Ryan scanned the horizon, adjusting the focus as he looked out over the water. "Any of them could be a match, but I see a Greek flag on one of them. I think we can rule that one out. There's also a supply ship, country of origin unknown, but it doesn't match the description either."

"How do you know it's a supply ship?"

Ryan handed the binoculars to her and pointed to the one in question. "You see the massive fuel hoses hitched to those mechanical arms?"

Beth shifted her gaze until it came into view. "Yes."

"Those are used to refuel other ships. The design features change from class to class, but all supply ships have those refueling lines."

"Well, that's two down, three to go. What do you think we should do?"

Ryan let out a sigh and watched the choppy waters dip and sway to some unknown, jittery rhythm. "We can watch for movement. If Graham has people coming to meet him here, then they'll need to take a smaller boat to them. Those ships can't get any closer without running aground."

"You want to sit and wait?"

"It's better than going nuts trying to determine who's who out there. At least until the rain dies down."

Beth didn't like it. There was something about sitting on her hands and doing nothing that agitated her. Maybe it was the lack of action? But Ryan made a good point. The enemy could lead them straight to where they were hiding if they didn't know they were being watched. It was worth a shot.

"Fine, but if we don't see anything in two hours, I want to get a closer look."

"If we don't see anything in two hours, then I'll let you pick the boat I steal for you," Ryan replied.

Beth smiled. Chivalry wasn't dead.

CHAPTER TWENTY-THREE

The Osprey hovered down to land on an airstrip at a joint base outside East Berlin. Thanks to Gunny Shade's resources, a secondary transport was waiting to carry the team the rest of the way. Once Wills had a signal, he had reached out to Beth who had ordered them to come to Lisbon. He hadn't mentioned their guests, but introductions would have to wait. After a lengthy conversation with Beth's contact, Han, Wills was convinced they had a solid plan.

"I have arrangements for you and Adriel to stay in a safehouse in the area. It has enough supplies to last several months, so there's no need to venture out. Will you two feel safe while we're away?" Wills held Tian's hand as he spoke. He expressed a gentleness that betrayed the trained killer Ames had watched on the battlefield.

"We can do what's needed," Tian replied softly. She was exhausted but had refused to sleep on the plane. Her brother hadn't been as stubborn. He had slept nearly the whole way, lulled to sleep by the droning of the engines. Ames grew concerned to see the large abomination twitch and fit about. He assumed that was why Tian had stayed awake, holding his massive hand in hers.

A blacked-out moving truck waited at the airstrip to transport the sibling refugees. Wills and Ames helped them board and watched the truck haul them away. Their good deed left more heartbreaking questions than answers, but they would have to peel that onion later. They were needed elsewhere.

"Time to go," Wills said as the truck rounded a corner and disappeared from view.

Ames nodded and followed his partner into the small jet. It boasted seating for six, but the two of them crammed in like sardines in a can. Both men were large before the super soldier program, but between the cybernetics and the serum used to facilitate healing and growth to support the machinations, each of them was practically the breadth of two men now.

That came more into focus when they piled into confined spaces like this.

"So, what's in Lisbon?" Ames asked. The plane began to taxi the airstrip in preparation for takeoff. It was a much smoother ride than the Osprey had been, but then again, they weren't off the ground yet.

"Beth thinks Graham is meeting some people there. She believes one of the ships anchored out is the one you saw in Dubai."

Ames counted on his fingers. How many days had it been since he failed his mission? Four...maybe five? "It would be tight, but if they traveled at full speed a ship like that could make the trip," he said. "I think."

Wills smirked. "Beth already checked the math. It's plausible."

"Good." Ames couldn't find the words to express what he felt. There was guilt eating him alive from the botched Dubai trip. A man was dead because of him, and the attack on the carrier may have hurt more people had they not already been at a defensive posture.

The dopamine hit of leveling a Russian base to free more than twenty victims from hell and torment was already waning. How many lives were lost in order to rescue them? How many of those men defending the base had no idea what they were defending? He related to being in the dark, not just with Graham, but during his time in the Marine Corps as well. Low level people were never properly informed before they were let loose to kill.

It was morally wrong to place people in those positions, but it was exceptionally effective for those in charge.

By the time he left his thoughts, the plane was already climbing in altitude. Ames peered out the window and looked over the ever-growing metropolis. Berlin had been split up nearly a century before following World War II. It wasn't until 1989 that Berlin had been unified, only to split once more less than forty years later. At least this time they didn't have a wall between them. The split was purely political and the civil conflict that caused it had spread like wildfire through other major cities in the region.

They might speak the same language, but they didn't identify as the same people. That much was clear.

Ames settled into his seat and tried to relax. Their expected flight time was just shy of three hours. Any other time he'd doze off to sleep, but it eluded him. Every time he closed his eyes, he saw death. It carried the same weight as the dreams he'd had following the strike that tore his body apart.

"I'm going to have to seek help," he muttered under his breath.

"What?" Wills asked, opening his eyes slowly and looking over to Ames.

He hadn't meant to speak it out loud. He imagined Wills could relate. Every warrior could to some capacity, but he shrugged off the notion and denied saying anything.

Ames didn't like lying, but sometimes facing the truth was worse.

The Duke of York, Prince Frederick, bastard son of Prince Andrew arrived via helicopter. Graham held himself steady as the prop wash billowed down. Even with a helipad fit for standard, single engine helicopters, the duke's craft was nearly too large to fit.

The young man departed; his silk shirt splayed open near the top to display his chiseled, perfectly smooth chest. He was manic about his appearance, more so than the German Under Secretary. There were whispers that the two men were an item. Whispers muted by the crown at every turn. But whispers were hard to muffle when actions screamed that something was afoot.

Kaiser was a solid fifteen years older than young Frederick. The duke was barely above the age of consent when Kaiser first latched onto him. British reports made little of it at first, stating the German Under Secretary served as a mentor to a man seventh in line for a crown he would never wear. The burden of politics for a duke might not lead them to a throne but could well lead them to being a diplomatic ambassador for the kingdom.

It was for the good of England and Germany that peace between the nations was maintained while civil unrest blossomed out of control within their own borders.

In truth, the reports covered up the fact that grooming of young royalty had gone on for generations. It was just that Frederick was out in the open with his exploits that anyone seemed to notice what Kaiser had done. But Frederick had used Kaiser just as much as the older man had used him. Both men were eager for power in any form.

"Frederick, it's good to see you," Graham said, taking the duke's hand in his.

Frederick flashed a smile. It wasn't hard to see Prince Andrew in the young man's eyes. The boy's mother had been no one in particular. Simply an opportunity the former duke hadn't turned down. Andrew had been wrung through the mud over abandoning his son, the one whom he knew nothing about. Tabloids boasted that it was fortunate the Queen had past, for the news would have truly killed her.

It was doubtful that she was in the dark over the many misdeeds of her son. The woman had been stronger than most people gave her credit for.

"Thank you for the invitation, David. Is Stefan here?" He used the Under Secretary's first name and the question fell with a heavy burden of thirst.

Graham gestured with a curt nod towards the entrance into the ship. "He's waiting for you. Dinner will be in a few hours. We'll get to business then."

"Perfect. Thank you," Frederick replied as he left the American standing in the rain while the helicopter rose from the deck and disappeared into the grey sky.

Graham held onto the rails and looked out over the bay. Five nations were represented by the new alliance he planned to form. His new acquaintance, Xian, from China would arrive later. His personal nuclear submarine was still several miles away. The man had the authority to control an army consisting of a billion men. All he needed was incentive.

Graham had that in spades. A billion super soldiers constructed using the best technologies that the American tech giant and Russian military science had to offer would be unstoppable. The Order would fall away like an unpleasant afterthought.

Then Graham would rule the world.

He scoffed as he thought about his years of conniving against those who thought they controlled him. They were close to finding out, even sending Zero to come kill him. But they were stupid, believing that he would offer them the keys to his super soldier program. They would have used it to police the world. Instead, he would use it to destroy them, seize the world, and mold it in his vision.

It was time for a revolution. It was time to deny border-controlled nationalism. It was time to lift the veil and expose the separatists for what they were, an obstacle for a single, unified world.

It would be beautiful.

And it would all be his.

"There it is," Ryan said. He handed the binoculars to Beth and pointed at the ship on the far right as a helicopter came in for a landing. "There's no way that helicopter was designed to land on that ship."

"I think you're right," Beth replied. Her heart raced. She had been right, Graham did come to Lisbon, and Under Secretary Kaiser was likely there with him. She studied the markings on the helicopter and noticed a familiar seal marking the fuselage. "That's the Duke of York."

"You sure?"

"Yeah, I met him when he was about twelve years old. His father had died, and I attended the funeral as part of their security team. He was a nice kid, a little creepy, but what else would you expect from someone who didn't have a real family?"

"I guess that's the burden of life in the public eye. It has to have an effect on you."

"It's sad that he got roped into this. He was more likable than his cousins. Probably because he was born of a commoner before the scandal hit the papers." The duke exited the helicopter and met someone. His back was to Beth, so it was hard to tell, but she wanted to say it was Graham. She bit her tongue. It was foolish to say anything unless she was one-hundred percent certain.

Ryan cleared his throat. "The boys should land in the next hour or so. We should set up before it gets too dark."

Beth agreed and scanned the horizon for the best place to do so unseen. "There's a fishery across the way. I'm sure we can utilize one of those boats."

"It will have to do," Ryan replied.

The closer it got to go time the more Beth questioned what they were getting into. It would be simple to call down an airstrike and blast the ship out of the water, but that wouldn't facilitate accomplishing their primary mission. They needed answers. They needed a way to infiltrate the Order on their terms.

Graham was the target that would accomplish both. Shut down his operations and the Order.

It was logical.

Then why was it still gnawing at her like she was missing something?

Beth looked down at her watch. They had two hours of daylight left. Two hours to plan an attack on a ship they were unfamiliar with. Two hours to put into action what she and Ryan had spent years contemplating and fixating on.

She should be happy.

But she wasn't.

She was scared as hell.

"Do you think we're doing the right thing?"

Ryan cut his eyes at her as he put the car into drive to head towards the fishery. "Why wouldn't we be? This is what we've been planning since we discovered the truth. We just needed the right players involved to make it happen."

"Something isn't right," she said. "My intuition is that we have it wrong."

"I've had that feeling before. It's hard to shake it, but you have to ignore it. That's the fear talking."

She wanted to accept that. She really did. "What if it's more than that?"

Ryan eased the car onto the road and sped up to match the flow of traffic. They drove in silence for a long time until he pulled into the fishery lot and cut the ignition. He leaned toward her, his lips inches from her ear. "I'm scared too. Don't tell anyone, but I spent most of my adult life afraid. If not for the anger pumping through my veins, I would clam up and not be able to function. As someone who has felt that every day of his life, believe me when I tell you that fear is a liar. You're doing the right thing."

"Maybe you're right," she said. She willed herself to believe him. It was all she could do.

"Of course, I'm right. I listen to you," Ryan said as he climbed out of the car. The burden of his weight leaving the vehicle caused her side of the car to droop a couple of inches. His words and simple physics elicited a smile from her.

"Do you really believe that?"

"That's the only thing I know is true in this world," Ryan replied. "So, let's push fear aside and do this. It's time for the good guys to win for once."

Beth nodded. Indeed it was.

CHAPTER TWENTY-FOUR

Rain fell like buckets as the small jet landed in Lisbon. Water streaks blistered across the windows, bubbling before flicking away as the air rushed over it. It was mesmerizing to watch, a dance for his eyes only as he stared blankly.

Sleep eluded the former Marine, but he knew it would. Instead, his exhausted body lay sprawled across two seats as he tried to rest his aching back. His age and injuries were catching up to him, and no amount of cybernetic augmentations could completely alleviate everything. If they could, then he would no longer be human.

What would be the point of existing then?

Wills stirred across the aisle from him and glanced out the window. "Already?"

"You sleep well?" Ames asked without looking away from the window.

"Enough, I suppose. I kept seeing weird stuff in my dreams. I wish I could turn my brain off sometimes."

Ames grunted his agreement. He had the same thought for months. Ever since the strike that nearly took his life. His dreams were haunted by the faces of those he lost. The men who depended on him.

Wills pulled his cell from his pocket and scrolled through his messages. "I got news from Beth."

"What kind?" Ames asked. He hoped the news was that it was over, and he could collapse guiltlessly into the deepest sleep of his life.

"They're holed up in a fishery by the bay. They have some weapons for us to use and Ryan stole a boat."

"Of course, he did," Ames replied with a smirk. "When do they want to deploy?"

Wills kept updating his cell, shaking his head, "I don't have anything more than that. Just what I mentioned and the address."

Ames groaned as he shifted his bodyweight back to a normal seating position. What he wouldn't give for a chiropractor and a massage. "How are we getting there?" He asked as the plane rolled to a gentle stop near a gate at the terminal. All the lights were off on this side of the terminal to help conceal them.

Small favors went a long way sometimes.

Wills scanned the area through the window on his side of the plane where a van was waiting, hazard lights flashing. "I think Beth made the arrangements for us."

"Are you sure?" Ames peaked over his partner's shoulder. "That could be for anyone."

"I can't say I'm certain, but I'm more than willing to commandeer the van if it means getting this mess over with." His words were void of any joking tone. Wills was as fed up and tired as Ames. It was an easy presumption the same was true with Ryan and Beth.

They were all itching to get even with Graham and stop whatever evil the Order had planned. This was like Syria all over again; hurry up and wait, keep waiting, convince yourself nothing will ever happen, then boom...go time.

The men called it "hesitation whiplash". He called it "politics over results". They were both right.

Ames followed Wills off the plane and headed towards the van. A local exited the vehicle and opened the side door for them. He said nothing, simply gestured towards the open seats inside.

The soldiers each took their own seat and let the man close the door behind them. Once the driver returned inside, he looked back and said, "Baia Fishery?"

Wills answered, "Yes, please."

"You men don't look like fishermen." He put the van in gear and slowly eased it out of the lot and onto the near empty street. The windshield wipers groaned under the strain of the heavy rain. The passenger side left streaks making it hard to see through though the glass.

"We're more fishers of men," Wills replied. He wasn't wrong, but the context was. They were far from missionaries and Ames didn't want the driver to get the wrong idea.

"I see. I served in the army during the revolta conflict. I lost my left leg in a firebomb incident." He turned the van down a larger, busier road before continuing. "I found my faith after that."

Wills exchanged a guilty glance with Ames. "I more meant we find people, not converting them to our religion," Wills corrected.

Ames felt like a heel just being in the van with him, but the sensation eased when the driver laughed.

"I don't mean to be rude, but I don't imagine you would have great success talking religion with people. You're very intimidating looking."

Another series of turns put them in view of the bay. It was a wash of grey as the sky and water met under the overlay of gushing rain. Within minutes the driver eased the van to a stop and let them out at the fishery.

"What do we owe you?" Wills asked as he exited.

"It was already paid for. Thank you."

Wills pulled a wad of Euros out of his pocket and handed them to the man anyway. "Thank you for your service," Wills said and placed a hand on the man's shoulder.

"Thank you," the driver replied and ran back to climb into the driver's seat.

They never caught his name, and Ames felt bad about it. He struck him as a good guy just trying to make an honest living. He had turned his torment into a life of hope. The man claimed to have faith and in such a miserable world that was an accomplishment.

The door to the fishery opened and Ryan leaned against the frame with his arms crossed over his chest. "It took you boys long enough. We've been getting antsy."

"You could have started without us," Wills shot back.

Ryan turned his nose up at that and laughed. "Beth said you would say that. Come on in and dry off. We have plans to show you."

"This is what we have." Beth spread a map over the table with a stapler placed on it to represent the frigate. "The ship is anchored out with a camel attached to the aft section. The water is a bit choppy and there's someone standing watch. There's no way we can get there unseen, so we need to approach at the bow."

"That's nearly thirty-feet above the waterline. We'll have to climb and try not to make noise doing it," Wills said.

"Right," Beth stated. "I propose using electromagnets to climb the hull. You don't have to engage the magnet until it touches the surface. It should reduce the noise."

"What do we have for weapons?" Ames asked.

Ryan stepped over with two duffels and set them on the table next to the map. He pulled out small arms and laid them out in neat little rows. "It isn't the superior firepower you may be used to, but these should get the job done. Especially in close quarters."

Ames pulled one of them off the table and inspected it. "I wasn't expecting .40 caliber," he said. "Nine round magazine has its limitations, but unless they have dozens of people firing at us at once, we should be able to hold our own." He set it back on the table and took a seat across from Beth. "What I don't understand is why they have people coming to the ship. Why not meet somewhere out in the city? They have the money and the means."

"Control of the environment?" Wills suggested.

"That's what I was thinking," Beth replied.

"If you can control who's coming and going, then you have the means to determine who walks away on their own and who disappears because they're a threat to you. Graham is smart," Ryan said.

It was a decent enough explanation, but it still struck Ames as odd. There had to be something they were missing. "Who all has arrived that we know of?"

"Under Secretary Kaiser from Germany. A man we believe is a biochemist from Russia. And Frederick Duke of York. Plus whatever crew he has on the ship. It could be tens of people or hundreds. We don't really know," Beth said.

Her estimation of personnel on board let some of the air out of their sails. They wanted to go in four strong and seize an entire ship. That would be next to impossible if they were overwhelmed in a firefight. The confines of a ship provided excellent cover, but it could also be a trap in case of a fire. You could choke to death from smoke if you couldn't find your way out.

"Do we have any drones, or the ability to call in for air support?" Wills asked.

Beth let out a sigh. "No. We're at the mercy of our limited numbers and resources. The only thing in our favor is we know where the target is and have the element of surprise."

"Presumably," Ames fired back. "He could be waiting on us."

"Fair point," Wills said. "Ryan said it himself, the man is smarter than we would like. That makes him dangerous."

"What do you suggest? We've been working towards this for years. The pieces are finally out in the open. We may not have the whole Order in our sights, but we have enough heavy hitters to cause real damage. Do you want to give up when we're on the cusp of doing what's necessary?"

Wills leaned forward and draped his arms over the table. "I'm not suggesting we do nothing. I'm just stating the fact I think we may be walking into something designed to lead us into a trap. I think we should consider that in our plans."

"What do you propose?" Ryan asked.

"Enter from two different areas of the ship. Two of us take the bow, the others sneak towards the back, take out the watch, and we essentially meet in the middle once we're all on board. We can sweep the area, lure some distractive firepower if necessary, and not have all our assets bottlenecked at a single entry point."

Ames hadn't meant to say anything out loud, but the words poured out. He hoped he wasn't out of line, not that he would apologize for stating the truth. He owed them enough to speak up. It could save their lives.

"I didn't want to fire first," Beth stated, "But you make a good point. If we all go in and they're waiting for us, then casualties to our cause could end the mission before it even starts."

"I was trying to sound a little more positive than that," Ames replied. His response elicited a laugh from the group.

No one could deny what they were going into was less than ideal. If they had a dozen people with every level of tech available to them, the risks would still be sky high. But the sad truth was no one would ever be willing to go against these people. The persuasion of power was too much. It was like literally fighting a giant with nothing but your bare hands and resentment.

It would have to be enough.

"As positively as I can spin this, I think your point should be considered in our plan of attack," Beth stated. "So, who wants the bow and who wants the stern?"

"Ames and I will take the stern. We can move about with less noise than Hercules over here," he gestured towards Ryan with a sideways glance. "He would probably shoot the guy and sound the alarm himself."

Ryan cleared his throat. "All I heard was you think I'm a Greek demigod. Everything else that poured past your lips was gibberish," the old man joked. "But you guys can have your fun. We can handle the bow. It'll probably be more fun anyway."

The team snickered at their antics. They were hours away from jumping headfirst into what could be their last mission together. It was a suitable response. Pretend the danger isn't there so your fear doesn't stunt your forward momentum. Every service had a way of teaching that response. It always delved into laughing at the danger, making it feel smaller, easier to swallow should you be the unfortunate one to take your last breath.

"Then it's settled," Beth said as she folded the map in her hands. "Let's gear up and get ready for war."

Graham had waited for this moment for a long time. Most of those assembled before him were on board with any plan he would concoct. But first, he had to vet them, prove their trustworthiness. Ensure there were no traitors amongst them.

"Do you believe the Order works to the benefit of those at all ranks of the organization?" Graham asked as he poured glasses of wine for those seated around him. The wardroom of the frigate had been covered in tapestries and candlelight bounced off the walls in a slithering dance.

"I believe their decisions are made to benefit those at the top. Anything beyond that is happenstance," Frederick boasted. He sat next to Under Secretary Kaiser with his shirt unbuttoned down to his navel. His hair was messy and the first appearance of sloppiness in his voice sounded Graham's internal alarm. Either the young man was already drunk or drugged. Still, there was something about what he said that rang true.

"The same can be said for any governing body. I'm asking for specifics, not apologetics," Graham replied, passing the glasses around before hesitantly pushing the half-filled glass to the duke. "I'm questioning their intent."

"Frederick is right," Kaiser said, holding onto the younger man's shoulder, gentling nudging the boyish duke closer to himself. "The Order makes decisions for those in power. If I am not worthy of their respect, then I get no say in decisions made with my position, or my resources."

Doctor Timur nodded. "They work me like a slave. The money is useless to me. I have no way to enjoy it in my lab toiling away with whatever scheme they desire."

"What would make *you* happy, Doctor?" Graham asked.

The disheveled man shrugged. "I suppose I never gave it much thought. I would like to try my hand at manipulating brain waves to remove fear...or project it to its fullest extent."

His words brought smiles to the other men surrounding the table. All but Graham. He knew what the Russian would do with it. He made a mental note to not allow that to happen. "What about you, Frederick?"

"Happy?" Frederick asked, his grin stretched from ear to ear. His cheeks flushed as Kaiser nuzzled his ear. Sweat beaded his forehead despite the chill circulating in the room. "I don't believe in happiness. I believe in power. The powerless are always unhappy. The powerful are always unfulfilled. There is no middle ground."

Graham second guessed his assumption that the duke was intoxicated and instead wondered if Kaiser had slipped him something else that hadn't reared its head yet. There was a reason the German was not favored by the Order. He thought with his hormones instead of his brain. Still, he was useful in his own way. He had connections that wrapped around the world twofold. Graham chided himself for contemplating his early dismissal.

"And you?" Graham directed his question to Kaiser.

The Under Secretary smiled coyly. "A world without borders. A world without consequences. A world without judgement." His eyes practically flickered when he spoke. There may have been a light inside of him, but if there was it burned with lustful darkness.

"None of those things can be promised," Graham replied. His tone was void of emotion. He spoke as a man of science. He spoke as a man with vision beyond what others were capable of seeing.

"Then a world without the Order," Kaiser said, stifling a laugh to keep from choking on his wine.

"Now we're talking," Graham said, raising his glass.

A chirp of the com rang overhead and Anacleto said, "The Chinese are approaching. They will dock with us within twenty minutes."

"The Chinese are involved?" Doctor Timur asked. If he tried to hide the indignance in his voice, then it was lost on Graham.

"They are. How else do you suppose we cut ties with the Order?" Doctor Timur grumbled something under his breath, but Graham didn't bother asking what. "They are what we commonly refer to as a necessary evil. They provide the means for our emancipation."

"At what cost?" Under Secretary Kaiser asked. His otherwise cool demeanor splintered. The Germans had a tough history with China. If not for the Order interceding, Germany and most of the eastern region of Europe would have collapsed into Chinese authority less than a decade prior. Kaiser likely believed he was letting go of the chains of one master only to serve another.

He was right, but Graham wasn't going to say so.

"What would you give to get out from under the Order's rule?" Graham stepped around the table and approached the German. He didn't try fighting the scowl forming on his face. He let his inner rage come to the surface, just close enough to bare his teeth and reveal what he hid from most of the world. "Am I wrong in hearing you tell me you would give up your wealth to have the opportunity to usurp the Order? Did I mishear you?"

Kaiser swallowed hard and slunk back in his seat. He narrowly pushed Frederick off his lap as he cowered before the American tycoon. "No. I said those things."

217

"Did you mean them?" Graham practically hovered over the man. His menacing shadow fell across the horrified German's face. "Did you mean what you said?"

"Ye...yes." Kaiser answered.

Graham smelled his fear. He placed his hand on the German's face and lifted his chin to meet his gaze. "That's what I thought," Graham said, his voice smooth and cold. "So, let's play nice with our new friends. Shall we?"

No one had the gall to say no. Not that he would accept no for an answer anyway.

CHAPTER TWENTY-FIVE

"Talk about inconspicuous," Wills said as he handed a large duffel over to Ames. "I wouldn't be surprised if the owner of this boat paid Ryan to steal it."

Ames smiled at the joke. He'd seen his fair share of equipment that had seen better days, but the small craft looked as if it came off the assembly line by mistake. The welding bead going along the centerline looked like bubbled glue, and he tried not to pay attention to the holes rusted through the metal near the railing.

"I'm pretty sure it was abandoned," Ryan said. "I didn't want to steal a yacht and grab anyone's' attention."

"You won't be getting any attention in a heap pile like this," Wills replied, continuing his over the top antics to get a laugh. It worked, until it didn't. The weight of what was coming did a more than adequate job of snuffing out their lighthearted attempt of masking what they felt.

Silence fell upon them like a heavy blanket. They riffled through the duffels and secured their loads as the choppy waters jostled the small craft. All that held them to the pier was two rotting ropes tightly wound through the cleats built into the wooden platform protruding from the pier.

The rain had died down to a slight mist, but fog clung overhead, diffusing what little moonlight peeked through the roaming storm clouds. Only the city lights provided any illumination.

In the distance the mast lights on the frigate shone in a dull yellow. The camel platform at the rear of the ship had a blue spotlight shining over the top that blinked in and out. When it was fully on the beam spread out over several hundred meters. They would have to hug the shoreline until they got past the ship, then backtrack to avoid detection.

"Are we ready?" Beth asked as she approached. She carried with her a small tablet. The glow from the screen shone up from beneath her face and framed her pale face with a red halo as it reflected off her hair. Her eyes were puffy, but no one mentioned it.

They all had their rituals.

"As ready as we'll ever be. I guess it's time to put this puppy to the test. Sink or swim, boys," Wills said as he patted his hand delicately on the side of the boat.

"I think I'm going to sink like a rock if it comes down to it," Ryan replied. "This arm weighs as much as the rest of me." He lifted his cybernetic arm with a grin.

Ames smiled, but it quickly faded. He'd never tested his ability to swim after the augmentations were in place. He had to pass a swim qual in the Marine Corps, but his body was wholly natural back then. He didn't want to make the unfortunate discovery that anything had changed at a time like this.

"I don't think I'll have a problem," Beth replied. "I'll be sure to call for help." Her tone was flat, but the smile she forced on her face was proof she was at least attempting to make a joke. Everyone chuckled, more out of respect than the humor of it. The night was growing heavy and keeping a jovial attitude was too demanding. They settled into their collective mission-focused mindset. It was automatic for people accustomed to this sort of life.

Wills rose from his seat and loosened the mooring lines while Ryan cranked the motor. To everyone's surprise it worked. Ryan said he had tested it, but he said a lot of things.

"You weren't kidding," Wills said, speaking what everyone else was thinking.

"I never kid about boats," Ryan replied.

Wills and Ames pushed the boat away from the pier and Ryan operated the small outboard motor. The hum of the engine was barely louder than the water cresting over itself like a sloppy, boiling broth. Ryan maintained a steady speed, letting the motor sit at a comfortable RPM so the sound sort of faded into the ambience of the sea.

After several minutes, Beth spoke, "I think we have more company."

Ryan released the throttle and let the boat drift and he knelt lower into the boat. "What do you see?"

Beth held the binoculars up to her face and studied the scene. "It's a sub tying to the port side of the frigate. There're no identifying marks, but it isn't an American ship. It's a warship but it looks too refined."

"What does that mean?" Ames asked.

"It means I think it might be a personal submarine with military capabilities. It's designed to not look like what it is."

"What makes you think it has military capabilities?" Wills asked, pulling his own binoculars up to examine it.

"There's a gun mount, and someone is posted to it."

"Well, that makes things more difficult," Ryan said. "Can we still approach from the other side of the frigate and avoid detection?"

"We're going to have to. Let's just hope they don't post more watches around the frigate. We'll be seen before we're close enough to mount an attack."

Ryan grunted and advanced the throttle. The boat began its slow crawl over the water, keeping to the shadows and out of sight.

Ames narrowed his eyes as he watched the frigate. Somewhere

inside was evil unmatched by anything he'd ever seen. And that evil had company. He swore under his breath. Each step of this mission to take down the Order had come with more hardship than he could imagine. How could someone like him hold so much power?

The boat swayed slightly as a heavy gust of wind swelled in the bay. They were past the frigate, out of the view of the spotlight when Ryan turned port and headed straight for the bow.

"This is it," Ryan said. "The end of the line."

The submarine loomed closer, barely poking out of the water. The Portuguese sailors stood by, mooring line in hand to assist with the docking. Graham couldn't tell what they were saying, but at least they were working as a team. It was more than he could say for the men he'd left in the wardroom. The only thing working between them was hormones between Kaiser and Frederick.

He shook his head of the thought and focused on his last guest. The one who held the keys to a billion soldiers for his disposal.

The sailors tossed lines to their counterparts and used the cleats and bitts to pull the submarine closer to the frigate. There was a significant difference in height above the water, but as the ballast tanks emptied, the submarine rose higher.

Once the ships were properly tied off together the Chinese sailors secured the brow between them and manned the rails. Someone piped and rang a bell as their leader exited the submarine and stood tall at the foot of the brow. It was a display of military authority. It was a show to bolster the man's ego.

It seemed to work.

Xian Chen stepped aboard the frigate like he owned it. His support staff, armed to the gills, followed behind him. Of all places to wear a cape, the Chinese propagandist chose the tight spaces of a ship to stomp around like Lord Vader. All he needed was ominous music and he would mostly look the part.

"Welcome to the *Valoroso*, Xian," Graham said with an extended hand. The man took it, gripping Graham's hand tightly, but barely shook it. "You're right on time."

Xian nodded and gestured for Graham to lead the way.

The American sighed. He knew Xian could speak, he'd heard him on many calls, but the man clearly chose to play the part that his masters in the CCP paved for him. Graham didn't blame him; he had been chosen to serve a role as well. Once it played out, the Order wanted to kill him. It seemed there was no retirement plan in this kind of life.

Graham led Xian and his men back to the wardroom where his other guests waited. Kaiser had a scowl on his face when the men walked in. All eight members of Xian's support staff flanked the room, standing guard for their leader. The room immediately felt a bit stuffier. Not at all the way Graham had planned. This was supposed to be the first magical step at a brighter future. Even he had to admit that it felt more like a sentencing.

"Gentlemen, this is Xian Chen of the CCP. He is here to aide us in our march towards a new alliance."

"In what hole did you dig this guy out of?" Frederick asked. "He looks like a comic book villain."

Xian glared at the duke, his stoic expression more than enough to stifle the bravado the young man felt bolstered enough to spew before knowing any better.

"I've known Xian for many years. There is a comradery between us that lends itself well to bridging our perceived differences and moving forward together."

A scoff sounded from the Russian, but the doctor looked down at his feet, another coward with an opinion.

"My people look forward to our arrangements with all of you," Xian said. He sounded like a robot, emotionless.

"He's a liar. Do you know how many of their own people they've killed?" Kaiser spewed vitriol.

"And how many of your people have you violated, tortured, and killed?" Graham shot back. "Do you believe us to be saints?"

"I'm just saying that there is a certain decorum involved in what we do. It does not align with the communists' ways." Kaiser tugged at his tie and rose from his seat. He placed his hand on Frederick's shoulder and continued, "If this is the path towards a new alliance, then I favor not breaking from the Order. If it isn't broke..."

Graham cleared his throat. "Xian is my guest. I made the arrangements. This is not a negotiation."

"Maybe you should have vocalized your plan with the rest of us before inviting someone from the other side?"

"If this is not settled, then perhaps I should explore my options elsewhere," Xian said, eyes forward, staring a hole into Kaiser's soul.

The German looked at him, his lips quivering as much with fear as with anger. "You should. You have no business with our affairs. You will just as surely betray us as you would your own people."

Frederick shifted in his seat, the confrontation between world powers growing in intensity.

"What the CCP does with its own people is not your concern. What the CCP does to its enemies may be your concern." Xian didn't flinch. He didn't blink. He just stared like a predator.

"Are you threatening me?" Kaiser rose and slammed his fists on the table. A yelp escaped Frederick's lips. Even Doctor Timur stirred, shifting away from the tension in the room. "I will destroy you."

"Gentlemen, please," Graham said. He raised his hands trying to persuade Kaiser to take his seat, but the German wouldn't listen. His eyes flickered with rage.

"Go to hell, Graham. And take your nonsense with you," Kaiser spat. "I'm done here."

The boldness of the Under Secretary unsettled the room. The air was thick, choking. Any way toward negotiating was diminishing by the second. Xian seethed in his silent, stoic way. Kaiser's nostrils flared. If looks could kill, then both men would combust in flames.

"What did you say to me?" Graham said.

Kaiser cut his eyes at Graham. "Do I need to repeat myself?"

"Yes."

"Fine, you can go to hell and take this entire charade with you. I'm done."

Graham's lips curled ever so slightly. "That's what I thought you said." He pulled a gun from behind his back and fired across the table. Blood and brain matter spewed across the room, painting the tapestries clinging to the bulkhead. The dull thud of his head slamming against the tiled deck set silence ablaze in the tight room.

It wasn't until the blood pooled around the German that Frederick chose to speak. "Why did you kill him?"

Graham holstered the weapon, gave a knowing nod to Xian, and glared at the young duke. "Do you not know why you're here? Are you too stupid to realize that things are already in motion that will disrupt the core of this modern society?"

"He didn't have to die," Frederick muttered through sobs. He fell to his knees on the deck next to his former lover. He reached out but didn't touch the dead man. Instead, his hand lingered over his lifeless face.

"He served no purpose if he refused to work with us. Turn off your emotions and get with the program, or you can join him," Graham said stoically.

Frederick turned to face Graham. Fear was a stench that mixed heavily with the blood in the air. He slowly rose to his feet, wiped the tears from his eyes, and reclaimed his seat. He sat, eyes forward, ignoring the death right next to him.

"Good. Now we can begin," Graham said as he gestured towards a seat across from where Kaiser had sat.

Xian took it and pulled himself up to the table. "With Germany out, we will be required to provide more resources. I expect to be compensated with his portion."

Graham agreed. It was only fair. "Doctor Timur will travel with you to help prepare your facilities with our technology. He assures me it will work well with your current program. I believe each of our technologies will provide a much-needed piece of the puzzle. We will be unstoppable."

"What of the Order?" Xian asked. "They will try to intervene."

"I have that under control," Graham replied. "The super soldiers at my disposal will inhibit the Order."

Xian scoffed, breaking character. "I have received word that your super soldiers are rogue agents, Mr. Graham. My sources tell me that the Siberian base was attacked. They lost their own assets. Was that part of your oversight?"

Graham clenched his fist. He hadn't received that word. Doctor Timur had been pulled out to attend this summit and Graham assumed all was well on that side of the world. "Life has its distractions, but as long as Doctor Timur is available to us, that is all that is important."

"Integrity is important to us," Xian said. He rose from his seat and doffed his cape, letting it fall to the deck. His black uniform was adorned with several medals over his chest. But none of that distracted from the weapon holstered under his left arm. "Your business is failing because you are too weak-minded to do what is necessary. We do not have confidence that you will not be a weak link in our business dealings."

Frederick pushed his chair away from the table. Graham's shoulders slumped. It wasn't supposed to go down like this. "What if I gave you my portion as well?"

Xian gawked at him, his confused expression drawing attention from Frederick and Doctor Timur. "I don't understand. Why would you give up your stake?"

Graham narrowed his eyes at him and said, "I had integrity until I let fear rule over me. I'm done being afraid. I have enough money, what I want is authority. I want to topple the Order and bring it burning to the ground. Anything beyond that is just icing on the cake."

Xian smiled, a wicked curl to his lips. The knowing expression in his eyes suggested he never had any intention of walking away. He simply wanted to apply pressure to see what he could walk away with. But what was done was done. Graham would have to live with it.

At least for now.

"I accept your terms," Xian said. "I'll do what's necessary to see that this new alliance succeeds."

"Good," Graham replied. "Because I want to start tonight."

CHAPTER TWENTY-SIX

Ryan cut the motor and let the boat drift towards the frigate. The choppy water slowed the drift considerably, and Ames and Wills used paddles to finish their trek. Idle chatter from the other side of the ship alerted them of a presence onboard, but so far, they were undetected.

"You first," Ryan whispered, gesturing to Beth.

She nodded and made her way to the front of the boat. Beth reached out with the electromagnetic handles until they contacted the hull. She used them to climb up to the weather deck and slowly climbed over the railing before lowering the handles down to Ryan.

He hoisted a duffle over his shoulder and began his climb. Once over the rail he waved off Ames and Wills and settled behind a large deck box next to Beth. He opened the duffle and pulled out a claymore. "If things go awry, I don't want to die without leaving a surprise," he said, keeping his voice low.

Beth nodded, noting the placement before she scooted along the deck below the bridge. She couldn't see if anyone was up there looking down, but if they saw her, they weren't sounding the alarm.

Likely the angle of the windows didn't allow anyone to look straight down anyway, so she figured they were safe...for now.

They moved slowly, deathly quiet. A hatch on the starboard side sat open, latched onto a doorstop to keep the wind from slamming it shut. Red lights shone from the interior, making it hard to see what waited inside lurking in the shadows.

Beth stopped, staring into the abyss, listening for anything that could be waiting. "I think it's clear," she whispered.

"I'll go first," Ryan said, brushing past her and towards the hatch.

Beth held her weapon up for coverage, anticipating gunfire. Once he crossed the threshold, she followed, darting into the ship and staying low. They stayed in the doorway for a short time to let their eyes adjust before going deeper into the ship.

Beth took point again and led them through the narrow passageways. Up the ladder to the right would be the bridge. A few feet on the other side of the passage was a ladder leading down into more darkness. That would be where most of the spaces within the ship would be.

She turned to Ryan and pointed down the ladder. He nodded and moved towards it, careful not to make a sound as he stalked down the ladder well. Beth followed once he disappeared deeper into the space.

They were in a berthing no larger than most single car garages. It was pitch black except for two red lights overhead on the other side of the space. She led them towards it, stopping at a metal door with an exit sign glowing dimly on the surface.

"Should I try it?" She asked, gesturing at the door.

Ryan nodded, "Careful, they tend to pressurize and slam on you."

Beth approached slowly, turning the doorknob before pulling it towards her. The pressure on the other side kept it closed at first, then she broke the seal and a rush of air passed. The slightest creak sounded from the hinges and her fear piqued. She held her breath, waiting for someone to rush towards them, but no one did.

Ryan moved past her, leading them deeper into the unknown ship. They hugged the bulkhead as they moved, crouching and stepping lightly. Every ten meters or so they had to step over a knee knocker, its silhouette marked by the dull, green glow of reflective tape. Further into the ship the sound of a television program squawked. Someone laughed, clapping their hands and stomping their feet. The smell of booze wafted in the air around them.

"Another berthing," Ryan whispered. "Keep going?"

Beth pointed towards a cut in the passageway moving more towards the center of the ship. "There."

Ryan moved forward, stepping over another series of knee knockers before stopping by the turn.

Placards on the bulkhead had number and letter systems like the American ships, but none of them stated what the spaces were. At least not in a way Beth was familiar with. It was like being lost in a maze in the dark. Everything looked the same...mostly.

A door opened behind them, and Beth shoved Ryan towards the corner and into the crossing of the passageway. They stood there a moment, eyes locked, listening for danger. They were in enemy territory, at a disadvantage, and one wrong move would bring attention their way.

Beth hesitated to say what was on her mind, that this was a mistake. It would have been better to call in an airstrike and be done with it. What had she hoped to accomplish traipsing in here?

Nothing that seemed relevant now.

Footsteps approached. Drawing their attention, and their weapons. It was a man, likely the one who'd been watching television in the other berthing. He was humming something to himself when he stopped, chuckled to himself, then turned to walk the other way.

"That was close," Ryan said.

"Too close," Beth agreed.

"Let's just hope the other guys get in position soon. Once it starts, we can get it over with."

He had a point, but once it started, that was when people died. And likely not all of them would be on the other side.

Ames paddled the boat towards the stern, fighting against the choppy waters while Wills kept the boat from knocking into the ship. Moving in the dark, with only the shine of light coming off the shore helped cloak them, but the closer they got to their entry point the harder it was to keep the current from pushing the boat into the frigate. Any knock or squeak would reverberate around the ship and potentially alert the enemy.

This was a job requiring finesse. Once people started shooting at each other then he could let his hair down.

"A little closer," Wills whispered. Ames could barely hear him over the sloshing water. He eased up on how fast and hard he paddled. The blue spotlight on the stern was angled away from them, but the light still illuminated the space they planned to board. "A little more."

Wills was on his tiptoes trying to see over the deck of the ship to find the watch. The frigate's stern had a sudden drop from the main weather deck, down two levels to a smaller platform leading into the skin of the ship. It was designed for personnel to leave and board the ship while anchored, but also for a watch stander to keep an eye out for sailors falling overboard.

This was the easiest spot to board physically, but also the easiest to be spotted before the fun began.

Wills waved a hand for him to stop. Ames pulled the paddle from the water and eased it down into the boat.

There was movement casting a shadow in their direction. It shifted in and out of the light as the person paced the deck. The shadow loomed larger, then it stopped and grew smaller as the watch stander moved to the other side of ship.

Wills grabbed hold of the mooring line and hauled himself up the side of the ship and above the watch platform, lurking in the shadows. Ames held the boat close to the frigate and waited, his eyes on his partner.

Wills extended the blades from his arms and leaped. He brought three hundred pounds down onto the unsuspecting sailor and stabbed the man through his back and out his chest. The watch stumbled lifelessly towards the handrails and drooped over the side.

Ames looked up, thinking he was seen, only to see the blades pull out from the body before Wills sent the man over the side.

It was messy, but effective.

Ames tossed up their duffle then boarded himself. "Did we have to kill him?"

"Would you prefer a negotiation next time?" Wills asked.

Ames shrugged. There were casualties in every war, but most of the time the soldiers knew they were in a battle. This felt different somehow, he couldn't put his finger on it. Perhaps it was the lackadaisical approach these men stood their posts? They weren't ready for battle. They weren't ready for what was coming.

"We're in position," Wills said softly into his com. He checked his watch and nodded to Ames.

It was time.

Ryan and Beth looked knowingly at one another. Wills had checked in and their assault on the frigate was a go. Within the next two minutes someone was going to know they were there. A few seconds after that people would start dying. That's how it always went.

Ryan moved first, heading towards the other side of the ship down the cross-connecting passageway. He stopped short, glanced around the corner, then continued in a swift, quiet pace.

Beth followed, keeping her eyes and ears open. There were sounds coming in all directions, hushed by the constant whir of air circulating through the ship. The pressure built up in her ears and she tried getting them to pop, but it didn't help with her hearing, though it did relieve the pressure.

Ryan held up a fist and she slowed to a stop behind him. Voices carried down the tight corridor, foreign, jovial. Not the sound of men knowing what was coming.

That was the point.

Beth moved past Ryan. Her smaller stature would help her stay concealed as she moved past the open door. Blinding, white light poured out of the space and onto the deck. She hadn't realized how quickly her eyes had adjusted to the dark until this moment. She paused, careful not to make a sound. The men were close, maybe twenty meters on the other side of the thin bulkhead.

She looked down as shadows shifted on the glistening tile in front of the door. It was waxed to a mirror-like finish and showed the reflection of a man standing just inside the doorway. She got enough of a view to know he was there but couldn't tell which way he was facing.

There were at least three other voices in the room. One of them was either drunk or obnoxious, likely both. He spewed a flurry of words she didn't understand and elicited as many groans as he did laughs.

Beth looked back at Ryan, her eyes asking the burning question racing through her mind. He shook his head. Stand fast...but she couldn't stand there forever.

He moved forward, stepping lightly. She focused more on his movements, willing him to not make a sound and give them away. She didn't see the shadow in the doorway shift. She didn't feel the other presence in the passageway until it was too late.

"Quem é você?"

Beth's eyes darted up to the man standing there looking at her. Chairs shoved out of the way, scraping against the deck as his friends moved in to join him.

The sailor reached out to grab her, but Ryan was already moving in.

The American snatched the man up by the neck and held his

233

head in his hands. The sailor's feet kicked, and his arms flailed as he tried to fight off the stronger opponent. Broken Portuguese phrases were cut off by his whines and groans. The harder Ryan pressed, the higher in pitch the man's voice trailed until his body went limp and Ryan dropped him to the deck.

Beth took a guarded step back, pulling her weapon as the other three men rushed out the door.

Ryan met the first one with a heavy punch to the face. The crunch of bone reverberated as the man collapsed to the deck. A second man took a swing, connecting with Ryan's cybernetic arm. The clink of knuckles on metal was accompanied by his wails. His hand was broken. His body was next.

Ryan yanked him up and spun, slamming the sailor into the steel bulkhead. His fist sunk into the man's chest, caving it in.

That left the fourth sailor, standing and gawking at them with horror etched onto his face. He stammered, stepping back, holding his empty hands up in surrender.

But there would be none of that this night.

Ryan grabbed the man by his neck, lifted him, and squeezed. The man's face turned blue as Ryan held him up in the pale light. The man grabbed hold of Ryan's arm, gripping it tight, but flesh was useless against metal.

He stopped breathing several seconds later, the light in his eyes faded, and his arms glanced off of Ryan's and dangled limply next to his body. Ryan kept squeezing until he was sure, then dropped the man into his pile of victims.

Two minutes into the mission and they were discovered. A few seconds later, people died. Just like she knew would happen.

But it wasn't over yet. Footsteps approached. Running towards them.

Ryan shoved Beth into the room where the sailors had been and stepped inside himself. His eyes narrowed and he breathed heavily. He was strong but moving his massive body with all the cybernetics installed took its toll on his cardiovascular system. He couldn't keep fighting like this. He didn't have the stamina that new versions of the same super soldier program had. It was as if he was designed to fail. Ryan just refused to cooperate.

The movement stopped short of their position, and this time the people speaking weren't Portuguese. They were Chinese.

Ryan leaned back, took in some steady breaths, then looked down at Beth.

She was ready, whatever he planned on doing. She gave him a nod, then watched as he darted into the passageway, nearly knocking the door off its hinges as he rounded the corner.

Beth jumped out of the room and took aim, but Ryan took up most of the space. She didn't have a clear shot as he bowled over four men. Shouts and screams emanated from the squad, but that wasn't her concern. But that soon changed with a gunshot blast.

CHAPTER TWENTY-SEVEN

"This New Alliance is the birth of a true, one world government. We will remove borders. We will replace inefficient government. We will annihilate the parasites. Utopia is within our reach," Graham said as he raised his glass to toast.

"Here. Here." Their chorus of agreement met his ears with a satisfaction he had only dreamed of. He was a natural born leader. His success was less a factor of the Order's involvement, and more with what he was capable of. In truth, the Order was just as much a pond of leeches and parasites as those who lived off the government teat.

But soon they would be over.

"I know you want to celebrate this achievement, our unification, but all things must be symbolic if they are to hold any meaning," Graham stated. He turned around and grabbed a box for each member of his alliance and passed them out. "The symbol of our unity is found within. It is for our protection."

Frederick tore open the box first and pulled out the contents. He glanced back at Graham. His puffy wide eyes lost in tears, but also confusion. "I don't understand...a mask?"

"Look closer," Graham replied.

Frederick did so and pulled the facial part around to closer examine it. "This is your face."

"What is this?" Xian asked. "We are to be equals. We are not your puppets."

"Every empire needs a leader. I told you I didn't want the money. I want the authority. I want the power. You agreed, did you not?"

Xian nodded, his eyes daggers as he realized what Graham had done. "You planned this." It wasn't a question.

"Of course, I did. It was Sun Tzu who said, 'Plan for what is difficult while it is easy, do what is great while it is small'. I spoke plainly. I didn't deceive you. I am not at fault for your misunderstanding of what was happening, but I'll ask you, is there a problem?" Xian shook his head. "Good," Graham continued.

The Chinese had a small, but well-armed force. Just the eight men in the room could kill Graham before he had the chance to call for help, but they stood still as statues. If the man was threatened, they might act. Graham had no reason to make them, though. This was going according to plan, as well as it could have, anyway.

"These masks represent your commitment to me. You are my shields," he looked to Frederick. "You are my swords," he looked to Doctor Timur. "And you are my armies," he said to Xian.

All three men pulled the masks over their faces. It was like looking in a mirror, only when they spoke a different voice came out. The ritual was nearly complete, and Graham would soon have what he was after.

He stepped around the table and knelt next to Kaiser's body. He dabbed his finger in the blood and pulled it to his lips, taking it in.

"Warriors used to consume the blood of their enemies. They believed a part of their spirit would bond to them, to make them more powerful. Kaiser was our enemy. Consume him." He dabbed another finger into the blood and put it to Frederick's lips, then to Doctor Timur, and finally to Xian. The man was resistant at first, then gave in.

In the end, everyone bowed to their superior. They did as they were told, and with the blood ritual complete, Graham had all he needed.

Authority.

The witchcraft he'd used on them would ensure he was well protected. Anything he said, they would do. A sinister curl to his lips formed as he looked at his minions. His reign was only just beginning, but soon the world would cower to their new leader.

As images of world domination flooded into his mind, the outside world appeared to serve a different master. A gunshot rang out, then the klaxon sounded. At any other time, he would have been nervous, but he had an army on board. His victory simply hadn't happened yet.

"Go out and bring me the intruders. Do this for the New Alliance," he ordered. The men scrambled to their feet and exited the room. Graham reclaimed his seat at the head of the table and drummed his fingers along the surface. His authority was supreme. Those men would die to protect him.

They belonged to him now.

"Do this for me," he whispered, remembering the words that enslaved him to the Order so many years ago. But now he was free.

The klaxon wailed no further than two feet from Ames's head. The piercing clanging of a bell ringing at full blast caused tears to well in his eyes. He stumbled a step before bracing himself against the bulkhead, his head swimming.

"You all right?" Wills asked, but it sounded like he was underwater.

Ames shook his head, wincing before he put his hand to the device controlling his hearing and disengaged it. It had been months since he went without hearing and it brought its own kind of torment, but deafening silence was better than the klaxon turning his insides out. He held himself up a moment, watching for movement and seeing Wills lips move as fast as the klaxon bell clanged.

Those words fell on deaf ears. The heightened senses he'd been giving were now a curse. He noticed it during the battle in Siberia, but this was worse. The frequency was like driving a nail into his forehead.

Wills stomped around, agitated, arms flailing like a character in a silent film. Then, he extended the blade from one of his arms and stabbed it through the klaxon. Sparks flew from the box, and the super soldier's hair lifted slightly from his head, but the smirk and thumbs up was enough for Ames to risk turning his implants back on.

The clanging continued, but from somewhere deep in the ship. The wave of nausea was gone. The disorientation was gone. But his anger remained like a companion in the night.

"You good now?" Wills asked.

"Yeah, thanks," Ames replied.

Wills led them inside, weapons drawn and ready. The stern opened to a narrow passageway in the center of the ship. It led forward several meters before splitting. There were small spaces on either side of the passage, most of them open and containing small machine rooms for HVAC, water sanitation, and other ship services. Once the path split, it was solid white bulkhead stretching to both sides.

"Which way do we go?" Ames asked.

Wills mumbled to himself before addressing the question. "I was thinking we could split up and cover more ground. Either of us hits a snag, we call for backup."

Ames didn't like it. The ship seemed empty now, but that was largely due to the klaxon covering the sound of anyone running up and down the passageways. He would have to silence each speaker to keep his bearings. That would likely lead someone straight to him.

"I don't know man, this is a two-person job," Ames said after a moment.

"Then follow me," Wills replied and took the starboard route.

The further into the ship they went, the harsher the tone was coming from the klaxon. The disorientation was returning, but not as overwhelmingly as it had before. The two stopped before the turn and Ames charged up one bracelet, stepped around the corner, and blasted the speaker right off the wall. It erupted in a shower of sparks and clanked onto the deck in pieces.

"My way was cooler," Wills said with his nose turned up.

"My way didn't shock me and make me smell like burnt hair," Ames replied.

Wills scoffed at the comment, then smoothed his hair back.

Bootheels slammed against the deck several meters ahead. They sounded like they were moving away, so Wills stole a peek. Three men darted down the passageway as they came down the ladder well nearby. A fourth was at the bottom and spotted him. He shouted something indistinguishable to the American, which made a lot more sense to his friends. They immediately turned around and leveled their weapons, firing like madmen.

Wills pushed Ames back around the corner as a chunk of steel splintered behind him. Both men turned to look at the destruction then back at each other.

"What the hell kind of weapon is that?" Wills asked.

"The kind that we don't want to get hit by," Ames replied, pulling himself off the deck before helping his friend. Back on their feet, they ran for the other passageway on the port side to regroup. This fight was just starting and already they were fleeing. It wasn't looking good for a seamless takeover. At least not from their position.

Ames just hoped Beth and Ryan were faring better.

Her ears rang and the smell of spent gunpowder clung to the air around her. Beth swung her body back around, diving into the empty space from which she came, sprawling out over the floor. She flipped her body around and aimed at the open doorway, waiting for the enemy to spring.

Instead, Ryan filled the doorframe, lumbering towards her, hand over his chest. When he pulled his hand away, blood poured from a wound where his cybernetic arm met the organic portion of his body. He took a stumbling step, the fell over like a log.

She wanted to scream. She may have, but she didn't know for sure. What she did know was that the high pitch wail in her head matched the overwhelming terror flooding through her body. She reached out for him and checked his pulse.

"Thank God," she whispered as she clamored to her feet.

She wasn't about to go down without a fight.

Beth leapt from her position and pounced towards the first sign of movement she saw. She whipped around the dark-clad man and pressed her pistol against his head. Without remorse, she pulled the trigger, looking away just in time to keep the splatter out of her eyes.

The ringing continued, this time worse, but she wasn't going to stop.

Another soldier sprung towards her with a menacing grin. He was armed with a rifle too long to be useful in such a tight space. He took four long strides towards her before she capped him in the knee. The .40 caliber round took out enough flesh that he wasn't going to be a threat anymore. He howled in pain, a satisfying wail.

A softer side of her wanted to pity him, but sympathy for the enemy was weakness. He brought it on himself. Besides, she needed someone to get answers from.

Beth yanked the man by the hair of the head and pulled him into the space with Ryan. "Who do you work for?"

He glared at her, his eyes full of tears. Snot and blood poured from his nose, but he tried desperately to look defiant.

Mostly he looked like an idiot defending a monster.

She pressed the pistol under his chin, pushing the barrel hard enough to dig into his skin. "I'm only going to ask this once... Who. Do. You. Work. For?"

"Perhaps I can answer that question for you, Ms. Browning," a voice said from the passageway.

Her eyes darted to a man dressed in black. He stepped into the light, revealing the marred flesh of a man who'd seen hell and lived to talk about it. He wore a bowler hat and pulled it off when he entered, dragging one leg behind him as he clutched his hat with both hands in front of him. If he had any fear at all, he didn't show it. He was as cold as anyone she'd ever seen in a lifetime of fighting winless wars.

"Who are you?" Beth didn't bother pulling the gun from the soldier's chin. She held his life in her hands and would spend it any way she desired.

"I go by many names, but none of them are relevant right now," he said. He spoke eloquently, like he was playing a part in a school play instead of stepping on scene into a battle. "I believe we have a mutual interest on this ship."

"What would that be, walking off of it in one piece?"

He smirked and it somehow made him more terrifying. She wanted to look away but couldn't. "I'm here for David Graham. You're here for David Graham. I think you can see where this is going?"

"Enlighten me," she said flatly. She didn't know anything about this man and the fact he knew her name wasn't enough of a reason for her to listen to what he had to say, much less trust him. If anything, it did the opposite. Besides, she wasn't about to stop killing bad guys because he seemed to think they could form an alliance. Her role in this was to execute anyone associated with the Order. Not potentially help them. And something about this man screamed "the Order".

"Ah, a skeptic," he said as he walked to the other side of the room and sat in one of the folding chairs along the bulkhead. He placed the hat on his lap and clasped his hands together at his waist. "I'm here to kill him because he is a maniac who is unfit for the position he held within an organization I'm part of."

Bingo, Beth thought. Nailed it. "So, you want me to kill him for you?"

A smile tugged at his thin, scarred skin. "Far from it. I want the honor. I simply want you to walk away and let me carry out my orders uninhibited."

"That sounds sketchy to me," Beth replied. "Why would I do that? Our interests begin and end with Graham but giving up my stake doesn't advance my cause."

His smile turned off as quickly as it came and eyes burning with hatred stared back at her. "You're making a mistake," he said.

"The mistake is letting you speak when you're part of the problem," she shot back.

"Is that a fact?" He rose from his seat and placed his hat onto the chair before turning to face her. "Then perhaps we should do something about that?"

Beth took a step back. For an unarmed man, he had a way of evoking terror just by looking at him. This psychological war was as haunting as any physical war could be. Her palms were sweaty. Her heart raced. "Let's do," she hissed, trying to sound intimidating despite her trepidation.

His ugly yellow teeth showed as the burnt flesh pulled away in a smile. He was a spawn of hell. She had no doubt about that.

He nodded ever so slightly and said, "Let's."

Out from the relative darkness of the passageway a dark blur caught Beth's eye. She moved to dart out of the way but had very little room to maneuver with Ryan passed out on the deck and her would-be hostage kneeling next to her, his leg half-ripped off at the knee.

A hard fist caught her shoulder with enough force to send her stumbling backwards. Beth grabbed hold of a chair to help balance herself but didn't have time to regain her footing before the blur appeared again. This time she caught enough of a glimpse to realize it wasn't a man who'd struck her.

The woman looked up at her from a crouching position. Long, dark hair in her face obscured most of the details, but the bright red lips and dark eye makeup against pale skin made her look like the bride of Satan himself.

"Urio is like your friends...only better," the man said with a sneer. "And I love to watch her work."

The femme fatale leapt from her crouch and extended a leg in a high kick towards Beth's head. She tried to dodge, blocking with both arms, but it was like getting hit by a truck. The kick landed low, directly below her shoulder on her upper left arm. Her head whipped forward as her body craned back against the bulkhead.

Beth's eyes blurred as the woman stalked closer. Tears welled in her eyes. Death was coming and she was powerless to stop it. She boldly stared ahead for as long as she could maintain consciousness.

It wasn't enough.

She never saw what was coming.

CHAPTER TWENTY-EIGHT

Ames never ran from a fight, but this time was different. His legs moved as fast as they could as he bound over each knee knocker positioned every ten or so meters. It was as if the shipbuilders were paid extra per obstacle. He cursed their names under his breath as he darted around another corner and down a passage that led back across the ship.

He'd lost Wills. He'd lost his situational awareness. And he had no idea where he was other than "Frame 76". That might mean something if he knew exactly where Frame 76 was in relation to the bow and stern, but it was just a number out of context.

"Think. Think. Think." He hissed each word as he racked his brain. This mission had gone way past failure quick. He'd lost coms with everyone. No one was shooting anymore, but he presumed that was because his friends were dead, and now the enemy was hunting him. That was the only logical conclusion.

Ames sucked in heavy breaths and tried to calm down. His heart thudding in his ears was a distraction he couldn't afford. He needed to listen for approaching bad guys. He had to steady himself so his gasps wouldn't clue them in to where he was.

He had to do a lot of things if he wanted to step off this boat alive.

Ames pulled his weapon from its holster and held it in his hands. Nine rounds of .40 caliber bullets were great on the range but weren't effective in closed quarters combat with moving targets. Especially when you're shooting while running.

He was a trained killing machine. He should be able to wipe the floor with them, but at least one member of the squad had a weapon with the destructive power of a missile. His eyes fell to his wrists and the bracelets he wore. He always thought like a Marine. Every Marine was a rifleman. He was still a Marine, but he was also so much more now.

Ames charged the bracelets with kinetic energy and watched as blue electricity balled around his fists like miniature suns. The hairs on the back of his neck stood on end.

Then he heard footsteps.

He faced the direction the sound came from and waited until he saw the tiniest bit of movement and fired.

It was a miss, but the scorch mark in the bulkhead was far more satisfying than the little ping marks his bullets made at the same distance.

Additionally, the shriek that followed gave him a renewed sense of power.

"Don't move," Ames barked as he stomped towards the man who'd fallen on the deck. All he saw was feet scrambling away from him, but they weren't fast enough. Ames turned the corner and aimed down, right into the face of the man responsible for all this. "I said don't move."

Graham held his hands up over his head, his jaw slack. "Don't shoot!"

Ames's eyes betrayed him. It looked just like Graham, but the voice was different. The clothing was different. And the visible signs of weakness were glaringly evident that this person was far from the tycoon who created the super soldier program.

Whoever this man was, he was a tenth of the man Graham was.

"Who are you?"

"Don't shoot me," the man replied.

"That all depends on whether you answer my questions or not. Who are you?"

"I can't tell you, he'll kill me," the man said. The expression in his eyes betrayed the face looking back at Ames. Whatever technology was used to construct this mask was beyond what Ames thought was possible. That meant any number of encounters may have been with people who weren't who he thought they were. That sent a chill down his spine.

"Take off the mask," Ames ordered. The man tried scooting away, until Ames reached down and yanked him off the deck by his shirt collar. He held the whimpering man up, his feet dangling limply. "I didn't say leave. I said take off the mask."

"I can't."

"Why can't you?" Ames voice was a low growl. His anger bubbled just beneath the surface. He was more than ready to let it out.

"He'll kill me," the man replied.

"You said that already, but what makes you think I won't?" Ames asked. He charged one of the bracelets again and held the arching metal fist to the man's face. Terror-stricken eyes widened, followed by a scent of ammonia. Ames looked down at the piss dripping down the man's leg. "Tell me what I want to know. Who are you and where is the real Graham?"

The response came in stammering bursts. The relevant information wasn't that Ames was responsible for a member of the royal family wetting themselves, but that Graham was located in the wardroom one deck above.

"Thanks," Ames said before dropping the coward to the deck. "I suggest you not leave this ship unless you want to hang by your testicles. If I have to hunt for you, I'll make sure it's worth my while. Do you understand?"

Frederick nodded and scampered away like a little rat.

That left Ames to do what he came for...to kill Graham.

Beth came to in a dark room, lit only by dim candles. Her head ached and her whole body felt like she'd been run over. She clenched her eyes shut and willed them open hoping she was dreaming. If so, it was a nightmare.

The scent of blood hung in the air, and it reminded her that Ryan had been shot. She slowly turned her head and saw him lying next to her, his eyes closed, his chest slowly rising and falling. At least he was alive, for now.

Voices spoke just out of line of sight. There was a table obscuring her view, but she recognized two of the voices. One was Graham. The other was the maniac with the scorched face. Neither of them were on her friend list.

"I told you I would reclaim the weapons if you gave me time," Graham said. His voice held a tinge of fear to it. Beth understood why. It was like looking at a monster. To meet him was the thing of nightmares.

"And I told you I would come for you if you tried to run. I'm a man of my word. Besides, your work here was not for the Order. It was to boost yourself into a position of power."

"I do what's necessary to get the job done, Zero. You of all people should understand that." Graham raised his voice. Beth didn't know if it was a fear response or if he was simply trying to be intimidating, but she doubted either would work in his favor. But Graham's success wasn't what caught her attention. It was the name he had said. Zero. She'd heard that name before but couldn't recall where.

She racked her brain while they continued to talk at length. Then she remembered that "Zero" was the callsign of an operator with the SAS. She had met him at Prince Andrew's funeral years prior. He had spent years working for the royal family, but after the funeral no one had heard from him. Beth always assumed he either retired or was reassigned.

The truth, as it turned out, must have been much darker.

"I'm claiming these weapons of yours and delivering them to the Order. But I'm also doing what I should have done last time we met—"

There was a shuffle of movement and Graham came into view as he backed away from Zero. Beth closed her eyes enough to see out of slits, hoping she wouldn't be discovered.

"I want you to meet someone, David. I want you to meet the perfect weapon that you could not create. I want you to meet Urio."

A black boot stepped over Beth's head, startling her, but no one noticed as the walking death machine approached Graham. This was his show and anything involving she and Ryan would wait until Graham ceased the breathe.

It was only a small consolation. Hell was coming one way or another.

The door crashed open, slamming against the bulkhead and dislodging a section of tapestry strung along the ceiling. Beth turned to see Ames step in, his fist glowing a bright, cobalt blue. Arcs buzzed around his hands as he approached, murder in his eyes.

"And the prodigal son returns," Zero hissed. "Urio, show David what you're capable of."

She turned on her heels and faced the former Marine. Claws extended from her fingers, tiny sharp blade-like talons glistening in the candlelight. Urio didn't say a word. There was no emotion in her face. Even the way she narrowed her eyes before pouncing was void of any humanity.

Urio leaped. She drove straight towards Ames like a bullet, her talons extended towards his face.

He waited for her to close in, then snapped to the side and slammed a kinetic blast into her ribcage. The strike sent the small woman propelling into the bulkhead. She hit with enough force to pull the entire wall of tapestries down and knock over the line of candles. Fire caught along the deck as she rose slowly and stepped back into the fray.

"You can take a hit," Ames said. "Let's see how long that lasts?" He bolted towards her. This time she mimicked his defensive strategy and waited until he struck, quickly moved out of the way, and dealt a counter blow. The slash of her talons met the flesh of his real leg and sent him reeling. He collapsed into the licking flames and struggled to hold himself up as the fire grew beneath him.

Blood poured from the wound. She'd struck an artery.

Zero stepped over and knelt next to Ames. "The poison laced talons have an active coagulant. The effects are almost immediate. As your blood pumps, the coagulant seals the wound, trapping the poison. Eventually it gets to your heart, but it isn't in a rush. The effects are slow. But the incapacitation works immediately because an enemy who cannot fight, cannot kill."

He rose and faced Graham. "The future of warfare will be battle-fields strewn with bodies slowly dying from the poison. One soldier like Urio can take out hundreds. Conventional weapons will have little effect. She feels nothing. I tried to warn you that you had outlived your usefulness to the Order, but you didn't listen."

Graham stammered. Beth watched as his face grew paler and sweat beaded along his forehead. It may have been fear or the rising temperature in the room. She looked back at Ames as the fire grew. He struggled to back away. Then her eyes moved to Ryan. The bleeding had stopped, and she wondered if Urio was the one who'd inflicted the wound. She thought it was a gunshot, but maybe not?

Urio stood behind Ames, watching the fires rise. She was like a tin soldier, poised in deathly elegance. If she couldn't feel, then she would stand there until the fires consumed them all.

"You forgot something," Ames choked out. Beth didn't know if it was an effect of the smoke or the poison, but his defiance showed his warrior spirit.

Zero turned to the fallen Marine. "What is that you're saying?"

"I said you forgot something."

"Like what?"

Ames grunted as he pushed himself up off the deck. "We aren't conventional weapons," he hissed. Ames charged his bracelets and fired both kinetic blasts into the deck, sending himself up and back, crashing into Urio. Beth turned to face the other direction to see where they fell and watched Ames grab hold of Urio's neck.

Urio lashed out with her talons, but they could only reach so far. His cybernetics protected him. Ames recharged his bracelets as he held onto her throat with both hands. Despite his injuries, he held her up and out of reach until he was ready. Blue light erupted around her head as he sent every bit of force into one point.

Urio's head snapped back. Her body went limp. Ames discarded her with a throw towards the open door, then collapsed to the deck, out of the fight.

A surge of pride rose in Beth's chest. They fought like a team. They unified against a common enemy. Even if it was over, she was proud of what they had done. They chose to fight true evil, and it would always know that good people existed.

That would have to be enough.

Graham stood and watched his life's work fall at his feet. He didn't deserve to be here. He didn't deserve a lot of things, but that didn't change reality.

The Order had been onto him from the beginning. He thought he was crafty enough to allude them, but somehow, they were three steps ahead and developed a super soldier program that superseded his efforts by decades.

What was worse was knowing his alliance with China was a ruse. The Order had already formed their own alliance. Xian's presence here was simply to destroy what Graham had tried to build. He did so by providing the best super soldier he'd ever seen. Urio was a killing machine. Ames might have taken her out in the end, but he was dying along with Ryan. He had no defense against Zero or the Chinese still aboard the ship.

They would surely string him up into the masthead as an example of his disobedience. His corpse would rot as it dangled from thick ropes as a display harkening back to the anti-piracy times with the British Navy.

He didn't deserve that either, but it was coming.

Zero turned to face him, his yellow teeth bared. "Ames proved an efficient solder. I'll admit I thought he would have given up as soon as the poison entered his body. He was clever too. Unfortunately, he wasn't clever enough."

Graham's heart nearly stopped beating as Urio rose from the deck. Her hair was disheveled from the voltage spike Ames had used against her, but as she stepped forward, she looked none the worse for wear.

She strode over, her gait as feminine as he'd ever seen, but she wore the scowl of a predator.

"If you're going to kill me, then just do it already," Graham said through his teeth.

Zero smirked and stepped out of the way as his machine of war drew closer. "You should feel honored," Zero said. "You inspired this design."

The words fell deafly at his ears. His focus was on Urio and those talons extending from her fingers. She didn't anticipate her pounce. She didn't give a warning. She simply swiped, digging into his chest until he felt her touch his heart. She drew closer, holding him up as his legs went limp. There was nothing else in the room except the two of them. A disgraced man and his killer in his final moments.

She pulled him closer. Their lips almost touched.

Somewhere between the pained beats of his heart he heard the quietest of whimpers. He thought it was him until he saw the tiny movement of her lips. She repeated it...

"Help. Me."

Graham's eyes grew wide. Everything Zero had said was a lie.

She did feel. She did speak. But whoever made her kept her prisoner in her own mind. He may have been a bastard, but whoever did this was much worse.

He tried to speak. He tried to find words to comfort the woman trapped inside. They were both victims of the Order. In another life they may have been able to work together to thwart it, but in this life, he would die, and she would continue to suffer.

It was the cruelest of jokes.

Maybe he did deserve it.

As he drew one more painful breath, he kept his eyes locked on hers. It felt like time stood still while eternity waited. He wanted to apologize. He wanted to end his life doing one good thing, but he was powerless.

He had always been powerless. He just refused to acknowledge it.

He reached out for her but lacked then strength. She lowered him ever so slightly, allowing his hand to rest on her cheek. Urio held him there for just a moment, then she punctured his heart, inserted the poison, and it stopped beating.

David Graham, like everything he had ever touched, was dead.

CHAPTER TWENTY-NINE

"Grab Ryan and Ames," Zero said. "I'll carry Browning." He knelt next to her, brushing his gloved finger across her cheek. Her response brought a curl to his lips. "You can't pretend to be unconscious after I saw you watch what happened here."

"Maybe I was hoping I was dead," Beth fired back. Her blood boiled. Watching your friends die did that to you. She didn't really want to join them in death, but neither did she want to live through whatever torture the Order had waiting for her.

"Maybe you don't have to wait much longer," Zero said. There was a sadistic twinkle in his eye.

The innuendo wasn't lost on her. Beth's eyes darted to the woman who had killed Graham. He planned on using them to make more solders like Urio, but there was no future in being part of their walking dead army. "I'll kill you before you can do that me." She meant every word, but he was unshaken.

Instead, he hauled Beth up to her feet and latched onto her arm with an iron grip. For a man deformed by fire he was as strong as anyone she'd ever come up against. Part of her wondered if he was privy to the program that made Urio. If that was the case, they didn't go all the way with him. She still had to endure his talking.

"I think you'll like Harbin this time of year. It's cold and bitter, like you," Zero said as he led Beth out of the room. Fires crawled up the bulkheads of the wardroom, but out in the passageway the temperature difference was night and day.

Beth tried dragging her feet to slow him down. She didn't want to leave. Staying here and burning to death on this ship would be a moral victory if nothing else.

"Keep moving or I'll drag you by your hair," Zero threatened.

She walked normally but focused on the zip ties binding her wrists behind her. If she could break free, then she could...do what? Get killed by Urio?

Beth let out an exhausted breath. She didn't want to admit defeat, it wasn't in her nature. But fighting seemed a moot point. She had watched what Urio did to Ames, and he had two-hundred pounds over her. In any other situation he would have had a decisive victory. Instead, the smaller opponent dragged Ames and Ryan behind her like they were stuffed toys.

Three Chinese sailors stood at attention next to a ladder well leading up to the weather deck. Next to them stood another man adorned in medals. He had a stoic expression. If he tried a little bit harder, then he would look like he smelled a fart.

Beth recognized him from the news. He was the chief propagandist for the CCP. His face was plastered nearly as many places as their president. China always played the role of isolationists. It appeared that was as much a lie as the reports they let leave their country.

"The weapon worked perfectly," Zero said.

"What of Graham?" Xian asked.

"Deceased, and my hands are clean."

Xian nodded, his face void of expression. He gestured towards the ladder well, towards their escape from this evil place. Two of his men darted up the ladder.

"By all means," Zero said. "You go first."

Xian moved ahead and Zero waited for him to be out of earshot. "You can never trust a man who doesn't smile," he whispered. "Let's go."

"Wait for me," a voice called from around the corner.

Beth stared in the direction it had come from to see Wills crawling on the deck. Both his legs were gone along with one arm. He looked like death warmed over as he panted. She wanted to call out to him, to warn him that he should have stayed hidden, that a fate worse than death was coming. But she couldn't find her voice as her heart was in her throat.

Zero turned to the Chinese sailor and instructed him to fetch the wounded American.

"Keep your CCP claws off of me or I'll splatter your brain all over these pretty white walls," Wills barked. His usual bravado was tinged with pain. He was dying and he knew it, even accepted it. But he wasn't going alone.

The sailor spat something back at him, a taunt or warning. Beth couldn't tell and she doubted Wills could either.

"Shut up and go to Hell," Wills replied, swinging the stumps that were once his legs around. Beth saw something skid across the deck before Wills reached for it. The sailor stopped and a moment later a blast erupted and took half of the man's torso off between his chest and waist. The man collapsed dead, and Wills howled with glee. "Woo! Take that you filthy animal."

Zero turned to Urio, his smile faded into worry. "Kill him now!"

Urio dropped her load and sprinted towards Wills. She jutted between misaimed shots, jumping onto the bulkhead and using it as a springboard to carry her to her next leap. She moved with deadly precision and ghostly silence.

Wills waited with defiance etched onto his face like stone. He was covered in blood and Beth wondered how much of it was his and how much came from the people he had to kill to retrieve that weapon.

256

Urio closed the gap between them, talons outstretched, she leaped, then exploded as the weapon penetrated her body and scattered her along the overhead. A red mist poured onto the deck as clumps of organic tissue and metal fell from the air.

Their weapon was dead and there was no coming back this time.

Beth wanted to smile at their victory, but the fight wasn't over yet. Far from it.

Beth pulled away, but Zero's grip was like a vise. She struggled, using every bit of strength in her legs to push off the rungs of the ladder.

"I'm not leaving here empty handed," he seethed. He held onto the railing with a death grip. His eyes flickered with hate.

Above, one of the Chinese sailors called down to him, but his words were lost in the fight. Zero momentarily let go of the railing and came down with a fist, slamming it into Beth's forehead like he was driving a nail with a hammer. Her neck snapped back, her legs limp noodles, her eyes welled with tears, but she continued to fight despite the bleak hopelessness she faced.

"I won't let you turn me into that," she spat, fighting through the knot in her throat. Her friends were dead or dying. She had surrounded herself with what she thought was the future of modern warfare, the first super soldiers, only to find that their superiors were made in secret by a foreign enemy.

Every bit of intel she'd used to construct this mission was based on a lie and she was responsible for their deaths. But she wasn't losing soldiers. She was losing family.

Her rage boiled over. If she was going to die, then she was going to do it right here.

Beth let her knees bend as Zero pulled her towards him. She drove her knee into his groin, sending him doubling over. She didn't back away. Instead, she met his nose with the top of her head. His grip loosened.

Not by much, but it was just enough to count.

She propelled herself backwards, kicking her booted foot into his chin and driving him back. A satisfying crack snapped his head back and sent him limply onto his back.

Beth met the deck below with a thud, knocking the wind out of her lungs, and crunching her hands under her bodyweight. A whimper escaped her lips as she gasped for air.

Teary eyes watched Zero's body droop down the rungs until his feet touched the deck. He looked unconscious, but only for a moment. Burnt flesh turned into a sneer over yellow teeth as he hauled himself up.

It was like fighting the devil in her dreams. There was no stopping him.

Breathlessly, she scampered back on her heels in a feeble attempt to further the gap between them. She couldn't get past the bulkhead and Ryan's body before Zero was on his feet and stalking his prey.

He loomed over her, dragging his dead leg behind him. He was the monster under the bed that Hell itself couldn't contain.

"If you're going to kill me then get to it already," she said, her voice weak.

"I have much more planned for you than that," he said as he reached for her.

Beth closed her eyes, willing herself to keep fighting until she breathed her last. She anticipated his touch, expecting him to yank her off the deck and haul her away like she was a bag of dirty laundry.

Instead, she heard a familiar voice.

"Hey, Freddy," Ames said, his voice like gravel. Zero looked down at him, his eyes slits of impeccable darkness. "See you in Hell."

Ames took hold of the man's ankles and charged his bracelets. They glowed blue as electricity coursed through his hands. Zero struck at the Marine, but a solid object met an unmovable force. Neither man would relent.

Beth broke free of his grasp and backed away. The arcs and sparks were as bright as a welder's torch. She winced as it flashed but couldn't take her eyes off it.

Flames caught Zero's pantlegs, and he fought to put them out.

For the first time, she saw fear in his face. She would have felt sympathy if she didn't know any better. Instead, a surge of elation filled her. He deserved this as much as Graham deserved what happened to him.

Ames roared, his voice soaring over the frantic whines coming from Zero's scarred lips. The blue energy burned brighter and hotter. She felt the heat coming off it like she was sitting next to a furnace. Her own voice joined Ames's as if she could channel her energy into his. She couldn't stop screaming even if she wanted to. She willed the energy to crawl right up the former SAS agent's body and consume him, to send him back where evil like him belonged.

Beth didn't blink. She didn't breathe. She simply watched as Zero burst into flames. His screamed made her skin crawl, but only for a moment. In a flash it was over. The flames consumed him, and the fight left him before he could truly suffer.

She could only take solace in the fact that if there was a God, then Zero's punishment was far from over. It would last eternally.

Ames let go and pulled away from Zero's fiery remains. He had held on so long that his cybernetic arms had begun to wilt and melt. They appeared to function, but not fully.

"You saved my life," Beth said.

Ames looked up at her, exhaustion and pain in his eyes. "You saved me first."

"This isn't over," she said. "The Chinese are getting away."

Ames moaned and tried to force himself up. "If we stop them then at least we can say we did something," Ames croaked.

Beth rose to her shaky legs and tried to help the former Marine. He chose the bulkhead to support his weight, then used a knife to cut the zip ties binding her wrists. She ran over the Wills and checked for a pulse. It was weak, but present. She grabbed the weapon he had used against Urio and charged for the ladder well.

"I can't get up there in time," he said. "I'm too weak."

Beth wiped tears from her face and said, "I'll come back for you. I promise."

Ames nodded, then fell back to the deck.

She was on her own.

Just like in Stuttgart, but that was another life ago.

She cracked her neck and ran up the ladder ready to finish this.

———

The cool night air was an immediate relief. It was easier to breathe, and to think as clean air hit her lungs. It took a while for the smoky smell to be replaced by the fishy scent of the bay, but it was a welcomed change.

Beth exited the ship on the wrong side and had to cautiously make her way to the port side undetected. She remembered where Ryan had placed the claymore and was careful not to get too close. The Chinese sailors were already tossing off the mooring lines holding the submarine to the frigate by the time she arrived.

Xian was nowhere to be seen, and only a few sailors were visible on the narrow weather deck atop the vessel.

She stayed hidden, not wanting them to see her and return to the frigate to finish what Zero had started. They yelled at one another in a foreign tongue, but Beth detected a sense of franticness to it. They weren't leaving because the mission was done. They were fleeing.

That made them desperate.

Beth looked down at the weapon Wills had used against Urio. Parts of the female solider were cybernetic just like her crew, but most of the woman's body was organic. What the weapon did to her was disturbing beyond words, but it was effective.

She wanted to board the submarine and take out everyone involved in this horrific nightmare, but that lacked efficiency. She was nowhere near one hundred percent after the night she'd had. She needed something less subtle. She looked around and found the .50 caliber mounts. Part of her doubted the rounds would penetrate the submarine's hull, but she had to give it shot.

The sailors disappeared down into the depths of the submarine and closed the hatch. Now was her chance.

Beth ran for the nearest weapon mount as the submarine drifted away from the frigate. The ballasts filled with seawater and the vessel began its slow descent under the choppy waves. She placed the unusual weapon onto the deck, took hold of the .50 cal, and waited, timing it just right before squeezing the trigger.

The .50 caliber cannon roared with three-round bursts. Each round glinted off the surface of the submarine with an audible ping.

Her heart sank. It was armored. The rounds were as useless as tossing rolls of toilet paper at a brick wall.

"The Tzar will sink that vessel," a voice said behind her. It was laced with a thick Russian accent.

Beth turned, expecting another attack. Instead, she saw an older man with disheveled hair standing with a mask in his hand. "Who are you?"

"That's not as important as the fact that the Chinese are getting away. You'll miss your opportunity to sink them."

The mysterious man was right. She knelt to pick up the unusual weapon and took aim. She fired a succession of rapid bursts. The force exiting the barrel slammed into the hull, biting chunks out of it with each blow. It worked as well on metal as it did flesh.

The submarine immediately took on water and listed to one side, rotating rapidly until the ship was on its side. Bubbles rose to the surface as it disappeared under the dark water. She waited a long time to see if anyone broke the surface, but there was nothing but cresting waves rolling over one another.

Ultimately, she turned to face the man still lingering behind her. He stood in stock silence. He let the mask fall to the deck before looking to meet her gaze and speaking, "I wasn't always a bad man. I wanted to help people. I wanted to cure ailments and help the poor. That's why I became a biochemist." he sniffed and wiped at his nose. "I was forced into this life that I never wanted. They made me do things I'm ashamed of, but that shame doesn't negate the fact that I did them."

Beth took a step towards him, "What did you do?"

"That super soldier they brought with them was far superior to the designs I used. I tormented and mutilated those poor people to develop a soldier that was strong and resilient, but uncontrollable." He stopped speaking and fell to his knees crying. Beth wanted to say something to encourage him, but if he did the things he said, then he certainly didn't deserve her sympathy, whether he did it willingly or not.

"What's your name?" Beth asked.

"I'm Doctor Timur, the Frankenstein of Russia."

She'd heard of him, but always assumed it was a story about a facility more than an individual. What images were leaked were the kind that kept you up at night. Torment and mutilation were far too general of statements to attest to what he had done.

Beth lifted the weapon and leveled it at him. He didn't look up. He didn't plead with her. He simply knelt there and waited for what the whole world knew he deserved.

"Beth, wait."

She looked up to see Ames hobbling towards her. He dragged himself into the light before collapsing next to the Russian doctor. He panted, trying to catch his breath before speaking again. "Did you take part in the experiments in Siberia at the base on the foot of the mountain?"

Doctor Timur turned to face him. "I did."

"I saw what you did to those people." Timur didn't speak. He didn't even budge. "One of those victims you experimented on helped us fight the soldiers there. We freed everyone trapped in those tunnels."

Doctor Timur sobbed harder, but it didn't sound like sadness. "Russia will kill me for my failure, but I think it is a good way to fail. It means the human spirit does not easily lean towards evil. Perhaps there is hope for them?"

Ames caught his breath. "Can you fix what you've done?"

The doctor shook his head. "I wish I could, but the grafting technique used would still leave them deformed and disfigured. I had to use obsolete tools to do what they asked of me. It was terrible for them. Many died, but I tried to convince myself that they were better for it. I tried to let them go peacefully when I could."

Beth's heart broke. He was a madman. No amount of guilt could make up for that. She moved towards him, lifting the weapon once more.

Ames held up a hand to stop her.

"Is there anything you can do to ease his suffering?" Ames asked.

Doctor Timur wiped away more tears and inhaled sharply. "I would certainly try."

Ames cut his eyes at Beth. His expression said everything she didn't want to hear. Then a thought occurred to her, "Do you know what kind of poison they used for Urio's blades?"

The Russian nodded. "It is a slow acting poison, fatal if left in the blood stream too long, but easily nullified."

"Help me save my friends and I won't kill you," she said.

He looked up at her and nodded. "I would help you even if you did."

It was a bizarre reply, but strangely she believed him. "Then get to it," she said. "We haven't got long before the authorities arrive."

EPILOGUE
EAST BERLIN, TWO WEEKS LATER

Ames muttered a silent prayer as he held a small Bible against his chest. Even with every reason to hold resentment for what he'd endured going through his mind, he only felt thankfulness. It was the first time in as long as he could remember that he was truly happy. *Perhaps this is what peace feels like*, he thought as he closed his eyes.

A knock at the door pulled his attention from his thoughts and he smiled as Beth rolled Wills into the hospital room in a wheelchair. Ames's partner in crime had lost three limbs from the "super weapon" the Chinese had brought with them. It took them three tries to stop him, but ultimately Wills got his hands on the weapon and used it to end their ordeal on the *Valoroso*.

Beth sported casts on both arms from fractured wrists, but the dark bruises around her eyes had faded to a dull yellowish purple.

"Here to break me out?" Ames asked.

"Definitely," Wills chimed in. "You guys will be on the run, but I don't know what to call what I'll be doing." He gestured towards the stumps where his legs had been with a goofy grin. The pain meds were working well, and his loss hadn't done much to stifle his sense of humor. Ames found it better to laugh with him then agonize over what he'd lost, no matter how hard it hurt to see him in that chair.

"If I have to keep pushing you then you'll be on the run too," Beth said. "I'll be your legs."

Wills laughed at that then looked up at Ames. "Are you ready?"

Ames glanced at the hospital bed he'd been confined to for most of their stay. The poison treatments saved his life, but the rest of the time the room had been used as a cell while Interpol sifted through information to determine what crimes to charge them with.

As it stood, they were allowed to leave the hospital, but were limited to East Berlin, more specifically the safehouse where Tian and Adriel were holed up. It was a compromise, but it was worth it. Freedom came with a price, and it was one their team agreed to collectively.

Though, the more time went on, the less likely it appeared they would even face charges. The team was media darlings who even coined a name for them, "Damaged, Incorporated". The name caught on when people learned they were wounded warriors turned into cybernetically modified super soldiers. The term was trending on most networks and gave them a bit of positive publicity. Of course, freeing over twenty people who were trafficked from all over the world was bound to bring some attention.

Ames rose to his feet and took his first steps as a free man. He didn't let the fact that his freedom was pending a final decision from Interpol hold him back. "Where's Ryan?"

"Outside in the grove. He wanted to watch the wind blow through the trees," Beth answered.

Ames nodded and followed them out towards the elevator. Armed guards roamed the halls, not to keep them in, but to keep the public out. Most of the hospital was cordoned off and only a few staff members were allowed to work with the team.

"How are we getting to the safehouse?" Wills asked.

"Han is driving us."

"Public enemy number one?"

"Yeah, that reminds me; don't freak out when you see him. He's wearing the mask we found with Doctor Timur."

Ames cringed at the thought that someone was wearing Graham's face. The world still didn't know he was dead, a fact purposely with-held by the European governments. That was far from the only secret, but it was the one that bothered him the most. The media still hadn't mentioned that Frederick, Duke of York was missing, or that all the bodies had yet to be recovered from the sunken submarine. He supposed some truths might never be revealed as slow as bureaucracy moved.

They made it to the van where Han waited in the driver's seat. Sure enough, he looked like a dead man, but the mask concealed his identity. According to Beth, he liked to live dangerously, so driving them around would be right up his alley.

Ryan walked slowly to meet them, his head hanging low.

"Everything all right, boss?" Wills asked.

Ryan nodded. "I just don't like the idea of going from one cell to another. The safehouse is well-stocked, but it isn't home."

"You guys have me," Han said, thankfully not with a voice anywhere near Graham's. "I can bring you anything you need."

"We appreciate that," Beth replied. "It's probably best we get a move on. They want to reopen the hospital for new patients."

"Yeah, let's climb in, everybody," Ryan said.

"How insensitive," Wills spat. He gestured towards his stumps and continued, "How am I supposed to climb when I don't have any legs?"

Ryan groaned. "How about I toss you in? After all, you're half the man you used to be." His jab lifted everyone's' spirits. All except Wills who only partially feigned offense.

"That's a good one," he said. "Mean...but good."

Ryan laughed and lowered the wheelchair ramp for Wills to get into the van. "I didn't mean anything by it."

"I know," Wills said as the ramp lifted him up. He shifted the wheelchair into place and Beth helped strap it in. "What's on the agenda?"

"Taking Doctor Timur to help Adriel," Beth said.

"Oh, they didn't shoot that jerk in the head while we weren't looking?"

A man cleared his throat, and everyone turned to see the Russian being led out in cuffs by two guards. "No, they did not shoot me in the head while you weren't looking, but I'm sure they wanted to."

The guards uncuffed him and the man shoved himself into the back of the van in stoic silence.

"That's too bad," Wills said under his breath. He locked eyes with Ames. Neither of them liked the idea of the doctor "helping" Adriel. According to the Russian's own words, nothing could really be done. Still, Beth was insistent that he try. The fact he helped treat Ames and Ryan from the poison was supposed to prove he wasn't all bad.

In Ames's opinion, the man was an opportunist. Of course, he helped them, it kept him alive. He just hoped they weren't making a mistake reintroducing him to Tian and Adriel. If anyone was to be harmed by this idea, it would be them.

"Everyone ready?" Han asked.

They all agreed, and Han honked the horn with two short bursts. The escort vehicle in front of them moved out first, then their van followed by another escort. Most of the ride was in silence. Not that there weren't many conversations to be had, but the fact that Doctor Timur wasn't one of them and they didn't want to include him.

By time they arrived at the safehouse the tension started to dissipate. Han let them out and led them into the safehouse, guarding the doctor as they entered. Tian and Adriel waited. They had been briefed on what to expect, so they faced it together, locking hands.

Tian wiped tears from her eyes when she watched Wills enter in a wheelchair. Her brother moaned his sympathy. They were good people who endured horrible things but didn't focus their energy on hating Doctor Timur. They spent it on sympathy for the team that helped save them.

Ryan stepped up to them and extended his hand. "My name is Michael Ryan. It's an honor meeting you. My guys told me you helped save a lot of people."

Adriel took his hand then pulled Ryan in for a hug.

Ryan laughed at the child-like gesture. Adriel may have looked like a monster, but he was far from what he was created to be.

Ames had a thought and spilled it without hesitation. "If there's no hope of restoring his life to what it was, then maybe he would make a good part of the team? You should have seen him work in Siberia. It was incredible."

Beth met his gaze and whispered back. "I think that's a decision they would need to make, but I think you're right. We can discuss it with Ryan later."

"I know you remember Doctor Timur, but he's not here to hurt you. We asked him to help you," Ryan said after their hug fest. "Do you understand?"

Adriel nodded and gave an audible affirmation.

Ryan turned to the doctor and whispered, "Don't betray my trust or Hell will sound like paradise after I'm done with you. Understand?"

The Russian said yes and stepped before his creation. "I'm sorry for what I did to you, Adriel. I don't deserve your forgiveness, but I hope one day I no longer warrant your hate."

Adriel stared down at him for a long moment, then lifted a giant hand and touched the doctor. The man flinched, but nothing happened. It was just a simple touch.

It wasn't forgiveness, but it was a start.

Ames sucked in a breath and wiped tears from his eyes. He hadn't realized he was crying, but he couldn't help it. He saw hope in the way Adriel looked at the doctor. Despite the man doing him wrong in so many ways, he still had a heart of compassion. It was beautiful.

"Darkness cannot overcome the light," he whispered, remembering that he'd read that somewhere.

It was true. And he believed it with every fiber of his being.

ABOUT THE AUTHOR

Drew Avera is a Navy veteran, musician, and the bestselling author of the Dead Planet series and the Alorian Wars.

He was born and raised in rural Mississippi and grew up with a deep affection for comic books and science fiction movies and television shows. His love for comics inspired him to pursue a career as a comic book artist, but an injury to his hand ended that dream permanently.

Still, he was inspired to create in one medium or the other. He picked up a guitar at fifteen years old and began writing songs almost immediately. That "obsession" as his parents called it put him on the path to rock stardom...in his bedroom.

It was when he turned sixteen and bought the novel "What Savage Beast" by Peter David (The Incredible Hulk) that he caught the bug to be a writer. Unfortunately, it would not come to fruition until fourteen years later.

Drew enlisted in the US Navy as an Aviation Electricians Mate at seventeen years old. He served twenty years and deployed on four combat deployments to the Persian Gulf. During those deployments he would spend his free time reading books. He loved reading books in a series and that inspired his journey to becoming a fiction author.

In November 2012, at the age of thirty, Drew began his journey as an author by participating in National Novel Writing Month (NANoWriMo). He published his first book in March of 2013 and the rest, as they say, is history. With more than twenty books published in the space opera, military science fiction, cyberpunk, and dystopian genres, he has built a backlog with something for everyone who enjoys science fiction adventures.

After retiring from the Navy, he began an exciting new career in the simulation field. with more than twenty titles under his belt, Drew has plans for an all-new space opera and military science fiction series as well as new collaborations with other writers.

The best is yet to come!

To learn more about Drew and his books, visit www. drewavera.com.

Made in the USA
Monee, IL
04 October 2022

15236254R00154